THE HARVEST IS PAST

A NOVEL

HUGHES KEENAN

This book is a work of fiction. Names, characters, places, and incidents either are products of the author's imagination or are used fictitiously. Any resemblance to actual events or locales or persons, living or dead, is entirely coincidental.

ISBN: 1467909122
ISBN-13: 9781467909129
LCCN: 2011960307
CreateSpace, North Charleston, South Carolina

DEDICATION

For Patrick and Seig - *Commilitones in bello Fratres*
and for my children: E.E., Jack, Libby, and Tom

"The harvest is past, the summer is ended, and we are not saved."
—Jeremiah 8:20

PROLOGUE

As promised, on the first weekend after his tenth birthday, his father took him to the hunt club to teach him to shoot. "Double digits" is what his father always said. As soon as Em hit that milestone, he was ready. Not before. His mother didn't argue, not that it would have mattered if she did. Hunting in their family was a rite of passage, a part of their heritage, and any disagreement by her would mean endless taunting and sarcastic comments from her brothers during family gatherings. Beyond that, she risked the icy stare of disapproval from her father. The former she could tolerate; the latter she could not.

Learning to shoot was an event Em had looked forward to since the first time he remembered seeing Father (it was always "Father," he wasn't the kind of man you called "Dad" or "Pop") in the basement, cleaning his shotguns after a weekend of hunting. He would spread out a large sheet of chamois on the workbench, its surface stained with the oil and solvents from years of cleanings. Then he would arrange the guns, the cleaning rods and brass brushes in a very specific manner. Some of the swabs he used for cleaning the guns had been cut from Em's old cotton baby diapers.

The basement was a world his mother would only enter to do laundry, and even then only on the rare occasion when the "help" was sick. She never went near the workbench and never interfered, interrupted, or disturbed his father when he was cleaning the guns. Em was allowed to sit on the bottom set of steps; and he could smell the tobacco, solvents, and oil as he listened to the slide of the brushes inside the gun barrels as they removed the debris of shooting. He would sit there for a long time, until the cold of the concrete floor worked its way through the thin padding of his slippers and the bones in his feet ached. His father's back was always to him. Only once, during what seemed like years of observing, did Em remember his father turning to acknowledge him there on the steps. His long face stared flatly but approvingly at Em, the ever-present cigarette angled slightly at the corner of his mouth.

Em imagined that learning to shoot would suddenly make him older, and that mastering the firearm would propel him to a level equal to his father. Then he would join him at the bench. He would unroll the chamois and arrange the cleaning materials. They would sit side by side, not bothered by anyone, cleaning the guns, smoking cigarettes, and maybe talking about the hunt or other worldly things.

First, Em would have to learn to shoot. With all his nervous energy, he was up early Saturday morning. Father was already out in the garage, preparing for the drive to the club, which really was a private game reserve his grandfather had bought cheap during the Depression. At various times, it had been farmland, a small open-pit lead mine, and even the site of several minor skirmishes of the Western campaign during the Civil War. Quantrill's Raiders had used the land as a hideout from the Jayhawkers, too. All of that was exciting for a boy who wanted to be in the land of gentlemen's violence. It was a place where mothers, maids, babysitters, and nuns were not allowed.

In the kitchen, still in her nightgown and bed jacket, his mother packed up a lunch of sandwiches, consisting of thick slabs of meatloaf between heavily buttered slices of white bread, a single leaf of lettuce, and a mayonnaise and ketchup concoction she spread over the cold meat. A full Thermos of fresh black coffee was on the counter, and next to it, a single can of soda. As it was Saturday, Em was allowed a soda. Vess black cherry was one of his favorites. That was his allotment, his mother said, one soda a week. She didn't know that Elvina, their maid, would sometimes sneak him a bottle of Coca-Cola on Wednesday afternoons, which was her ironing day. It was her bribe so he would keep her company. Em would sit, nursing his Coke, and listen to her tell stories about the jazz days in town and about her half-brother, a famous musician who, she said, gave Count Basie his first break. She would ramble on, and he would listen, until she started complaining about her work. Elvina said that of all the housework, she hated ironing the most. Mother said Elvina didn't have to tell anyone how much she hated ironing; they only need see her ironing to know.

Father drove the station wagon, a monstrous yellow Plymouth with big fins on the back. Billy O'Connor, Em's best friend, said his parents thought it funny that they owned such a big car for having only one child. Billy's family had eight kids and they packed everybody into a Buick, which was a pretty big car; but it didn't look so big when they drove to church on Sundays and all those kids were piled in, screaming or crying as they wrestled with each other for more space to breathe.

On the drive down Highway 71, they stopped at the Rich Hill general store, a run-down building clad with asphalt roof shingles and a single, old, green Sinclair gas pump out front. Inside it was dark and smelled like stale food and kerosene. It had a basic selection of foodstuffs. In Em's eyes, it was a derelict of a store compared to the well-lit, well-stocked, and operating-room-clean supermarkets where he would pick out his can of soda. You could get Vess in singles at the supermarket, but every time he reached for the black cherry, his eyes were always on the six-pack of eight-ounce bottled Cokes in the red cardboard carton. Someday, he promised himself, after he learned to shoot, he would buy a whole case of Cokes and sink them into a big tub of ice; and Billy, Leo (his other best friend), and he would drink them as fast as they could and then burp until their throats were sore.

Father bought a new pack of Lucky Strikes, which he put in the top pocket of the brown corduroy shirt he always wore to the club. He also bought several boxes of 20-guage shells and a pumpkin. There were hundreds of gourds outside the store, all put in neat piles in wooden crates ready to be shipped out to the city, most likely, where they would be sold at the downtown market or on street corners.

The road to the hunt lodge passed over several creeks, of which only one was bridged, and that one only by a rickety old structure made from railroad ties turned into pilings. In the fall, depending on several factors, the area was pretty much a swamp that could usually be navigated, but if the water got too high, it flooded quickly and ruined the duck hunting.

The lodge wasn't so much a lodge as it was a house on stilts, which were actually a dozen or more legs of cinder blocks filled with concrete and rebar. Em never heard of anyone inhabiting it when the water was high, although the tree house construction kept it safe from any flooding, and there was always a canoe under the house. A long, angled wooden stairway led up to an extended porch partially covered by the roof. A walkway with railings wrapped around the entire house.

Huge sycamores surrounded the place, which at that time was painted a mawkish green that was the result of a "deal" one of his uncles got on Army surplus paint. Unfortunately, there wasn't enough olive drab to cover the house, so he stretched it with flat white.

The lodge had remained that color for years, except where peeling areas revealed a light blue undercoat. The only recent improvement was new gravel along the road leading up to the cabin and the parking area, which was hard to see because the sycamores had shed early. The leaves were big and leathery and reminded him of elephant skin. They made a soft sound when he walked on them, not like the crunching of the maples that had already turned color, died and had fallen like scarlet and yellow snowflakes onto the green, meticulously trimmed yard at home.

Through the naked branches of the giant trees, the sky was a crystal blue that only comes with fall. Although the sun was just clearing a grove of old cedars, it was a very warm day for late-October, and he could hear bees skimming through the air.

The tractor starting up startled Em as he watched a blue heron, its wings folding and unfolding like a swimmer. The tractor was an old Allis Chalmers, nearly rusted out but in fine working order, pulling a two-wheeled flatbed with a pair of long, mismatched car seats bolted to the wooden deck. The tractor burned a lot of oil, and every time the engine was revved a fresh plume of black smoke erupted from the stack and stained the sky.

There were three duck blinds at the club. Two were on either side of the large swamp on the southern end of the club that connects to the Marais de Cygne, when the seasonal rains are heavy. The northwest side of the parcel was dotted with several potholes that were scraped from the earth by the failed lead-mining operation. Of these, the deepest and largest was known as the Old Pothole. It was the favorite and most hunted of the blinds, because there was always water, and it was not subject to the vagaries of an occasional drought or the U.S. Army Corps of Engineers.

There was little rain late summer and even less through September, so the ruts in the crude road that led to the Old Pothole were deep and hard as concrete. When it was muddy, the large tractor tires slipped, and the driver would have to gun the engine and spin the wheels until they caught, sending showers of mud clods high into the sky.

The jostling of the road kept Em busy. To keep everything from being thrown off the trailer, he held the shotgun cases to the floor with his feet, cradled the ammo box of shells between his ankles, and kept the Thermos upright in his crotch. With one hand, he held onto the lunch basket; with the other hand, he kept a tight grip on the top of the seat.

The stretch of road through the large meadow that opened up into the Old Pothole was the worst. There were no trees and only the thick bluestem grasses to protect the soil from erosion. In some places, the ruts were as deep as the tractor axle, and Father had to position it and the trailer in a balancing act on the top of the ruts while carefully negotiating both vehicles through the only fence opening.

Father cursed one of Em's uncles who had promised over the years to backfill this part of the road. It was an open joke among his uncles that his father had complained ever since the promise had been made—and that it would go on as a broken promise as long as he complained.

They cleared the fence and came to a stop about twenty yards from the blind perched on the eastern edge of the pothole. Cattails swayed in a light breeze that accentuated the dryness in the air. Em jumped off and started to arrange everything on the back edge of the trailer.

"You remember what I taught you?" Father asked, handing him the 20-gauge and a shell.

"Yes, sir."

"Load it," he said, standing back with his hands on his hips and a lit cigarette in his mouth. "Take a practice shot at the stump over there. Remember…"

"If you're red, you're dead," he answered, checking the safety to make sure it was on.

Em shouldered the gun and squinted down the barrel toward the stump. Without thinking or breathing, he jerked the trigger and waited for the noise and recoil. Nothing happened.

"Pay attention," Father scolded. "Your safety is still on."

Frustrated, angry with himself, and afraid he failed his test, he frowned at his father and turned back to the stump. In one motion he clicked the safety off, raised the gun, and pulled the trigger. He heard the gun and felt the kick in his right shoulder.

"Better," his father said, handing him another shell. "Next time, try to hit the stump."

Em passed a few more shells through the gun and peppered the stump pretty well before his father went to the tractor and brought back the pumpkin. He took a black marker from his pants pocket and walked over to the stump. He stood there, his back to him, and began to draw. When he returned to where he was standing, Em could see that the pumpkin had two eyes and a mouth. The eyes were big and dark, and the mouth was crude and flat, with no hint of either a smile or frown.

Em was caught by surprise and almost fell to the ground when his father grabbed the shotgun away from him, put a shell in, and fired. The pumpkin exploded in a shower of orange chunks and creamy strings of seed-speckled fibers. With his ears ringing and the taste of gunpowder in his mouth, his father led him to where what was left of the pumpkin was strewn about the ground and high grass.

"Bad things can happen with a gun, that fast," he said. "Do you understand?"

"Yes, sir," he croaked, still shaking inside.

Em spent the next half-hour shooting at rusty beer cans they found around the blind until he ran out of shells. Then they ate lunch and he helped his father cut and bind grass for the roof of the blind. It was the most glorious day he had ever had, better than drinking Cokes with Billy and Leo and burping. He was part of the club now and would be allowed to attend the fall hunting weekends with his father, uncles and cousins.

It was the world of gunpowder, meatloaf sandwiches, coffee, and cigarettes. His cousins were all older, so he was the last of the line until they started to marry and have sons who would also be taught to shoot when they reached double digits. After that day, each hunt was an event of men: a camaraderie of shared smells, tastes, and sounds. And there was his father, with his deadpan face and cigarette.

In the early fall of his sophomore year at Stonefield Academy, Em was suffering through geometry when Father Munro stood in the classroom doorway and quietly informed the teacher that "young Morley" should be excused from class to accompany him to the office. Munro was an old-breed

Jesuit who wore a long black cassock, which he tied off above his potbelly with black braiding and a large rosary. Em and Billy had lit a string of Black Cats and thrown them into a freshman gym class days earlier, and he thought it was finally catching up to them—though he swore nobody had seen them, and neither of them bragged of the prank. Billy wouldn't break, and neither would he. They were routinely pulling students from class to grill them about the incident.

That was what Em thought as he walked silently beside Munro—that is, until they passed the disciplinarian's office. As they turned into the principal's office, the priest put his hand on Em's shoulder, as if to convey some sort of comfort. Standing in the office was his cousin, Denton, dressed in his army uniform. Even though he was a good ten years older, Denton was the cousin closest in age to Em and always made it a point to be nice. He had graduated from Stonefield and gone on to West Point. Earlier in the summer, Denton had returned from Vietnam and was temporarily stationed at Fort Leavenworth.

As they left the great circle drive at the school, Denton told Em the caretaker at the hunt club had found his father sitting in the blind at the Old Pothole. He had gone down over the weekend to clear some brush, and when he didn't return, his mother called the caretaker to look for him.

For several days leading up to the funeral, Em thought his father had died of a heart attack, but then he overheard one of his uncles talking. The caretaker had found Father with the barrel end of his shotgun resting on his chest. He pictured his father's brown shirt and the broken pumpkin on the stump, and he remembered the taste of gunpowder.

Skin so black, it's blue in the early morning sun and humidity. Sweat glistening off Heavy Hat's face, half covered in the shade of his campaign cover. The Recruit marvels at the color of his skin. So black. Inky black. Darkest Africa black. Black as night. Black as the end of the world. An eternity of black. Heavy Hat is screaming from the bottom of his stomach up through his chest and finishing with a hurricane of coffee-smelling spit. Jarhead Deluxe. Ooooorah, motherfucker! Parris Island in late spring. Orange ball just below the tops of the pine trees outside the squad bay. The big yolk threatening to suck the Recruit dry before it hits its apex for the day. Noses and lungs swollen with pollen. Pass the motherfucking chlortrimeton. Big green giants all over, the pines welcoming you with cool shade, then shitting their yellow clouds into your mouth and nose. The heat. The heat. The heat. Cranking out more bodily fluid than piss from an elephant. Feeling hard as rock and loose as blubber. Bodies that can't move without pain. Aspirin is for pussies. Take the pain. Love the pain. Make the pain your friend. Pain is the Recruit's best buddy. Pain keeps you alive. Pain tells you you're alive. Pain is life. Relish every pang, sting, and burn. Ain't even had morning chow yet. No sleep. No appetite. Will puke it out anyway, big chunks of whatever got shoveled down the pie hole getting left behind in a mud hole, foxhole, rope hold, or toilet bowl. Sometimes the Recruit just opens the top of his blouse and pukes inside. Smell bad. Feel good. Keep it tucked away. Keep it close to your chest. No sharing private shit. The Recruit ain't private. The Recruit ain't shit. Heavy Hat reminds the Recruit. The Recruit is a puke. Less than a puke. But try not to puke. The Recruit is one organism. Get it in the Recruit's head. Your "you" is dead. You are us, we. Semper Fi. The Boot Shit Recruit on the far end passes out. Hits the ground like a redwood. Timber. Goddamned Gomer Pyle. Heavy Hat is screaming. Boot Shit makes a sick sound when he hits the asphalt. "Who the fuck gave you permission to faint on me, you piece of shit?" Not a flinch. Keep ranks unless otherwise ordered. Fuck that guy. Eyes forward, chest out. The Boot Shit still passed out on the asphalt, Heavy Hat standing over him, dripping his clear, cool sweat on the Boot Shit. Gimme some of that. Looks good, uh-huh. Feels good, uh-huh. Smells good, uh-huh. Sound off. Heavy Hat's tirade of spit pouring out from the blackest, most starched and polished Marine the world has ever seen. Heavy Hat has performed a miracle. Lord have mercy. The Boot Shit is back on his feet. Sir, yes, sir. Heavy Hat in full-tilt boogie scream. "I've been shot, I've been blown up, I've fallen out of airplanes, I've died a thousand deaths and come back to piss kidney stones without blinking. I know what pain is, and this Recruit faints in the cool morning breeze? Faints?" He's so far into the Boot Shit's face they become one. "Recruit, what kind of person faints?" "Sir, I don't know, sir." "Women faint. Are you a woman?" "Sir, the Marine is not, sir." Electric scream, louder and clearer.

They hear the screaming louder and clearer on the moon. "You ain't no Marine. Do you know what you are?" "Sir, no, sir." "You are mung, recruit. Do you know what mung is?" "Sir, no, sir." "Mung is what drips out of pussy after an abortion. You ain't even an abortion, recruit. You're the aftermath. You are some nasty shit we have to wipe up after." The orange ball cycles once, and the Boot Shit is gone from the squad bay. Off to Pork Chop Platoon, never to be seen again. Square away time. The Recruit performs Divine Worship. Please Lord, the Recruit pleads, make Heavy Hat go away. The orange ball cycles again. Grass Week, and the Recruit is snapping in. The PMI goes fast. Up, down, right shoulder, trigger action, on your knee, butt shoulder, squeeze, go to prone. When the Recruit squints down the barrel, the world breathes relief. Noise abates. There is only the breeze in the top of the pines. A calm. More cycles of the orange ball. Firing Week. Ding, ding, ding downrange. The Recruit in his firing position, weapons free. Table 1. Call it out. Bull's-eye, 180 meters. Bull's-eye, 270 meters. Bull's-eye, 460 meters. Bull's-eye standing, kneeling, and prone. The Kill Hats watch and scribble on their clipboards. They buzz. Heavy Hat is jawing with the SDI. A big shit-eating grin on Heavy Hat's black-as-night face. The SDI squats behind the prone Recruit. "That's some real hillbilly shooting. Think you can do it again?" "Sir, yes, sir." The Recruit repeats. The SDI to the Kill Hats, "We got us a real-live Lee Harvey Oswald." No Pizza Box for the Recruit. Recruit earns a Big X. Heavy Hat grinning so big his teeth shine like keys on a piano beneath his campaign cover. Platoon gets the trophy. Platoon gets twenty-four-hour leave after the Crucible. The big orange ball cycles some more. Nine weeks gestation almost over. The Recruit is birthed a Marine. Honor, Courage, Commitment. June bugs and erections start to return to the squad bay. Eagle, Globe, and Anchor. A P F-fucking-C. Duded out in service uniform Charlie. Piss covers on our knob heads. Ready for the pass. Lined up on the asphalt. The Big X on my chest. Heavy Hat like the Heavenly Father, dispensing prophetic, prophylactic advice. "Pussy, gentlemen, is just meat on a bone. You can suck it, fuck it, or leave it alone." Ooooorah, Master Sergeant! The Buddy System. Billy and Leo and I head into Charlie Town. Hit the titty bars and get stunk drunk. Leo gets a hand job in a back room. Bitch is old as fuck. Swear she's missing some teeth. Nasty. We get drunk some more. Billy pukes on the hood of a car outside. Big red neon light on a strip mall. Strip mall. Strip bar. Strip down. Leo's bright idea, like the red neon light. We get tattoos. Motherfucker, that hurts, pass me the Jack. Left shoulder arms. G.H.M.F. below the Eagle, Globe, and Anchor. Brothers for life. Gung Ho Mother Fuckers. The orange ball cycles again. Head hurts. Arm hurts. We get our MOS. Billy to Combat Training to run a radio. Pussy. Leo gets SOI Geiger. Firing Week gets me SOI West, and on to sniper school. Pass Go, collect $200. "California, here I come…."

CHAPTER 1

The windows rattled, and the bedroom furniture was moved by the shock wave, sending the typewriter to the floor and setting off the return bell, as if to announce the start of the next round of a boxing match. Morley was sure the door to his room had been kicked open, though the darkness was proof it hadn't been. Exhausted after three long days of reporting, writing, and filing, he had taken a shower and fallen asleep covered only by a towel, which now lay on the floor. There he stood, confused, naked, and uncertain of his surroundings and situation, holding the desk chair over his head.

"Who's there?" he yelled. His vocal posturing responded to the threat, but the panic was unmistakable in his voice.

There was nothing. No answer. His eyes adjusted to the faint bar of light coming from beneath the door. He felt the beating of his heart in his eardrums and took a deep breath to try to slow his heart rate and relax his body. As he did, his peripheral vision discerned movement of another person in the room, standing near the dresser across from him. Instinctively, he snapped the chair back to swing at the intruder.

His eyes adjusted from the light coming from the window just before he swung. There, in the mirror of the dresser, was a scared, naked man, threatening himself with a chair.

"Jesus Christ," he hissed, feeling ridiculous and certain some joke was being played on him.

The flood of adrenaline dropped below his ears, its wake now just a warm wash in the pit of his stomach. He put the chair down but the uneasiness was still there. Was it a dream? Another flashback? He must have knocked the typewriter over himself when he started from his sleep.

He sat on the chair and tried to remember the dream. Parris Island seemed like a long time ago. The past was the past. You don't have to deal with it if you don't want to. Still, something gnawed at him. He put the facts together in his head. What woke him up? If it wasn't a dream, then what was it?

He sat there in a gauzy state of mind, somewhere between alertness and exhaustion, for what seemed a long time, replaying the dream, but the sharpness of the colors and sounds had already started to lose their freshness. He got up and went over to the window. There was more out there. He only needed to look. Through the flimsy sheers backlit by the lights of the city, perhaps a half-mile away, a faint glow rose from the ground like a distant campfire. Just as a single lick of flame illuminated the blast cloud rising from the landscape below, the sounds of the sirens began to wail.

Another surge of adrenalin pushed through him, this time born of excitement, not fear. Just as instinctively as he reacted to defend himself, he now acted with an urgency to perform. He turned the lights on, grabbed the phone and a fresh reporter's notebook from his bag, and placed a quick call to the London Desk to alert them of the blast—its approximate time, location, and general size, and that the authorities were responding.

"This is Emmett Morley, Dateline Belfast," he said, then dictated the headline and first two paragraphs of the snap to the copytaster on the other end.

"Very good," was followed by a pause punctuated by the sound of hard tapping on a keyboard at the other end of the line. "The snap is set up. Do you have an official verification?"

Morley hesitated for a moment, then decided to take the gamble. In the wire service business, being first got you the credit and the ensuing attention. Besides, he had felt the blast, seen the fire, and heard the sirens. Those were enough facts for him.

"Local authorities, the Royal Ulster Constabulary," Morley said. "I'll get you a name. Go ahead and file the snap."

There was a brief pause that made him feel that the copytaster wasn't buying it.

"Right, the snap is out, sending it A-wire as well. Ring us up when you get a new lead and a situationer if possible," he said. "We'll check with the Home Office here."

The line clicked dead, curtly, but Morley didn't waste time wondering about the abrupt end to the conversation. It was never worth it with the Brits. He'd worked with them long enough not to worry about their manners.

His luck was good, as there was an immediate answer at the constabulary station. He knew the constable on duty, who was rather breathless and anxious but steady as he told him the few details available. Morley could hear a furtive rush of activity in the background of the station, as he scribbled the information in his notebook. Flipping back over two pages of notes, he double-checked the time given for the explosion and read back the rest of his notes to the officer, stopping to spell out his name and rank. The officer thanked Morley but said he had to break off the call. *Cops*, Morley thought, *no matter what country, they always remember you taking the time to get their name right, if they wanted their name cited at all.*

Morley rang back the London Desk and was relieved when Bette, the senior night sub-editor, answered. She was very quick on dictation and sharp at rewrite. She was also much easier to deal with than the previous copytaster, who, he remembered, was actually from Chicago. On being transferred to London, he had developed a very patrician English accent and the same bad manners. Bette was Irish and, like her homeland, could be rough and delightful at the same time. He dictated five paragraphs to her and was about to end the call, get dressed, and head to the blast scene when she told him to hold on. He could hear her talking to someone else in the background.

"The Home Office is confirming a bomb and a warning call received two minutes before the explosion."

That caught him off guard.

"Two minutes? That's not right. They're playing us," Morley said. "The Provos give at least thirty minutes' warning, when they do give one. A two-minute warning makes no sense. What would that accomplish? Can you attribute the time on the warning to the Home Office in a direct quote?"

"No, it was a junior liaison officer," she said.

"Paraphrase it, then, but attribute it to the Home Office," he said. "I don't buy it. I think they screwed up, and they're covering their asses. I'll check it with sources here."

He hunched over the phone on the bedside table with his notes, still naked and anxious to get dressed. It was cold in the room, and he wanted to hang up and get to the blast site to get some color, but again Bette said to wait. There were more muffled voices in the background at her end and the rustle made by holding the phone to her shoulder.

"You're alone on this, Morley," she said. "Neither Brand X nor Grandma have filed anything."

"What about the Frogs?"

"They'll wait until next week to steal our copy," she laughed.

"Okay," is all he managed to say before telling her he'd head for the scene and call back with more details, color, and quotes as soon as possible. She said they would work the story from their end as well.

"I'll call Digger and let him know," Bette said, ending the call.

Digger was his bureau chief in Dublin. He was an Aussie. For some unexplainable reason, it seemed as if all Aussies were nicknamed Digger and liked to drink. Digger was a good sort, Morley thought, though Bette would pay hell waking him up at this hour, if she could wake him up at all. The image of his hungover bureau chief being awakened by a phone call from the London Desk in the middle of the night made him smile.

As soon as he put the phone in its cradle, a great ocean of doubt crashed over him. Bette had planted the seed of the fruit all journalists feared eating: inaccuracy. *My God,* he thought, *did I just dream this up? Did I just make up a story that didn't happen?* Nobody else had the story on the wires. Could it be that he had been dead asleep, woke up, filed a story that had gone across the world with his name on it, and it never even happened? He started fashioning a story kill in his head and his next career move before stopping himself. *Get back to the facts,* he cautioned himself. He could still see the glow of the fire through the cracked pane of glass. He had a confirmation from the constable on duty and the Home Office in London. Those were facts. It was a damn good piece of reporting, Morley allowed himself in a moment of satisfaction. Still, insecurity and self-doubt existed in all reporters like a cough they couldn't shake. He had taken a risk he shouldn't have, but it was calculated. The fact was, it was a lie at the time, and even though he knew it was a lie, he went with it—and it seemed to pay off, so far.

CHAPTER 2

The bomb destroyed a pub and part of a grocery next door in the mostly Protestant area of the Lower Shankill below Agnes Street. The concussion had been strong enough to crack a window in his room, topple the typewriter, and wake him from a deep sleep. Morley's hotel was near the city center; and his room on the sixth floor offered a decent view of the Protestant neighborhoods up Shankill Road, which snaked its way to the foot of a hump of a mountain called the Divis. The Falls Road Catholic neighborhood ran parallel to Shankill. The two areas were physically separated by the Peace Wall, which served as a kind of demilitarized zone, though its name held little meaning. As he looked out the window at the small fire and dim city lights and the black mountain that blotted out the sky, Morley noticed the crack in the glass ran almost straight along the line separating the two religious factions. For the moment, he appreciated the symbolism. The broken pane was new; the fracture had been there for centuries. He dressed, went outside, and hailed a taxi. The distant sirens had built to a crescendo that made him anxious. As he looked at the time on the large clock that hung outside the *Belfast Telegraph* building, his anxiety turned into agitation. It was 11:00 p.m. *Goddamn, never can get a break on getting a decent sleep*, he thought. He had managed only three hours after several grueling days of following up on the story of the kidnapping and murder of a wealthy local art dealer. Apparently conceived by the IRA as a way to raise money—they had yet to take credit for the crime—the kidnapping was an abject failure. A family had no father, and the Provos had no money. Still, Morley thought, it was a good story, and although tonight would be another long stretch, he would get another good story. Morley hoped to shag some quick quotes at the scene and gather a few more details that would satisfy London long enough for him to get some sleep. Depending on the number of casualties and how quickly he could file a first lead to the story, it should make the morning papers in the United States. Definitely, he thought, the handful of evening newspapers. The West Coast and Asian papers for sure. It was a twenty-four-hour cycle story. After that, it would be dead outside of Northern Ireland.

As enthusiastic as the driver was to get as close to the scene as possible, with the lure of a big tip from his fare, he was forced by the large presence of firefighters, constables, and military to let Morley off several blocks away. A perimeter had been established by the British army and personnel from the constabulary, and they were policing the cordoned-off area aggressively, as ambulances moved in and out of the site, their sirens and lights piercing the night air. Morley knew the area well enough, having canvassed the neighborhoods for previous stories, to navigate some of the back streets and alleys. Dodging in and out of dark sections of row houses and back passageways, he avoided two military patrols. Not that it was hard. The squawking of their radios and chatter on the nets could be heard half a block away. The cobblestones on the back streets of some of the older blocks were wet and slick in the cold night air, and he wished he had worn boots instead of leather-soled shoes. A stiff wind blew in from the Lough, and when he walked into open areas, the air turned markedly frigid and made his eyes tear up. His stealthy maneuvers, he calculated, had put him about a block away; exiting the next alley should place him right on the scene. His sense of direction was keen; however, to his surprise, when he turned the corner, he walked right into the back of a Saracen armored personnel carrier, its rear doors open. Milling about were heavily armed soldiers. The red and white hackles in their berets identified them as being from the Royal Regiment of Fusiliers. Several of the soldiers—mostly boys, Morley thought—were sharing a smoke. The surprise pedestrian startled them, and the butts dropped to the cobblestones. The cherries of the cigarettes hissed dead in the dampness, as the Fusiliers shouldered their weapons and targeted Morley. In another time, Morley would have been pleased with himself for getting the drop on them. They were sloppy. Scrubs sent to Northern Ireland to police "the Troubles." Their FAL machine guns had wood stocks, which the British army had begun swapping out for composite stocks during routine maintenance. That the weapons pointed at him had yet to get the change-out told Morley these guys were not a priority. Nonetheless, in the current circumstance, he was unarmed and uninvited. Luckily, he was a neutral, and it was his neutrality that he needed to communicate before one of the young soldiers squeezed their trigger just a little too tightly.

"I'm with the press," he announced, holding his arms in the air.

That the statement was delivered with an American accent tempered the soldiers' defensive posture, but only slightly.

"Credentials are around my neck. I should have worn it outside, but this cold," Morley said.

One of the tricks he learned early as a reporter was to disarm authority by playing dumb and innocent. It made them feel superior and made it easier to extract what he needed for a good story.

One of the soldiers shouldered his weapon and approached him. He pulled the chain with the press credentials badge from beneath the top collar of Morley's pea coat.

"Sergeant Major," the young soldier called out.

About two doorways up from the vehicle, the sergeant major had just finished urinating next to a trash bin.

"What is it, Conklin?"

"We snatched a reporter coming up on us from the alley."

"Well, shoot him, Conklin."

The other soldiers snickered at the sergeant major's humorous order.

"Can't, Sergeant Major; he's a Yank."

The sergeant major was medium-sized, but he carried himself with all the brass and balls of a much bigger man. There was no doubt he was in charge, and his men were delighted that he was, though at the moment he was chagrined at the lax behavior of his charges.

"I go to drop a P and you wankers are tossing about," he yelled. "Bloody fooking Provos could stroll right in here with a bomb, and you'd offer them tea and crumpets."

The men suddenly were red-faced and standing much straighter.

"Let me see here," the sergeant major said, looking over the press credentials still attached to the chain around Morley's neck.

"Not armed, are you, Yank?"

"No, Sergeant Major," Morley said with conviction, his hands still in the air.

The sergeant major was soon to reach pension, having been in service to the Queen for over thirty years, and knew how to size someone up in a start. He looked at the photo on the ID and at the man in front of him. Morley was in good shape, the sergeant major thought; mid-twenties, though he looked older; stood at proper attention, eyes forward; and there was no sign of fear. The small scars on his neck, face, and one wrist were signs of shrapnel. The man had seen combat, of that the sergeant major was sure; but had it been as a journalist or as a soldier?

"Why are you still holding up your arms, Mr. Morley?" the sergeant major asked, in a tone that implied the detained man was an idiot.

"I follow orders, Sergeant Major, and nobody's ordered me at ease," he said.

The response confirmed to the sergeant major that the man had been in the military.

"You shouldn't be here, Mr. Morley," he said.

"I was directed here," Morley bluffed. "I ran into two patrols earlier, and they pointed me this way. I'm looking for Major Brown."

Morley held his breath and hoped the bluff worked; he hoped the patrols he avoided hadn't called in to the command post and reported seeing nothing, but most of all, he hoped Brown was at the scene. He had talked to him only a few days earlier about the Kaitcer kidnapping, so the odds were good.

"How do you know Major Brown?"

"We met when I was stationed at the embassy in Dublin," Morley said, truthfully.

The sergeant major looked at Morley as if to ask for more details concerning his relationship with Major Brown.

"When my enlistment ended, I stayed on to go to university, and I just kind of fell into this business."

It was the truth, but Morley felt like it came out of his mouth like a lie—one that seemed to work. Morley could see in the sergeant major's face that he had just turned another reporter's trick. It was the one ace up his sleeve he could play with these guys, and that was that he was one of them. If the sergeant major didn't have him escorted away under armed guard immediately, then he had a chance to bond with the soldiers and get what he needed. They might even help him find a phone. If he were really lucky, Brown would be here.

"All right, Mr. Morley; wait here while I try to locate Major Brown," he said.

"Thank you, Sergeant Major."

"It is Sergeant Major Eames."

That was it. Morley was in, and Brown was around somewhere. Morley spent the next three-quarters of an hour talking with the soldiers behind the vehicle, sharing cigarettes and trying to stay warm. Anything they said was all off the record, and he let them know it. It was all off the record because they didn't have any useful information for him. They were young and dumb.

Across the street from them was the bombed pub, lit with portable floodlights. The firefighters had finished with the small blaze. From where he was situated with the soldiers, Morley counted three blue blankets covering what were either bodies or parts of them. It wasn't enough to get an accurate casualty count. He scribbled what he could observe in his notebook, absorbing the color of the scene. Now he just needed facts, verification, and a phone.

CHAPTER 3

"Morley, I would have expected you to be in the pub, not loitering about with this lot."

The Fusiliers gathered around the Saracen snapped to attention.

It was Major Brown. Tom Collins Brown, even though he was a single-malt Scotch man. Morley liked to tease him by calling him Major Tom, after the song. However, he respected the chain of command and liked Tom Collins Brown as a friend, and would never disrespect him in front of his troops with too personal a salutation. It wasn't right for the ranks. It wasn't what a friend would do. Besides, he wouldn't want to lose a good source.

"Sergeant Major Eames, how did you stumble upon this miscreant?"

Eames, at attention, turned his gaze to Conklin.

"Beg your pardon, Major, but according to Corporal Conklin, Mr. Morley stumbled upon us."

Morley could see Brown's demeanor turn serious as he walked to Conklin, who stiffened to an even higher level of attention. Brown faced the corporal but addressed Eames. Both men were about to feel the leather.

"Sergeant Major Eames, I can assure you that if someone of far less caliber and training than Mr. Morley were armed and fostered ill intentions toward the presence of British soldiers on this soil, there would more blankets to count," said Brown with a deadpan delivery that adeptly skirted above a raised voice but below a yell.

15

"Sir," Eames snapped back.

"Sergeant Major, get things tightened up," Brown ordered. "There really is a war going on. People really are dying, including British soldiers.

"Come with me, Mr. Morley."

As Brown and Morley walked up the street toward the remains of the pub and the four blanketed bodies, Sergeant Major Eames began addressing the soldiers well above a yell.

"Sorry about that, Emmett."

"I didn't want to say anything, Tom."

"The chaps get a bit knackered rather easily over here, and all sense of urgency and caution disappears. It's like home, but it isn't."

Morley knew that if he had been with the IRA and armed, the soldiers would all be dead. He felt foolish for not being more cautious. Maybe, he thought, it was an easy lesson for them to learn.

"I'll give you a quick look about, but then you have to go," Brown said.

As they walked around the debris, Morley chronicled the flotsam and jetsam of the blast in his notebook. It was a mélange of everyday life. There were some darts, canned goods, newspapers, and bread. A pint glass lay in the middle of the street, still intact with what looked like three fingers of ale in it. There was a sequined purse. What had been everyday items had become part of an absurd collage of violence.

Brown confirmed the count as five dead, and about a dozen wounded had been taken to various hospitals. Morley would check on their condition, but it would have to be tomorrow.

"Tom, there is a bit of a sketchy chain of events about the bombing," said Morley.

"Oh? Why is that?" Brown asked, as he stepped across a smoldering beam, the two of them picking their way through the debris.

"Home Office is saying there was a warning by phone right before the explosion," Morley said.

"Rubbish," Brown said, his demeanor becoming more somber as they walked closer to the shattered, smoldering pub.

"Think there's something wonky?"

"There's no Watergate going on," Brown said very matter-of-factly. "The Home Office simply got it wrong. There was a call right after the blast, but it wasn't a warning or claim of it being a political action. It was only to report the explosion. Likely just someone who lived close by. That's all."

The two of them walked the outside perimeter of the bombed-out building. The stringent smell of gunpowder and softness of the smoke struck Morley, as if one of the bricks on the ground had been thrown at his head. He was somewhere else for a moment. Walking on a beach. He could feel the sand underneath his feet and the warmth of the sun. He thought he heard the crack of gunfire when Brown stepped on a large piece of glass.

"Here, I want to show you something."

They walked around the front of where the entrance to the corner pub had been and onto a side street that Morley hadn't been able to see from his location with the soldiers. It had been cordoned off. There were no emergency personnel around. An empty lot across the street lent it a solemn and lonely appearance, despite the brightly painted political mural splashed on a building across the way, depicting some martyr of "the Troubles." The floodlights, which weren't directly focused on this side of the corner, produced a bluish hue in the shadows, though there was plenty of light to see. The wind seemed to pick up, causing a brisk rush of noise as it blew over the rooftops of the ramshackle row homes just down the street. Morley pulled up the large collar of his pea coat and wished he had brought his stocking cap. Brown appeared oblivious to the cold as he walked up to a single blue blanket. The plume on his beret fluttered in the wind and reminded Morley of a small bird with a broken wing.

"Tom, you said five killed."

"Right," Brown said, kneeling beside the blanket before lifting it back.

The woman was young, in her late teens or early twenties. She lay on her side, facing away from the pub, her face covered by long, dark hair. The blast had torn her blouse away, but a pink brassiere had stayed in place. Several long gashes had torn through her torso and contrasted with her pale skin. As he looked down at her body, Morley saw what Brown wanted him see: a small arm protruding from a large wound on the side of her extended abdomen.

"You can cover her up now, Tom," Morley whispered. "Please."

They both stood there for a moment, their eyes tearing up from the wind that blew in from the Irish Sea.

CHAPTER 4

Morley's urgency to leave the scene was hastened by more than wanting to file a new lead to the story. The excitement of covering a place like Northern Ireland came with a price. There was the obvious human cost he had just seen, and there was the cost inside of him. It was a war, and in war bad things happen to people, whether they are innocent or not. Nobody is untouched. He felt responsible in some unexplainable way. Guilt welled up inside of him, and his arms started to itch and tingle.

It don't mean nothing, he chanted to himself. *It don't mean nothing*. He tried to focus but couldn't. He needed to find a telephone and get the rest of the story to London. His hands were shaking inside the pockets of his coat. There was a hole in the lining of the right pocket.

Before he realized it, Morley had walked a good five blocks from the scene. The streets were dark. It was late and cold. Thankfully, there was only the damp, briny smell of the night. He could feel the throbbing in his chest and stopped to catch his breath. Across the street, a small cluster of people who had seen enough of the blast site headed back to their homes.

"Are you damaged?"

The question came to Morley from above.

"You appear to be in discomfort."

Disoriented, Morley swiveled his head back and forth, looking for the source of the question. He had been taken by surprise and tried to stammer a response. There was an old woman standing at the top of the stoop behind him.

"Are you all right, young man?"

I am not all right, Morley thought. *I am far from all right.* But the thought was fleeting.

"Do you have a telephone?" Morley asked. "I need to make a collect call to London."

The old woman sized Morley up. What she saw was something disarming in him, something fragile that needed to be tended, something from her past and his future. She motioned for him to come inside. The phone was in the hallway, and he made the call to London and filed the information he had collected. Bette signed him off for the night, and he was free to attempt to get some sleep.

Morley left a pound note under the phone for the old woman's time and stuck his head into the parlor where she was sitting. She had brought in a tray of fresh tea and some stale-looking cookies. The money wasn't going to be enough to get him back to the hotel so soon.

"It's frightfully chilly outside; please sit and have some tea before you go," the old woman said.

Her name was Mrs. Brennan. She had been born in Belfast. Her father had worked in the shipyards, as did her late husband, Oliver. She had no children. She had lived in the row house for most of her life.

She continued with her story as Morley politely sipped his tea. It was the one habit in the country that Morley did not like. Tea. He was raised on coffee. He liked it black and strong enough to eat the paint off the hood of a car.

The old woman had a pleasant voice, and hearing it began to make Morley sleepy. He hadn't followed a thing she said after she recounted the Germans bombing the city during the war; so he decided he should speak up and hopefully cut the visit short so he could get some rest. It was close to 2:00 a.m., and there wouldn't be any taxis. The walk to the hotel would take him at least half an hour.

"So you're a Protestant," Morley blurted out.

The old woman looked startled at first, then sat back in her chair and smiled.

"Oh, I've gone on too long, and you must be tired," she said.

Morley had hurt her feelings and knew he wouldn't be leaving quite as soon as he hoped.

"No, I didn't mean it that way," Morley stumbled through his words. "What I meant, as a Protestant and, well, having seen as much as you have..."

"Now I'm old, too," she teased. "Why do you assume I'm Protestant?"

"Well, you live in the heart of one of the most militant Protestant areas of the city, if not the world," he said.

The old woman let out a breath that had the effect of calming the room and putting Morley at ease.

"It is true that I'm old, but I'm not Protestant. I was born a Catholic and married a Protestant, but I haven't been anything formal for quite some time."

"Agnostic or atheist?" Morley asked, suddenly intrigued by the old woman.

"I'm present," she said. "It is the best one can hope for, especially with what time I have left. Being present lets me enjoy each moment."

"I'm not sure I follow."

"You're young, and it takes some effort."

Morley felt like a rocket just flew over his head. He had studied philosophy at Trinity—enjoyed it and thought he did well at it—but the old woman's words went right past him.

"Which side are you on?" she said.

Morley was flummoxed and processed the question for a moment.

"I'm not on any side."

"What do you mean by that?"

"I'm a reporter, an observer, an unbiased observer," he said. "I'm not supposed to have a side."

The old woman turned her head and smiled in such a way that the light from the small lamp by her chair appeared to tighten her skin and smooth the wrinkles on her face, and Morley could see she had once been a remarkably beautiful young woman.

"That's awfully convenient," she said.

"In what way?"

"In the way that you never have to make a choice. And in never having to make a choice, you don't have to take any responsibility."

The old woman saw the confusion in Morley's face. *The blissful ignorance of youth*, she thought, and changed the subject to the weather. They chatted through another cup of tea, but when Morley's stomach started to growl, as it did with tea, he knew it was time to thank her for her hospitality and excuse himself.

She walked him to the door, and as he turned to say a last "thank you," the old woman reached up to touch one of the small scars on the side of his face.

"Don't count on time to heal everything," she said. "Some wounds you have to treat yourself."

She had taken the pound note from under the phone.

"I want you to have this back," she said, pressing it into his hand. "You paid enough with your company."

Her insistence was firm and not up for debate. From her apron, she pulled a small gold pendant of three interlocking oblong circles attached to a thin chain.

"I want you to have this," she said, wrapping it around the pound note. Morley could see in her eyes that it meant a lot to her for him to have it, and he shouldn't make an attempt to protest accepting the gift.

"What is it?" he asked.

"It's a Trinity knot," she said. "For me it represents earth, fire, and water. I think for you, it will bring eternal love."

She slipped them into Morley's coat pocket, opened the door to the cold night air, and bid him a good morning.

Morley felt lighter, if a little conflicted, as he walked to his hotel. He tried to recount the old woman's words so he would not forget them. He knew they were important, like a lesson in school that he needed to memorize for a test. He also felt a little giddy. It was the longest conversation of any depth that he had had with a woman in a long time. Remembering how her face looked in the light, it was also the longest conversation he had had with a beautiful woman in a very long time.

CHAPTER 5

The *Belfast Telegraph* was, like many newspapers, a place where visiting reporters could squat at an empty desk in the newsroom to work. There were, however, unwritten rules for being a newsroom squatter: the visiting reporter's news organization would pay for any phone calls made, the visiting reporter would pick up the tab for drinks or a meal or two, the visiting reporter didn't stay for more than a few days, and the visiting reporter shared whatever tips he or she might have. Morley and his news agency had an especially cordial working relationship with the paper and its editors and reporters, largely due to Morley's sponsorship of trips to the billiards parlor around the corner for pints and the very generous stringer fees the Dublin bureau paid to several reporters every month.

Rested and feeling gratified with the big scoop from the night before, Morley had come into the *Telegraph*'s newsroom late in the morning and made a few calls, trying to shore up the erroneous Home Office claim regarding the telephone call warning of the bomb. He also tried a few sources with contacts in the IRA, which so far had not taken credit for the attack. Then he headed out with several *Telegraph* reporters to buy them lunch and a pint.

When he returned to the newsroom, Digger was sitting in the managing editor's office. Digger was his effusive self, gesturing with arms and hands while he conversed with the editor behind the glass that walled in the shabby office. The office and the title belonged to a middle-aged man who was a solid newsman but was, unfortunately, stuck with the name George Hacker.

That Digger was up from Dublin wasn't unusual. He and Morley took turns coming north when things heated up. Still, Morley's first reaction was dread. Did he screw something up? Was the Home Office pulling strings to get him sacked? Morley's initial unease subsided quickly, based on his having known Digger for the past two years. He knew the Aussie's body language and habits well; and furthermore, if it were bad news, it would have been delivered in Dublin, in private, and in a pub.

Digger, cigarette in one hand, spotted Morley and gestured with a big wave and smile for him to come into Hacker's office.

"Young Mr. Morley did quite a bang-up job last night," Hacker said.

Digger did what Digger did best; he delivered the hallmark of a senior editor—the backhanded compliment.

"He did indeed, great job mate, they are buzzing about you in London, made the Jakarta papers," Digger said. "But you could have filed that headline a lot sooner if you hadn't been sleeping in, and with an additional source or two as well. And why did that first lead take so long to file? Don't you think so, George?"

Morley rolled his eyes, and the three of them laughed.

"Just yanking on you mate, just yanking on you," said Digger.

Digger's jabs were followed by an awkward silence in the office.

"Well, I'll let the pair of you catch up; I've got a staff meeting," Hacker said, removing himself from the office and shutting the door with a rattle.

Morley bummed a cigarette off of Digger and regretted it the minute he lit up. Digger smoked menthols, and Morley hated menthols, as he thought they masked the flavor of the tobacco. It was like putting cream and sugar in coffee. What was the point, he figured. Vices should be pure and unadulterated.

"So, what's up, boss? We going to tag-team up here for a while?" Morley asked, exhaling the smoke with disgust almost as soon as he had drawn it in.

Digger shifted in his chair uncomfortably, took a long drag off his cigarette, and exhaled as he talked. "Look, mate, there's no best way to say this, so I'm just going to come out and say it," he said. "Got a call from the States last night. From your family. I'm sorry, mate, but your mother passed away."

Digger's delivery was so abrupt it didn't register with Morley right away.

"What?"

"I'm sorry, mate."

Despite the initial shock, Morley felt relief. He hadn't screwed something up. He wasn't being sacked. He took a long drag off the cigarette, held it and slowly exhaled the pressure that had quickly built up in his chest. For the first time, he appreciated the coolness of the menthol. Then he sat on the edge of Hacker's desk, took another pull and let his shoulders slump as he looked at his shoes. He felt like a child. He remembered getting the same news about his father in high school. He remembered the arm from last night. His thoughts began to spiral. He couldn't remember his mother's face or the last time he talked to her on the phone. Was it a week ago, a month ago? Certainly, it wasn't that long ago, was it? Hadn't she said she went to the doctor? Morley couldn't remember. The cigarette made him nauseous.

Digger didn't miss a beat and kept talking. Morley just stared at the floor, smoking a cigarette he didn't like, agreeing to everything his bureau chief said, though he wasn't really listening. It was all arranged. His family had booked a flight for him out of Gatwick that night. The agency was paying for him to take a shuttle from Belfast to make the intercontinental flight. He'd arrive in Chicago, then take another plane home. He would be home by dinner. Home? He hadn't been home in years. Not since the short stay at the VA hospital after Asia. Digger kept on. He would ship anything Morley needed from his flat in Dublin. On and on Digger went, not wanting to stop.

"Emmett, are you all right?" Digger asked, finally stopping, at the risk of allowing an opportunity for emotion.

That Digger called him by his first name woke Morley from his trance. He nodded and extinguished the cigarette.

"Listen to me, mate, the company thinks highly of you," Digger said. "I talked to the America's desk in New York. As coincidence would have it, there's a spot open for a correspondent in Kansas City. They sacked the guy a couple of months ago and haven't been able to fill the position since."

Morley looked Digger square in the eyes and nodded. "Go figure," he said. "Who would want to go to Kansas City?"

"It's a good opportunity to move up," Digger said. "I was going to have to kick you out of here soon, anyway. Get what you need to take care of done, and then check in."

Morley heard everything Digger had to say, but the same thought kept playing in his head like a tune that wouldn't go away, no matter how hard he tried.

I'm an orphan.

Midnight at the Oasis *is playing over and over. Jesus, someone turn that shit off. Is it on reel-to-reel? Christ, I hate that song. Not sending any camels to bed. I'm going to shoot one of them instead.* "Myrla, turn that fucking thing off." *Myrla is passed out on the bed, naked. She looks funny, but good for a Flip hooker. Amerasian. Taller than the indigenous Flips. Prettier. More expensive. Something smells bad. Is it Myrla? Is it Olangapo in March? Rained last night. The streets are a cesspool. My feet are in a puddle of vomit. Mine. The retching starts again. Nothing but bile. Stop after a while. What happened? The Oro, then the Queen Bee, then...? Don't remember. Last memory. Jackson with his non-regulation 'fro, yelling Eldridge Cleaver shit at some white swabs. Then the Shore Patrol. Beat it up Fields Drive. Oh yeah. Celebrating getting Lance Coconut promotion. Some paper-pushing fuck screwed up. E-fucking-3. More pay. We're flopping at Myrla's place above the Paddlewheel. That goddamned song is still bleating away. Has to be coming from the Paddle jukebox. Shit, stop it. Knock over empty bottles of San Miguel. The floor is sticky with beer and puke. Stumble across the room to get to the pipe on the table, and a rubber gets stuck between my toes. The smoke from the pipe curls into the room; its sweet smell wakes Myrla. Hear the beaded curtain make noise like cymbals. Myrla is making noise in the other room. Peeing in a bowl. Throws it out the window. The pipe helps. Head not hurting as much anymore. The tightness coming, then the deep breath, then the exhale. Better. The world slowly swirls instead of spins. Myrla floats down on the couch and purrs.* "You love me, Mowley?" "All time, baby." *Nod off. Been in Subic for months. Nothing to do but get fucked up, polish boots, and buy stereo equipment at the PX. Nod off some more. Floating. Breathing. Drifting.* My Soul on Ice. *The music gets louder and louder. The clouds are thinning. Louder. Clearer. Back in basics. Screaming. Meat on a bone.* Wake up! *I wake up. Jackson?* "Get up, you piece-of-shit honky!" "What the fuck, man? What the fuck are you doing, man?" *It's definitely Jackson, but the 'fro is gone. Head clean shaved like a black Mr. Clean. He's in his greens.* "What the fuck happened to you?" "Shut up, asshole, and get up." "Fuck you, why?" "We got to get back to the barracks, and you got to suit up." "Again, why?" "We got PCS." *No idea what the hell he's talking about.* "Permanent Change of Station, you dumb cousin-fucking cracker." *Still no clue.* "Combat, motherfucker! We got three hours to square shit away, and then we jump." *Pedi cab back to the base. Lean out and puke some more. Drink water. Drink coffee. Green as my fatigues. Squared away. The Dragon strapped to my back. Hog's tooth swinging like a big dick outside my flak jacket. PCS papers in hand. Getting it up. Motherfucking lean, mean, baby killing machines. Recon Marines. Find 'em, kill 'em, eat 'em. Play with the Ka-Bar. Wait on the tarmac. Jackson is reading Malcolm X. Three hours, four hours, five hours. Drones on. Eat LRPs. More water. Piss. Think of Myrla. She's probably fucking the camel by now. The air starts to vibrate. Hear it in the distance. Closer and closer. Chop, chop, chop. Big motherfucking Sea Stallion. Impressive. How do they fly? We hit the ramp like ants crawling up an elephant's back leg with rape on their minds. We're clean. Up in the air where it's cool. The infantryman's air conditioning. The humps all fall asleep.*

CHAPTER 6

The chimes of the grandfather clock in the living room worked their way through the house. Morley thought it was a hollow, lonely sound. He lay in his bed, looking at the ceiling, counting the hour gongs and hoping they would reach a number that would mark a decent night's sleep. A fourth chime sounded, and Morley willed a fifth, but he was disappointed. He rolled over on his side and sighed. He couldn't remember the last good night's sleep he'd had. Years, he thought. He recounted the dream the clock had woken him from and tried to calculate in his head how long it had been since the Philippines. Exhaustion made him work hard to do the math, despite its simplicity. Five years. In the measurement of a life, not that much time had passed. He felt old, but he was not old. He rolled over on his back again and stared at the patch of light, coming from the streetlight outside, that reflected on the ceiling above the bed. The pattern reminded him of high school geometry, and he tried to remember the name of the shapes floating above him. At first he concentrated on the patches of light and the geometrical names of their abstracted shapes, but after a while, his attention drifted toward the borders of the light made by the shadows from the panes of the window. They looked like prison bars to him.

For at least the next hour, the house would be free of sounds, aside from any he might make. He listened to his breathing. First he breathed heavily through his nose, but it agitated him. Then he tried breathing deeply and slowly through his mouth, listening for his heartbeat. The more he concentrated, the more uncomfortable he became. The room seemed to close in on him; the air rushing in and out of him became labored, and the pace of his breathing increased. A wave of nausea washed over him. Feeling like he would throw up and any moment, he jumped out of bed and ran to the bathroom.

The few steps it took to get to the toilet seemed to settle him. He took a deep breath in the darkness of the bathroom and felt better, though the blood still pounded in his temples. The knot that had worked its way to his throat retreated back to his stomach. In the ambient light, he looked at himself in the mirror. In the reflection he saw himself as a boy, the same boy who used to look in the same mirror for hours and wonder what he would look like when he was older. In the span of a life, he thought to himself again, reflecting on his reflection, not much time had passed at all. Yet, what time had passed had taken with it Morley's familiarity. Things survived. People generally didn't.

What was not unfamiliar to Morley was aloneness. Still, being by himself in the house he grew up in was uncomfortable, perhaps even a little terrifying. He continued to look at his reflection until he realized he wouldn't be able to get back to sleep. It was probably the jet lag, he thought.

Morley put on some jeans and a t-shirt and fumbled through his suitcase for a clean pair of socks. He had been home almost a week and had yet to put his clothes into the dresser.

When he stood up and turned toward the window to look outside, everything was white. It was snowing very hard and had been for most of the night. He could see how the thick blanket had softened everything it covered. The harsh shapes of nature and man were obscured, their original forms now rounded and exaggerated by the powdery accumulation. Color disappeared, leaving only the subtle contrasts of darkness and light and hues of grey. The only illumination came from the streetlights, which had icicles forming around their glass casings. The snowstorm muffled sounds, as if, he thought, a layer of insulation had been put down—or a bedsheet drawn over a face.

The house was a large white Colonial with black shutters; it sat on a corner lot. The front of the house faced west, toward the Great Park. In its time, the park had been the site of a Civil War battle, a private country club with a golf course, and, more recently, an international art event that involved covering the walkways with lustrous apricot-colored cloth for several weeks.

Morley's grandfather had built the house, one of the first of the Country Club development; and when he died, Morley's parents bought it from the estate. Morley remembered moving in when he was seven years old and being assigned the back bedroom. It was situated above the garage, which was built into the house and led into the kitchen. There were four bedrooms on the second floor and three more rooms on the third floor that were used as storage and as a playroom for Morley and his friends when he was younger. It was a lot of house for a little family. Morley's bedroom was the farthest away from the master suite, where his parents slept in separate twin beds.

Solidly awake now, Morley decided to go downstairs and start a pot of coffee. He made his way down the long hallway, leading from his back bedroom past two more bedrooms to the elaborately spindled main staircase. The décor and furnishings triggered in him a feeling that he was visiting a museum and not merely walking through his own home.

He stopped to admire the three Thomas Hart Benton prints, signed and numbered by the artist. His family knew Benton, who had even been to the house for dinner once. Past the second empty bedroom, toward the front of the house, was a pair of lithographs of old peasant women. Morley's parents had bought the lithographs on a trip to Germany. They hung on the wall outside the bedroom that led to the landing before you descended to the foyer and the large Persian rug that covered the floor.

Instead of going downstairs, he pushed open the door to the master suite and entered the large sitting room that led to the sleeping room behind it. It was the first time he had been in the room since arriving from Ireland. He felt like a spirit hovering above the floor, quietly and discreetly observing everything in the room but not stopping to touch anything. Some of his mother's belongings he recognized, and others he didn't. The two sitting chairs had been reupholstered in bright chintz during his absence. In the corner, facing a crucifix, was a *prie dieu* with a small but elaborately decorated Bible perched where one's elbows would rest during prayer.

Situated throughout the room were a good half dozen rosaries she had collected on her pilgrimages. It was the private quarters of someone devoted to her religion. It was a religion she had lived with her entire life, but only embraced with a quiet fervor after the death of Morley's father.

She was a good woman, Morley thought; a little distant, but capable of compassion and empathy when called upon. His father was emotionally absent, and Morley wondered if his mother had become more distant as his father drifted farther away. Morley guessed that her life did not turn out the way she had wanted. Within a two-year span, she lost both her husband—who had drifted away from her long before committing suicide—and her only son, when he shipped off to the Marines. Morley had returned home only once before her death, and then only briefly, to recover from his wounds at the local VA hospital. Even though he was ambulatory and his injuries superficial, Morley refused to stay at home out of embarrassment. His face, arms, and upper legs were fully bandaged, making him look like a mummy. From a practical standpoint, he told her at the time, there were too many dressings to change, and he didn't want to bleed all over the house. There had been a gulf between them since his father's death, a death that Morley had partly blamed on her when he was younger. And now, that gulf was permanent.

On a stand next to the sink in her bathroom was a collection of small fragrance bottles. The bathroom smelled dry and powdery, the way old ladies smell. She *was* an old lady, he remembered. He hadn't been born until she was almost forty. He was a miracle of sorts. Her miracle, she would say.

Morley held one of the perfume bottles between his fingers. It was a delicate object, long and thin, slightly bluish, and made by a renowned French glass company. He gently lifted the cap off the bottle, and his mind was instantly filled with a thousand electric flower petals. Looking out the bathroom window to the backyard, he could see his mother in her summer dress, delicately balancing a silver tray in one hand and a cocktail in the other as she navigated the clusters of guests, offering them appetizers with a smile.

He blinked, and she was sitting on one of the green-and-white-striped chases, smoking a cigarette held elegantly between two fingers. With her free hand, she patted Morley on the head and then cupped his chin and squeezed.

"Oh, my little darling, you are so strong and handsome," she said.

Morley dropped the perfume bottle, and it fell to the bathroom floor and broke into several pieces. The fragrance overtook the room, and his chest began to tighten; he couldn't catch his breath and started to panic.

He began to hyperventilate, and the confined space of the bathroom made it worse.

"I've got to get out of here," he said to himself.

He almost fell, coming down the main stairs to the foyer, but grabbed the railing for support with one hand while still clutching his chest with the other.

The house was closing in on him. He felt like the floors above had started to press down, and he would be squeezed into the Persian rug. His mind began to cycle. He didn't want to bleed all over the house if he were crushed on the rug. He thought of helicopter blades, swirling and chopping through the air, chopping through him. In the living room, there were a number of crucifixes hung on the wall that looked like blades. Then he thought of the homily the priest gave at her funeral Mass. How devout a woman Grace Morley was, and how generous her spirit. The priest recounted her generosity. She had taken him on pilgrimages to Lourdes and Madjugorje. Morley kept playing the homily over and over in his head, how the priest went on and on about the trips, but not once did he mention Morley or his father. Why didn't he mention them? Did she never talk about them? Did she hate them for going away? Did she not leave Morley behind? Was he not the surviving son?

He rummaged through the back of the large hall coat closet and found his old pair of snow boots. He jammed his feet into them before grabbing his heavy overcoat.

A voice in his head kept telling him, *get out, get out, get out!*

It was quiet outside. The voice stopped, and Morley could feel the cold spark of snowflakes as they pelted his face. The frigid air neutralized all sense of smell. He took a deep breath, exhaled it into a frosty cloud, and felt much calmer.

He stood for a moment under the half rotunda of the portico, which sheltered the front door. Before him was untracked snow for as far as he could see, which was only to the western boundary of the park.

Morley had no plan. Then he heard a whisper. The voice. *Get away.* Quietly, and without desperation, it spoke to him. *Start walking,* it told him gently. Morley had no plan, but he started walking. The depth of the snow reached to just below the tops of his boots, so he pulled his pant legs over them. He crossed the street and climbed the small berm that led up into the park. He turned around to see the tracks he had just made. The street had not been plowed, and his trail led, unbroken, straight back to the house. The snow was falling at a slight angle in the arc of light from the streetlight. The icicles were longer. He turned back toward the darkness of the park and kept walking.

As heavy as the weather was, there was little wind. The snow, the trees, the air, all of it was harmonious, he thought. He had walked, and the voice had stopped. Away from the harsh streetlights and well into the wide, sloping meadow of the park, the low clouds filtered all man-made light into a more natural illumination, subdued and contemplative.

It would be a beautiful death, Morley thought. All he would have to do is sit down and close his eyes. He could sleep a long sleep. One that he had not had for as far back as he could remember. Around him was darkness and light, beauty and death. Inside him was conflict and contradiction.

He looked around to get his bearings, turning in each direction. He was just north of the top of the meadow where he remembered the Confederate artillery had been positioned during the battle. West of him was the flat depression where a clubhouse once stood, and to the north was the warm glow from the shopping district that lay below the three tall apartment buildings. To the east were the tracks he had just made, which had now begun to disappear. He could make out the three dormers, jutting from the roof like a trinity, watching him.

He looked at his feet planted in the snow and then looked up at the sky. The snow peppered his face and began to fill his eyes, and a tightness formed in his throat.

He took in a tentative breath, hesitating at first as if he were underwater and could no longer hold his breath; then, without warning, he began to shake violently. He tried to fight it at first but surrendered quickly. First the tears came, then the sobs and soft wailing. He felt weak. Slowly he dropped to his knees and slumped into a sitting position.

In incoherent bursts, he looked up and cried, "I'm sorry, I'm sorry."

CHAPTER 7

Morley picked up the ringing phone in the kitchen.

"Em?"

Nobody had called him by that name in some time, and he wasn't sure who it was or how to react.

"Hey, asshole, it's Billy."

"What the fuck do you want?"

"Let's have some fun."

It was always Em, Billy, and Leo, from grade school up through Stonefield and into the Marine Corps. The three of them were inseparable. In grade school, the Monsignor often referred to them as the Father, the Son, and the Holy Terror. While Morley was the conscience of the three, and Leo was the most fearless, Billy was the charmer. He had good looks that made nature jealous. He was darkly handsome, with a demeanor that instantly made you put down your guard. Even Grace Morley thought Billy to be one of the most beautiful boys she had ever seen and always paid him the most attention when he and Leo were at her home. Men wanted to hang out with him; women wanted him inside them. Always the raconteur, Billy liked to party and could come across as frivolous and irresponsible, but when it was time to step up, Billy was the first guy in line to take a punch and the last guy to get stitched up.

The O'Connors lived two blocks—but several income brackets—away from the Morleys. There were eight O'Connor children, of which Billy was the oldest, packed into the small house on Wyandotte. His father was a district sales representative for a construction supply business, and his mother was a registered nurse. Financially, they only scraped by, but they always managed to keep a roof over their heads and their kids in private Catholic schools.

Ten minutes later, Billy was knocking on the back door, just as he did whenever he came by to collect Morley for whatever function or mischief they were up to.

Inside, they surveyed each other for the first time in several years. In ritual succession they shook hands, slipped into a soul handshake, hooked their fingers together like railcars, pounded their fists on top of each other's in turn, gave each other five, and held up their clenched fists.

"G.H.M.F.," said Billy.

"Don't mean nothing," Morley replied.

Billy sat in one of the chintz chairs Morley had moved from his mother's bedroom into his own and stirred the milk and sugar in his coffee mug.

"You're such a pussy, man. Why don't you just drink chocolate milk, instead of trying to make coffee taste like it?" Morley teased, as he moved several stereo equipment boxes around the room.

"I'm sorry about your mom, Em."

Morley looked at Billy and shrugged, acknowledging the condolence before opening one of the boxes with the pocketknife he found in the top drawer of his dresser.

Billy pulled a pack of Marlboros from the top pocket of his blue oxford-cloth, button-down shirt and clicked alive a flame on a red disposable lighter.

"Is it okay if I smoke?"

"Go ahead," Morley said. "It's not like we're going to get in trouble with anyone."

"Want one?"

Morley declined. Even though Billy didn't smoke menthols, Morley thought all cigarettes would forever taste like menthol. He wanted to quit anyway.

"I would have been there, man, but I had that interview in San Francisco," Billy said, and exhaled a cloud of blue smoke around him. "I really feel shitty about it."

"Don't," Morley said. "The priest was a boring asshole. Besides, I saw your folks at the wake anyway, and they told me."

"Oh yeah? They didn't say anything to me."

"So, Berkley, huh?"

"Yeah."

"What made you think of law school?" Morley asked.

"Women."

"Women?"

"They like prestige."

"Well, that figures," Morley said. "Here, give me a hand."

The two of them moved the coffee table that had been in the living room, situating it against the far wall near the bathroom and opposite the pair of sitting chairs. Morley pulled the stereo receiver and amplifier from its box, placed it in the center of the table, and began connecting cables from the two large speakers on each side.

"Where did you get all this shit?" Billy asked.

"PX, Subic," said Morley as he cut and spliced the plastic off the ends of the speaker cable.

"And you're just now opening them?"

"I'd completely forgotten about them," Morley said. "Bought the stuff and had it shipped back here. It was right before...."

"Don't mean nothing," Billy said, taking another pull off the cigarette. "You've got some good shit. Teac, Pioneer, Sony, Kenwood. How many watts a channel does that put out?"

"One hundred and twenty-five mind-blowing, skull-fucking, brain-melting watts," Morley said, remembering exactly how Jackson had said it when they were in the PX together. Then he wondered whatever happened to Jackson.

"Don't mean nothing," Morley said to himself.

Morley hooked up the cassette deck, the reel-to-reel and the turntable.

"Now all you need is a TV, and you have a real stoner's paradise," Billy said. "And this."

Billy reached into the pocket of the parka draped over the back of his chair and tossed a leather pouch used to keep pipe tobacco fresh. Inside was a small, elaborately enameled pipe and, wrapped in plastic, roughly two ounces of blonde Lebanese hashish.

"Like I said, Em, let's have some fun."

CHAPTER 8

The cacophony of clocks and alarms from the opening of Pink Floyd's "Time" startled Morley from his hash stupor, and with more effort than it should have taken him, he got up from the chair and turned the volume down on the stereo. Billy was asleep. Morley went to the window to open it and air out the smell of stale tobacco mingled with the sweet hashish pall from the room. Morley felt like it permeated every pore in his body and every fiber in the room. The odor and residual high triggered paranoia in him. He had not been stoned in some time, at least not without a strong base of alcohol to mask the effect, and he remembered the twitchy paranoia as the reason for quitting in the first place. Any minute, he joked to himself, the black helicopters would swoop down and police SWAT teams would surround the house. "No more of this at the house," he muttered to Billy, who woke from his own stupor at the sound of the window opening and was squirting eye drops all over his face.

Morley glanced around outside. Relatives continued to drop by unannounced, usually with casseroles in hand, under the guise of checking on him but really mostly to see when the appropriate time would be to start scavenging a lifetime of someone else's belongings, including the house itself. In the receiving line at the wake, in front of his mother's open casket, the wife of one distant cousin rudely broached the idea of buying the house "at a fair price."

Out the window, Morley could see what snow was left from the storm two days ago. The sun burned with an intensity he attributed to the hashish, and he squinted at the glare coming off the streets wet from the melt-off.

"Got anything to eat around here?" Billy blurted out, tears running down his face like a circus clown.

"You know, the idea of eye drops is to put them *in* your eyes."

"Yeah, fuck you," Billy said, wiping his face with his sleeve and offering the bottle to Morley. "Here, your eyes look like road maps."

Morley squirted a few drops in each eye and felt the burning sensation.

"There's a ton of food left in the fridge, but I'm sick of it. I'm sick of this place; let's go somewhere," he said.

Billy sat up, grinned his charming Cheshire cat grin, slapped his hands together, and spoke as if making a proclamation to the world.

"We shall go to Our Lady of Burnt Ends."

"Outstanding, Marine," replied Morley, with enthusiasm.

It took both of them to back the Oldsmobile Ninety-Eight out of the narrow garage, partly because they were both still a little stoned and partly because the beast of a vehicle barely fit into the space. Billy gave a thumbs-up when Morley cleared the door and ran around to jump into the front passenger's seat.

Morley had decided in those hours with Billy that he would sell the house when the estate cleared, but that he would hold on to the Ninety-Eight. It was a big old-lady car, what Billy called the White Man's Cadillac, but it was luxurious, and Morley knew he would need a good highway car if he was to be responsible for covering the Plains for the news agency. The land yacht would be reliable and comfortable to navigate. Like everything in his mother's life, except Morley himself, it had been meticulously preserved and cared for.

Morley paged through the afternoon *Star* while they waited for their orders to be delivered. They sat in the back booth with the rough, wood-covered walls and kitschy cowboy themed artwork and memorabilia. It was the same booth they frequented when they went to Catholic grade school just down the street, which is how the barbecue joint got its unofficial name. Instead of going to Mass on Saturday afternoons, he and Billy and Leo, and occasional followers, would instead hang out at the restaurant. It became such a habit that in eighth grade they skipped an all-school service to have a late lunch. When called before the Monsignor and asked where they had been, Leo said without hesitation that they decided to attend "Our Lady of Burnt Ends" for communion with the barbecue gods. Tired of having dealt with the three of them for nearly a decade, the Monsignor only rubbed his eyes, waved the trio away from his office, and said, "Maybe the Jesuits will do better with the three of you next year."

"Hey, I need to get a TV," Morley said, looking at the Jones Store ad in the newspaper. "Family-sized, Sony Trinitron Color, 19-inch, on sale for $579.95."

Billy made a rattling, slurping sound as his straw searched the bottom of the large, ice-filled Styrofoam cup for the last drops of pop.

"Damn, that's a big picture," he said. "Why do you need a big TV like that?"

"Work—and they're going to pay for cable, too," Morley said. "I've got to stay on top of things, like reading the papers. It's been two weeks, and I feel disconnected from the world. Besides, you know the wire service motto?"

"No, I don't know the wire service motto," Billy said, holding his cup up to the waitress for a refill. "Why would I know that?"

"No story is too heavy to lift," said Morley.

Morley continued to scan the newspaper as Billy worked on a second cup of pop. He looked for stories that he would need to know about for the financial and commodities-related side of being the new correspondent in town. There was an analysis of the Federal Reserve raising the discount rate a full percentage point to push the interest rate it charged to banks to 13 percent, as part of a strategy to ease inflation fears. As a result, the Dow Jones Industrial Average fell more than ten points in the first hour of trading after the move. Morley contemplated reaching out to the local Fed Bank for an interview with the president and also how to start linking outside influences into his coverage of the local Board of Trade.

He read about longtime CBS anchor and former Kansas City native Walter Cronkite's announcement that he would step down early next year and be replaced by Dan Rather.

A local attorney named Albert Riederer was running for Jackson County prosecutor. At a recent fundraiser for Riederer, the Jackson County executive made headlines for playing a saxophone for the crowd. "Politicians playing saxophone," Morley said aloud. "What is the world coming to?

"Hey, Billy, you'll like this," he said suddenly. "Penthouse filed suit against Eastman Kodak, saying it had no right to withhold 299 slides of Penthouse Pet Cheryl Rison. Says the company fears it would break obscenity laws if it returned the nude photos."

"Now that's the kind of law I'm interested in," Billy replied. "They have any pictures with the article?"

Morley scanned through the political section of the newspaper. It was a presidential election year, and the primaries were underway. The GOP hopeful appeared to be the governor of California, though there was a building controversy over one of his aides that could unravel his run for the White House.

"What do you think of Reagan?" Morley asked.

"Other than the line about him on the Woodstock album, not much," Billy said. "Old fucker, isn't he? I remember when I cycled through Pendleton right before my discharge; they all loved him on the base."

"Hey, catch me up on that," Morley said. "What happened? Mom was always vague in her letters or over the phone, and the whole Marine thing never set well with her. Fill me in."

"Funny," Billy said. "We all know what happened to you. You kind of checked out."

"Sorry," Morley said.

Their plates arrived. Two orders of burnt ends, Texas toast, pickles, beans, and sweet potato fries. Morley slathered the sweet and spicy sauce over the meat. The taste was what heaven would be like, he thought; hickory smoke flavor, crispy and crunchy on the tips, rich and moist in the middle, the meat warm and dripping with fat that tasted like butter.

Between large bites, and without looking up from their plates, Billy recounted his time in the Marines. As a radioman, he had been stationed on an amphibious landing ship in the South China Sea that participated in the evacuation of Saigon. Several weeks later, on his way down to the galley to get a cup of coffee, he slipped on the gangway and injured his back. The war was over, the drawdown of the military had begun, and he was offered an honorable discharge. He took the option and the GI Bill—which he liked to call the GI Billy Bill—went to college; graduated the previous May; and knocked around for a few months before deciding to apply for law school, which, he said, would start in late August.

"Why Berkley?" Morley asked.

"It's far the fuck away from here, and the East Coast schools were just way snobby for me."

To pick up some money before he left, Billy said he was now working with the men's clothier, Brooks Brothers, which would be opening its first store in Kansas City later in the summer. It was to be located in the old grocery store on the Plaza. Billy was helping them through the construction, inventory, and sales training, with the understanding that it was temporary. If Morley wanted, Billy could get him a discount on clothes.

Billy talked about his brothers and sisters, former classmates, girls, and, finally, about fishing.

"We should do some, you know," he said. "Have you done much?"

"Some, on holiday in southern Ireland, up the Kenmare River," Morley said. "All fly. I even picked up a few tricks. There is some good trout fishing in Ireland."

The two of them talked about the merits of different flies in different conditions and about the road trips they had taken together in high school to southern Missouri and Arkansas for fishing. It was agreed between them that they would take a trip to Colorado in the summer, once Morley had settled into work and before Billy left for California.

"What about Leo?"

Billy laid out Leo's story for Morley. Following basics, right out of infantry school, Leo was stationed at Pearl Harbor. It was all fun and games for Leo, up until the night he and a Marine officer drank too much at a local bar and decided to take on the entire crew of an aircraft carrier that had come to port after a six-month sea tour. Leo, who would never have been accused of being good-looking prior to the Hawaiian melee, had his face rearranged with a broken beer bottle. It took over two hundred stitches to put everything back together. The officer wasn't as lucky. He died two weeks later of severe head trauma. Despite the incident, at the formal hearing that followed, the Corps was impressed by Leo's dogged protection of the injured, unconscious officer until the Shore Patrol arrived. He even fought with the SPs to ride with his fellow Marine in the same ambulance. The vision of Leo, blood everywhere, his face hanging in shards, and his unwavering loyalty didn't surprise Morley in the least.

Leo was allowed to stay in the Corps; and after his enlistment was up, he returned home to help manage the family business. This was a small manufacturing company on the West Side that made metal hangers, which

Billy referred to as white trash abortion kits. Leo had been out of town buying wire from distributors and missed the funeral. Billy said Leo felt awful and a little timid about contacting Morley with his condolences.

"That's bullshit," Morley said. "Let's the three of us get together when I get back from Chicago."

"Chicago, what's going on up there?"

"I have training to learn how to write about wheat. I leave Monday for a few days."

"Good. Leo will be happy," Billy said. "This is good. Hell, it's going to be great. It's been a long time."

"Yeah," Morley said. "Seems like a lifetime of long time."

The two of them worked at the remains of food on their plates. Morley savored the barbecue he had not had for several years, but there was an awkward silence between him and Billy. There was the subject Billy didn't mention, and it felt to Morley that he was the one who would have to pick at the scab.

"What about Rhodes?" Morley asked abruptly.

Billy didn't look up from his plate as he sopped the last of his sweet potato fries in sauce.

"He's around," Billy said, looking up at Morley. "It's a small town, Em; you'll run into him eventually. Probably sooner than you want."

CHAPTER 9

There was a lot to like about the office suite. It was located on the third floor of the Kansas City Board of Trade Building, which was a short commute from the house. It had all the latest technology and tools Morley needed and an on-site technician to support them. It was across from the library, which made research easier. It was, essentially, part of the Plaza, which expanded the eating and drinking possibilities for meetings with sources. But what Morley liked best was that it was secure and private. A single, heavy mahogany door, bearing a brass placard bearing the agency's name, opened to a narrow hallway inside the suite. The first office along the interior hallway was assigned to a sales person who didn't exist. The second office belonged to the technician, a former AT&T guy named Hobart, who was almost never around and tended to work from his van when a service call came in. The last office was Morley's. There was no buzzer at the door, and with his office being the farthest away, it was impossible for any visitor to discern if Morley was in or not. Shutting the door to his personal office offered an additional level of privacy and silence. Because the suite was the local communications hub for the agency—the large bank of telecommunications equipment whirred away in Hobart's office—the front door was always locked. There was complete privacy, and that pleased him.

The Chicago trip had gone well. They were good people in that bureau, he felt. Very helpful, and also grateful that someone had taken the position in Kansas City, because it took a burden off the commodities desk. He had been indoctrinated to the mayhem and excitement of the Chicago trading floor, which made the Kansas City market look like a subdued gentleman's club. Morley had the parameters and deadlines he needed to make each day for his dispatches. Preopening comments had to be filed before 9:00 a.m., then another comment as soon after the opening bell as possible. A midday comment, if trading volume warranted it, should be filed by 11:00 a.m., and the closing bell comment would wrap up the trading day. To that he would add a comment about trading activity at the Minneapolis Grain Exchange, which required a single phone call. On a typical day, Morley would be done with the markets by 1:45 p.m., which left him ample time to work on news and feature stories.

It was evident to Morley why the previous correspondent had been sacked. The sales office was a repository of personal refuse. Dirty clothes were scattered about, and there was a scent of stale sweat and body odor that reminded Morley of taco meat. A hot plate and a toaster oven sat atop the large desk. The coffee maker was on the floor. A film of mold grew on the top of the dark liquid that Morley figured had been there for several months. Behind the desk, up against the window, was an old army cot and a dirty blanket.

As Morley had been told in Chicago, the previous correspondent was known for drinking—a lot. After being evicted from his apartment, Morley's predecessor decided to make a home in the bureau. How long he had lived in the office was still up for question, but his office domesticity ended when the building janitor found him attempting to bathe in the mop drain area of the service closet down the hall. The president of the Board of Trade immediately revoked his press pass and made a call to Chicago. It was part of a chain of events that had begun with the correspondent arguing with floor traders, with one incident resulting in punches being exchanged during a trading session, and ended with the locks being changed and the man being sacked. His belongings were unclaimed.

Morley made a note to get some plastic trash bags from the janitor and dispose of everything and to see if they could shampoo the rug to get the odor out.

The correspondent's office was laid out as he had been told it would be by Hobart when they talked over the phone. There was a desk by the window with plenty of room to take notes over the phone. On top of a small extension table, which formed an L with the desk, was the Monitor, a cream-colored box with a screen and keyboard. It was one of the new computers, directly wired into the agency's systems, from which he could write, save on floppy discs, and send market comments and stories. He also could send direct messages to other bureaus.

While he could send interoffice messages on the computer, reading them still had to be done on one of three machines that had to be constantly fed by rolls of paper that fit into brackets located at the back. The machines were lined up on a table on the wall behind his desk. One was the message wire, which printed out communications between bureaus; the second, the commodities wire that carried commodities coverage for the Americas; and the third, the international A-wire for breaking news and important feature pieces. The machines had been turned back on for almost a week and had flooded the floor of the office with a cascade of paper before the rolls ran out. Morley pushed the sea of pulp aside with his feet, pulled three new rolls from an open box on the floor, and reset the machines, which immediately started clicking at a high speed and spitting out more paper. The international wire machine needed a new ribbon, but Morley decided it could wait until he got the mess cleaned up and finished his inventory.

A note from Hobart was on the desk, outlining what each machine was set to deliver, where the key to the downstairs mailbox was, and, if Morley wanted to make changes to the news feeds, the number where Hobart could be reached. In most cases, the changes could be done remotely, without Hobart coming into the office.

Four clocks hung on the wall opposite the window, giving the time in London, New York, Chicago, and Tokyo. Beneath them was a chair full of back issues of *The Wall Street Journal, The New York Times, Milling & Baking News,* and various other news and commodities trade publications. A perk of the job, and of the bureau being located in a building of commerce, was that the *Journal* was delivered every morning. The *Times* came a day later via overnight air courier from Chicago. It had to be horribly expensive, Morley thought, but that he was among the exclusive few in the city that could read the *Times* on a daily basis within twenty-four hours of its publication made him feel important and above the crowd.

A press badge with Morley's name also sat on the table. He had about a half hour before he needed to file a preopening comment. He clipped the badge on the lapel of his jacket and took the elevator down two floors to the trading pits. Morley already had a list of traders whose names could be used for quotes, and he went around the phone-covered tables that surrounded the mostly empty trading floor and introduced himself. He collected preopening comments and price ranges for the day, which were given with humorous side comments about fighting, drinking, and bathing in the building, as well as promises of lunches and after-work drinks.

There was a glitch with the computer terminal in his office that prevented Morley from filing via the system. He called Hobart and left a message with the answering service, then called Chicago and dictated the preopening comments and told them he'd do the same with the opening comment until the technical issue was resolved. An hour later, the market opened slightly higher, due to support from commercial buyers and rumors of a grain deal with the Japanese. With the opening comment on the wire, Morley had very little to do until the midsession comment and the close. He sorted through the papers and the mail in no particular order and with no urgency.

At midsession, there was little activity on the floor, and contract prices remained unchanged. The Chicago desk passed on taking a comment, and Morley said he would get some lunch and check in when he returned to the office.

Standing outside the basement entrance on the north side of the Board of Trade building, where the Buttonwood restaurant and a barbershop were situated, Morley looked up at a slate gray sky of low, fast-moving clouds. The air carried an expectation of late-February snow flurries. Uncertain where he would eat, Morley began walking down the small hill and across the bridge that spanned Brush Creek and opened into the Country Club Plaza shopping district.

Digger had sent what clothes Morley had in his flat in Dublin. When they arrived, Morley was surprised at what little he had in the way of a wardrobe. Most Irish had very little, and wearing the same clothes almost every day was commonplace. But this was America. He needed to dress up more often to cover the wheat market. He also would be interviewing regional newsmakers and executives at *Fortune* 500 companies. Also, ties were required on the trading room floor, and currently, Morley only owned one tie, a regimental design he bought in London on a weekend holiday. He resolved to stop by Woolf Brothers before deciding where to eat lunch and pick up some shirts and ties. With his salary, no rent or car payments, and the fact that he would soon inherit a comfortable amount of money, even before selling the house, he gave himself permission to splurge a little on new clothes.

A half hour later, he stood on the corner of Nichols Road with a shopping bag of four new button-down shirts and five silk ties—one for each day of the week. It was a start. Still, the cost was more than what he thought he should spend; and he resolved to take Billy up on his offer of getting a discount at the Brooks Brothers store, which was under renovation just down the street.

Feeling accomplished and a little gratified, as shopping can make one feel, Morley looked up at the sky again, and a single snowflake fell and melted on his nose. With it came the smell of meat being roasted. The crisp air carried it from the German restaurant on the corner of the parking lot across the street from the men's store, and Morley instantly knew where he would have lunch. He crossed the street and walked past the fountain of a cherub who, in warmer months, would urinate into a seashell and collect loose change for a local charity.

The special of the day was sauerbraten, which he ordered with a Beck's. The lunch crowd was small; it was Monday, and it was winter. Still, Morley thought, a cold winter day was perfect for German cuisine. His plate came with sides of spaetzle, red cabbage, potato salad, and dark bread. It was more than he normally ate in a day, and he let go of the idea of ordering a slice of Black Forest torte in the dessert case.

The snow flurries had picked up their pace while he ate, and a small wind whipped and swirled them around the sidewalks and streets like small tornados. The temperature had dropped another five or ten degrees, harboring the chance for another big snow. Morley pulled up the collar on his jacket and stuffed one hand in the deep pocket. He had left his gloves in the bureau and now had to have one hand exposed to the chill in order to carry the shopping bag.

Walking down Nichols Road back toward the office, he smelled popcorn from the confectioner's shop, which brought back memories of grade-school carnivals, riding the Rock-O-Plane, and the carnies. A gust of wind blew a small cloud of snow into his face, stinging his eyes momentarily as he forced them shut. When the discomfort passed, he opened his eyes to springtime.

Disoriented at first from the tears running down his face from the cold, Morley squinted as if to clear the apparition from his sight. But it was still there. A very warm, almost severe light beaconed from one of the large display windows of Herons, an exclusive women's clothier. In stark contrast to the weather outside, bright colors exploded from the window: a carpet of lush, green grass; yellows and pinks from large paper flowers; and pastels of Easter eggs and elaborately decorated rabbits framed several well-dressed women wearing large straw hats. Two of the women flanked a third who sat on a swing suspended from the ceiling, the ropes obscured by large, impressionist clouds made from poster board cutouts. There was a fourth woman in the window—a live one.

Morley felt as if the street had suddenly been put on a steep incline that propelled him closer to the apparition before him. It took effort not to run toward the window, but he hesitated, feeling as if he had been seen. Suddenly shy, he stopped abruptly as if to admire the movie poster framed in the movie theater, announcing *The Jerk*, starring Steve Martin.

After a moment, and feeling like a jerk, he snuck a peek back at the storefront and realized he had not been spotted. In fact, the woman in the window appeared engrossed in her work and was oblivious to the world beyond the glass that encased her.

"The great Marine sniper, indeed," Morley said aloud, to no one but himself. "Can't even sneak up on an attractive woman."

Emboldened by the woman's lack of attention to what was going on outside and his obvious anonymity, Morley crossed the street in front of the entrance to the movie theater, walking toward the small courtyard and fountain nestled beneath the prominent bell tower that rose from the corner of Herons.

Morley absorbed every detail of the young woman as if sizing up wind direction, elevation, and air temperature at the firing range. She was tall and thin, with exquisitely shaped legs that led down to what his mother, he recalled, would describe as a "well-turned ankle." She wore brown patterned hose, a light brown tweed pencil skirt, brown leather heels that had laces in front, and a silk hunter green blouse that accentuated arms that had been carved from alabaster. Even in Ireland he had never seen skin so white and translucent. The blouse, though it set off her skin, presented an even more striking and complimentary contrast to her hair, which was an auburn color that had a luster and depth in which a man could lose his soul.

52

She kept her hair shoulder blade length. It was pulled back in a French braid to the left side of her head, with a hand's width left loose on the right side, covering part of her face.

Feeling conspicuous, Morley turned to move quickly past the window and back to work. As he passed directly in front of the window the woman bent down to retrieve a pair of scissors from the carpet of fake grass, and he caught a glimpse of the side of her face: the high cheekbones, full red lips, and, on the portion of her face not covered by the free shock of hair, a flash of sapphire blue in her eyes. He passed, he was certain, without her noticing that he was ever there.

He dropped his gaze to his chest and sunk his hands deeper into the pockets of his coat as a strong gust of wind blasted at him. His right hand ripped through the lining at the bottom of the pocket, and he felt something underneath his knuckles. It was the pound note wrapped in the Trinity Knot charm the old woman in Belfast had given him.

The afternoon crawled by after he filed the closing comment. Morley was distracted by the momentary passion he experienced on his walk back from lunch. It was a feeling unfamiliar to him. For the rest of the day, at least, he would enjoy the brief giddy, nervous electricity in his body. By tomorrow, he thought, he would forget about the red-headed woman with icy blue eyes and long legs, just as he would forget about a pretty face in a magazine as soon as he put it down.

CHAPTER 10

The snow flurries had moved through quickly, and the skies cleared by late afternoon, allowing a weak, waning light to paint the sky with muted colors at sunset. It was much colder, and the wind was blowing a little harder from the north when Morley left work. He had been given a temporary parking spot in the library lot across the street. As he crossed Main Street, the fading blue hint of sky hung over a world drawn in charcoal, with only shades of gray defined by dark heavy lines, giving definition to buildings, trees, cars and the few people leaving the library. The only sounds he heard was the harsh wind blowing through the bare trees and a mother encouraging her brood to move along quickly so they could get out of the cold.

The Ninety-Eight was parked at the far end of the lot. As he walked along the few cars that remained, Morley noticed a man hunched over the open hood of a small sports car. It was a green Austin Healy with a body that appeared to be rust-free, though its engine, or likely electrical system, was protesting the cold. Morley had the steep collar of his jacket pulled up high, covering most of his face, and a gray watch cap pulled down low over his ears, which made him unrecognizable. That he wanted to be unrecognizable at that moment, at least to the man tinkering with his car, made little sense at first. But the way the man carried himself, the way he moved his arms and muttered aloud, made Morley instantly uncomfortable. As he passed the man, he caught a glimpse of his profile. From a distance he would be considered good-looking, but up close his face had a doughy texture, and there was a telltale smirk. It was the kind of a smirk that is omnipresent, whether it be for pleasure or pain, truth or lies. Billy was right. Rhodes was around.

Morley moved quickly, but not so as to be noticed, hoping he would not be hailed to help out. He wasn't. He wasn't noticed any more than the wind in the trees or the crow cawing in the branches. As the Ninety-Eight warmed up, Morley gripped the steering wheel, the interior of the car illuminated only by the dashboard lights. Rhodes was still tinkering with his car at the far end of the lot. There he was, Morley thought—the prick, all suited up in his tailored topcoat, scarf, and calfskin gloves, driving his fancy but mechanically challenged import like some Edwardian English gentlemen. Morley had not thought much about Rhodes Whithorne in the years since the four of them were arrested and charged with stealing that car. The four of them, Morley protested to himself. There was only the three. Rhodes was a hanger-on that night, just as he had always been. Slumming with the bad boys to boost his reputation. And "that" car, Morley thought. Not "a" car, but "that" car, as if it had become a living entity that Satan sent to earth to ruin their lives. If it had not been for "that" car, life may have turned out differently.

Morley wiped that thought from his mind. Life, he knew, turned out the way it did for the reasons it did. Neither he, Billy, Leo, nor Rhodes were any more or less guilty than the other. Leo was shit-faced and would have done anything he was told to do that night. Billy always acquiesced to Rhodes out of fear that his father, who worked for the Whithornes' construction supply business, would lose his job. That night in the winter of their senior year at Stonefield, it was Morley, always the conscience of the group, who gave the go-ahead to steal that car—a stupid, fucking four-door Impala that they ended the night by pushing off a cliff in the Valentine neighborhood.

What seethed in Morley wasn't what they did, or how they arrived at doing it. What ate at him, what had eaten at him for some time but was only now surfacing by being back home, was the consequences of what they did. More to the point, he thought, the lack of consequence for Rhodes.

Morley took the column shift in his right hand and pulled it down to drive. He wanted to punch the accelerator to the floor and drive the behemoth right into Rhodes and his pretentiously impractical car. Instead, he quietly exited the parking lot onto 49th Street and drove home.

Like Billy said, Rhodes was around.

CHAPTER 11

The release valve on the steam-heated radiator whistled and hissed in Morley's left ear as he sat on the far end of the couch.

"Don't worry, it only lasts a minute or two, and it takes another hour to build up. But you can move if you'd like," Murf the Serf said. His delivery was precise; his tone patrician; and his accent subdued, educated, and barely discernable as coming from the East Coast.

Murf was Edmond Touhy. Murf was a dwarf. He also was a coke dealer.

He was Leo's friend, originally. Not through coke, though that was a benefit of being Murf's friend. Leo, who Murf called his Lion, had gotten Murf out of a bad scrape one night, and they had been tight ever since. Billy was friends with Murf as well, having been introduced by Leo. Morley, Leo, and Billy had been drinking at The Pike for a few hours when Leo and Billy struck upon the notion of Morley meeting Murf for a late-night toot. It was Friday night, and after all, what else did they have to do the next day? Morley was drunk, bored, and game.

"Do much coke, Morley?" Edmond asked.

"You don't see it much in the U.K.," Morley said. "It's expensive and hard to get. Only rock stars and royals can afford it. Still mostly smack over there. Fewer transportation issues coming from the Near East than South America."

"Not so much lately, with the Russians in Afghanistan, I would guess."

At the mention of cost, Leo put down several hundred dollar bills on the glass coffee table.

"The generous Lion," Edmond said, gently pushing the money back to Leo. "Tonight we are among friends. You are my guests. There will be no exchange of currency."

Razorblade in hand, Edmond scraped and tapped out eight lines from an ounce-sized pile on the table and handed Leo a sterling silver snorting straw.

"Bon appetite."

Miles Davis played softly in the background as the four of them took their turns snorting. For such a crude method of ingestion, there was a formal, almost elegant element to the ritual. In two quick moves, alternately pinching each nostril, Morley had the coke inside him. There was almost no sting or burning sensation.

"It's clean, isn't it?" Edmond said. "Pharmaceutical. And I can assure you, it's never been stepped on."

Morley sat back and let the coke take him. It felt good. The kind of good for which there were no words. One simply had to experience the elevation in mood and appreciation for one's surroundings.

Edmond laid out another set of lines, then went to the bar and brought back four snifters and a bottle of cognac.

The world outside melted away. There was only the apartment and the four of them, listening to the music, drinking fine brandy from crystal, and snorting really good coke. Morley got up and walked around the apartment. It was smartly furnished in Danish modern with a few well-placed antiques. Edmond had taste that was obviously inherited, not earned. The apartment, which was the second floor of a brick home that had been converted into condominiums, was a block from the art gallery and the art institute. It had a security gate, which Edmond had to buzz them through, and an elevator, which aided Edmond with any physical challenges that might crop up.

Morley was admiring a gold-framed oil painting as Edmond came along side to offer more cognac.

"That's a wonderful Kandinsky reproduction."

"What makes you think it's a reproduction?"

The comment took Morley by surprise. He was intrigued by Edmond, who let his response hang in the air for a moment before answering Morley's unspoken question.

"Reproduction. The original is in the Guggenheim. I have some Cubans; let's sit by the patio door so the place can breathe a bit."

On a glass table situated between a pair of Barcelona chairs, Edmond placed an elaborately crafted humidor inlayed with different woods. The chairs faced the sliding glass door leading to the balcony patio, which wrapped nearly around the entire second floor of the house.

Coked, drunk, and puffing on an illegal import, the two of them sat quietly for several minutes as the smoke drifted and swirled, carried by the breeze from the partly open glass door.

"I'd prefer to call you Edmond," Morley said.

"I'd prefer you call me Edmond."

"How did Murf the Serf come about?"

"The moniker, or the man?"

"Both," Morley said, exhaling.

"The nickname is leftover from prep school, a lighthearted attempt by some of my classmates to be cruel."

"Andover?"

"Choate, actually," Edmond said. "Good guess, but I would have really been impressed if you said Groton. But returning to your question, the emphasis was more on the Serf than the Murf, given my obvious challenges."

"What, that you have sandy-colored hair?" Morley said, sarcastically.

"*Touché*," Edmond replied.

"I didn't know we were *en garde*."

"Clever fellow," Edmond shot back. "And returning to the origins of Murf the Serf. You know, honestly, I'm not really a drug dealer at all."

"Certainly not, the mountain of cocaine on the table over there notwithstanding."

Morley felt he was on a roll, and the exchange with Edmond simpatico. Edmond laughed.

"Leo told me you were a reporter," Edmond said. "The facts, eh? Do they ever get in the way for you? For example, what is it you think people feel when they first encounter me? Not see, but feel?"

61

It was a rhetorical question; although Morley thought of an answer, he felt it impolite to even think it. Instead, he looked Edmond straight in the eyes and waited for him to respond to his own question.

"Disgust and fear," Edmond said, pulling his legs up and crossing them on the chair. He was becoming more comfortable with Morley. "I learned back in Choate that the best way for me to overcome those initial reactions and become part of the cool crowd was to have something they wanted and that they could only get from me."

"And that was?"

"The best drugs on campus."

The two of them laughed.

"So this is all about being back in high school," said Morley.

"Oh, make no mistake about it, we never leave high school."

"I don't know if I buy that," replied Morley.

Edmond smiled, took a long draw off the cigar, opened his diminutive hand and pointed it in the direction of Leo and Billy talking on the couch.

"Point taken," Morley conceded, and he thought of Rhodes.

"Accepted."

"So you're not a drug dealer?"

"No. Not in the traditional sense," Edmond said. "I'm more of a purveyor. Or I should say, Murf the Serf is. The coke is a key that opens doors for me that would typically be locked. Nobody wants a dwarf around. But a dwarf with good toot? I'm everybody's best friend. I'm an oddity with purpose."

"It pisses you off."

"No, it pisses *you* off. I've been this way my whole life. You've known me for about an hour."

"Why Murf the Serf—why not just be Edmond?"

Edmond reclined in the chair and took a few more drags off the cigar.

"That's simple. Murf the Serf is a jester, a charade. He's just a character I play purely for entertainment."

"For whose entertainment?"

"Mine."

"And Edmond?" Morley asked.

"Edmond is much more complicated," he replied. "Edmond is a Boston Brahmin of the best pedigree. Edmond, pause for surprise, is in his fifth year of a six-year medical program at the university down the street."

Morley inhaled the smoke from the cigar and began coughing. "Bullshit."

Edmond jumped up on the seat of the chair and cupping his hands over his mouth yelled out, "My Lion, Mr. Billy, what is Murf the Serf's day job?"

"Med school," they replied in unison.

Billy raised his brandy snifter and winked at Morley.

"I told you you'd like this guy, Em," he said.

"Come, come, let's get some fresh air," Edmond said, jumping off the chair and opening the sliding glass door wider.

The night air was cold, but not as bitter as the previous week. There was a slight mist settling on the limestone shelf of the patio wall. Edmond climbed a stair-step bench that had been built especially for him to enjoy his view, which faced south across the metal works department of the art school, toward the brightly lit Nelson gallery.

"A wonderful view," Morley said, taking a gulp of brandy to ward off the chill and settle the urge to grind his teeth.

"You will have to see it in spring, when everything is flowering," Edmond said.

"So, I still don't understand the drugs and med school. Coke is really addictive shit, and med school isn't junior college. And if you ever got busted..."

"Therein is the paradox," Edmond said. "The bent toward self-destruction is as much a part of the human condition as is the desire to be connected and the need to be autonomous."

"True."

"Be the reporter for a moment. How much coke did you see me snort?"

Morley recalled Edmond chopping lines and handing the silver tube to Leo. There were eight lines, but when it came his turn there were only two remaining.

"Leo the Lion..."

"Was Leo the Pig," Edmond answered.

"So you don't..."

"I can pass a drug test at will."

Morley was perplexed but determined. Edmond had opened a door, one that Morley had never before wanted so much to go inside and see what was behind it.

"Okay, I'm the reporter," Morley said. "What are you are doing?"

Edmond raised his finger in the air.

"Carol, let's see what's behind door number one," he said. "What I do is classes, clinics, and studies from Sunday through Thursday afternoon. You will never be able to reach me those days.

"The remaining nights are reserved for what I like to think of as my sociological field experiments. My study, if you will, on the behavioral effects of illegal substances on upper-middle-class, status-driven, social-climbing monkeys."

Morley couldn't stop grinding his teeth from the coke. He was anxious both from the drug and from listening to Edmond.

"Why Kansas City?"

"In medicine, it's not where you graduate from, but where you do your residency, and this program will get me a degree in the quickest time," Edmond said. "And as far as my sociology hobby with wealthy monkeys, the city is, well, like Paris in the '20s."

"That's a bit of a reach, isn't it?"

"You only need use your imagination," Edmond said, leaning closer, only inches away, close enough he could see the nicks and scars on Morley's face and neck.

"The damage goes far deeper than the skin, doesn't it, Emmett?" Edmond said, pausing for a moment. "I think you and I shall be friends. And that I shall be your guide."

Through the open sliding glass door, Morley could hear the shrill whistle of the valve on the radiator.

BOOK III

Seasick as shit on the Hancock. Lose track of day and time. Green light finally goes on, and we saddle up with a new platoon attached to the Two Four. Ready Group Bravo. Me, Jackson, some other shit, and the Chicano Indian. Calls himself Dee-nay from New Mexico. Father was a Windtalker. Mother a wetback. Says she's a "weech." "Your mother is a bitch?" "A weech." A witch. Dee-nay is a short fuck. Skin like fine Corinthian leather. Mean as shit. All mystical and crap. Carries an ice pick stuck in his flak jacket. Says it kills quiet. His mother sends him chants and spells. She's a weech, not a beech. Call her that again and get the ice pick in your eye. It's a cyclone on the deck. Rotor blast. A ballet of swab fucks in funny-colored shirts run around. "Them's they call grapes," Jackson screams. Seamen. Semen. Like olive drab sperm, we impregnate a Sea Stallion. All lined up on the flight deck, rotor blades spinning, they look like nasty-ass grasshoppers. Thumbs up and we're off. Leave my stomach back on the USS Hand Job. We're feet dry and in country in no time. It's green and brown as we follow the winding Mekong. It could be the Missouri or the Mississippi. Moon River is in my head. Start to make out buildings and street grids of Phnom Penh. The window gunner cranks and primes his X-Man Deuce. Some serious hurt on board. We circle. Three giant grasshoppers can land at a time. We start to descend, and the Stallion's asshole opens and pinches us out. LZ Hotel is a scrubby soccer field just down the road from the embassy. We bolt out like we're landing on Iwo Jima. Ooooorah! Gung Ho Mother Fuckers. Cherry fucks. New fucks. The rest of the Two Four laugh and stroll along like they are going for a smoke. Noise, dust, and heat. Clear the blades, and it's like we're just lost on the playground. Dazed. Nothing going on. No Japs shooting at us. No John Wayne. Disappointed. Master Gunny marches us off to the sidelines of the field. Heavily armed kindergarteners. Get the lay of the land. Set up a defensive perimeter. Indigenous personnel stare at us like, "What the fuck?" Vehicles block all access points except one. Master Guns spots the dragon on my back. "Lance Corporal, take a position on the corner of the wall. Eyeball those apartment buildings and shoot whatever shoots at you." Aye, Master Guns. Flip flop over to the corner of the white retaining wall that rings the soccer field. Find some shit to climb on. Shoulder the Dragon and chamber a round. Squint through the optics. Gimme something to hit. I wanna kill something. Shoot at me, you Khmer fuckers. Nothing but laundry hanging out windows. Start sweating through my ODs. It's pouring down my face. Feels like a frying pan on my head. Suck off big gulps from the canteen. The helicopters come and go, picking up embassy personnel. Small crowd of very white-looking people. Just another morning commute to work. They show up, get in, and go away. Just taking the bus to the office. No electricity in the air. All simple. Simple Simon. Who thought evacuating a country would be so easy? A sideshow, anyway. Not like the Big Shit next door. King Bird is circling above. Air Traffic Control. Oh-Nine-Hundred turns into Ten Hundred. Squint through the optics. Nothing. Ten Hundred cycles to just before Eleven Hundred. Whoosh bang. Whoosh bang. I just about shit my pants. One-Oh-Seven Mike Mike rockets. Hear them. Don't see them. Close. Don't see any smoke. People getting nervous. Marines getting jumpy. Humpy, jumpy Marines. Fingers on triggers. Thump, thump. Bang, bang. Mortars. Oh, fuck. Charlie's cousin, Kilo Romeo, is walking in rounds. The wall isn't so high anymore. The corner is the last fucking place you want to be. Just like a rat. Feel nauseous. The mortars stroll nearby. Whump. Whump. Nothing to shoot at. Jesus, give me something to shoot at. Give me something to kill. Trigger happy. Scared shitless slappy. Squint through my optics at the apartment buildings. Nothing but shirts and skirts hanging on lines. Peopleless. Got to look useful. A pair of Broncos gallop above the Mekong just behind the apartments. Nothing happens. Incoming stops. Heart beating in my ears. Catch a breath. Dee-nay is yanking on my ass. "C'mon, Morley. We didi." "Huh?" "Ex-fil, shitbrain." What? I ain't fired a round. It's over. That was quick. Master Guns is waving his arms like it's time to come in from recess, and I'm still hanging on the fucking monkey bars. Up the ramp. Up in the air. Well, I'll be Goddamned. A combat veteran.

CHAPTER 12

The bell signaling five minutes remaining in the trading session interrupted Morley's trance. He had been talking to Horace Barrett, one of
the senior traders, about the market, politics, and war. Horace was a dis-
tinguished gentleman of medium build, with a full head of silver-white
hair and a penchant for expensive ties and well-pressed shirts with gold
cufflinks. Horace had been on the floor of the Board of Trade for over thirty
years. He was half Seminole, originally from Oklahoma, but he had lived
in Kansas City most of his life. As a very young man, still practically a boy,
Horace was in the back of a smoke-filled room when Boss Tom told Judge
Truman he would be given a seat in the U.S. Senate. "That's how it happened," he said. During the war, Horace was the captain of a B-17 and flew
thirty-two missions over Germany in a plane called The Big Bitch. "I let
the boys name her," he said, with a smile that accentuated a scar that ran
from the middle of his right cheek to just below the top of his ear. He was a
real warrior, Morley thought, feeling humbled and in awe of the man. The
circumstances of how Horace acquired the battle wound was what had put
Morley in a trance. An explosion of antiaircraft fire over Schweinfurt sent a
large chunk of flak through the aircraft's windshield, a corner of it zipping
Horace's face open. His high cheekbone deflected the path of the shrapnel
into the abdomen of the top turret gunner behind him. "He hung there, in
his harness, dead. Most of his intestines were around his feet," Horace said.

"No skill, no courage, just luck. That's all it ever comes down to, luck." Morley was left feeling like he was bleeding from his own battle scars.

The sell-off in the pit was intense. There had been no fundamentals behind the previous day's rally that had pushed prices higher; and with no buyers today, prices plummeted 6.5 to 9.25 cents lower in the final minutes of trading. A cacophony of screaming accompanied the disjointed ballet of hand signals, as traders shoved and postured for position inside the pit. They made their trades, then furtively passed slips of paper recording the deals to the runners waiting outside the heaving circle. The runners sprinted, sometimes slamming into each other with an exchange of heated words, back to their respective trading tables and banks of phones to record the action as quickly as possible. Morley liked the frantic energy, the desperation in the faces of men responsible for exchanging large sums of money under intense pressure. During the harvest months, particularly in the soybean pit in August, it was not uncommon to see a young trader turn away from the frenzied pit and release his breakfast onto the floor. It also was not uncommon—though it didn't happen on as regular a basis in Kansas City as it did in Chicago—to see a trader one day, then never see him again; he was gone, having lost everything he had. Morley, awakened from his introspective slumber moments earlier, muttered Horace's words to himself, "No skill, no courage, just luck."

Morley hit the "send" button on the Monitor, and his closing comments were on the wire. Earlier in the day, he had attended a news conference at the TWA training academy, where the airline announced its intention to boost its order of new, wide-body jets to fifty from forty-five. His dispatch, phoned into the New York office, sent the price of shares of the aircraft maker higher and earned Morley praise from senior editors, who already were impressed with the young correspondent's recent interview with the local Federal Reserve Bank president. The snaps from that interview had moved currency markets sharply lower, and the story was exclusive to the agency.

Morley was quickly earning a reputation for both quantity and quality of stories, so much so that he had free reign to work on whatever enterprise pieces he could uncover. This afternoon, Morley was finishing up a story on maintenance problems with Titan II nuclear missiles, which were dug into hardened bunkers scattered throughout Kansas and northern Oklahoma. The rockets had a propensity to leak propellant into the air, creating a deadly red cloud that had recently forced the evacuation of sixteen farm families living within two miles of a missile silo.

Tapping away at the keyboard, Morley was less focused on the leaky ICBM story than on the night ahead. It was Thursday, and plans were set to meet Edmond, Leo, and Billy at Milton's Tap Room. Morley looked forward to the Thursday ritual with his friends. It was the one night Edmond wasn't distracted, though he would make his coke deliveries later in the evening; Leo wasn't on the road the next day; and Billy was still in the leisurely world of pre-law school, working at a store that had yet to open. It was great fun, great music, and great friends, and, for Morley, the closest he would ever come to the middle-class collegiate experience he didn't get in the Marines or at Trinity in Dublin. The camaraderie of Thursday nights, which often carried over to Friday nights, generated in Morley a feeling he had not had in a long time—perhaps ever.

⚮

Winter had turned to spring. With the vernal equinox, the light lasted longer and was less harsh, and the temperament of the Midwestern weather was softer, if no less violent with the approach of tornado season. Still, it was mid-April and a late spring bloom. As Morley drove the Ninety-Eight out of the garage, down the hill over Brush Creek, and past the clay tennis courts, the forsythia was in full bloom behind the Horse Fountain. The brilliant yellows exploded from the ochre-colored shrubs that had yet to give their hues of green, and scattered here and there were a few small dogwoods with delicate white blooms. A large tulip tree had started to shed its pink blossoms, waiting for one strong wind to strip the branches bare, scattering the pedals like snow. The scene was lighted by rays from the sun, piercing through orange purple clouds that made up the base of an anvil-shaped thundercloud that reached to the top of the sky to the west. The car windows were down, and the smell of earth was in the air, signaling to Morley that the storm was near.

He found a parking space at the corner of Main, next to the porn shop two doors down from Milton's, just as the rain began to come down in big pellets, increasing in intensity until sheet after sheet soaked everything and produced small, raging rivers in the streets and gutters. It was a stroke of luck to get the spot. Thursdays were usually busy at the bar; parking nearby was at a premium—even more of a premium right next to the adult video arcade.

The bar was warm from the humidity and sweat coming from its patrons and cool from the dim lighting and soft tones of John Coltrane playing on the jukebox. Morley shook out his coat like a hunt dog emerging from a pond with a fresh bird in its jaws.

Edmond sat on a stool at the end of the bar, holding court with the owner and an occasional customer. Edmond had made the first of his Thursday night deliveries and was being treated like a celebrity, which was usually reserved for famous jazz musicians, Count Basie among them. Edmond gestured for Morley to join him. Leo was hitting on a woman a good twenty years his senior, who danced at the Pink Garter. He winked. at Morley in passing, without diverting his attention from the stripper.

The scent of peat enveloped Edmond, who was drinking from a special bottle of scotch that was kept behind the bar just for him.

"Join me," he said to Morley.

"Bushmills, neat," Morley ordered, annoying Edmond.

"My scotch isn't good enough?" Edmond said, affecting a false hurt in his voice.

"I hate scotch," Morley said.

"Why do you hate scotch?" Edmond demanded, as if Morley were rejecting indoor plumbing or medical treatment.

"It smells like an argument," Morley replied, recalling the evenings of his childhood, his father and his mother in the living room, the sullen silence and occasional tears. Their marriage was like the chicken and the egg. Morley didn't know which came first. Did his father drink because his mother bitched, or did his mother bitch because his father drank?

Edmond laughed, and the two of them raised their glasses in a silent toast. The whiskey had a fruity aroma compared to the earthy smell of Edmond's scotch, and the golden liquid burned slightly yet smoothly going down, leaving a sharp film on the palate. Morley was relishing the first sips from his glass when he felt a hand on his left shoulder and a voice from the past. His body tensed, and he felt he needed to retch. It was Rhodes.

"The Prodigal Son returns," he said.

Morley took a breath, slowly turned around, and offered his hand to Rhodes.

"I'm the *only* son, Rhodes; you should have paid more attention in sophomore religion," said Morley, his open hand hanging in the air.

Standing next to Rhodes, but slightly behind him, was a blonde woman about the same age. She had a simple but pretty face and was nicely dressed. She smiled, obviously unaware of the history between the two men, and squinted with eyes that Morley thought had a bit of a spark in them. However, they were dark and almost predatory, and Morley had to look away almost as soon as he met her gaze. Standing behind her was Billy, who had a slightly confused and embarrassed expression on his face.

Rhodes wore a green tweed jacket with suede patches on the elbows. He held a pipe in his right hand that he switched to his left before shaking Morley's hand. Although Morley thought Rhodes made an attempt to grip him as if he were attempting to shatter a 2x4, the effort felt more like being squeezed by an eel.

"LJ, I want you to meet an old friend. We prepped together at Stonefield," said Rhodes.

Edmond was unable to suppress a laugh, which angered Rhodes, though only Morley spotted the flash of temper. Rhodes was the consummate chameleon, Morley recalled. He was always affecting a new air or attitude in an attempt to be someone he wasn't and never would be. Tonight he was a preppie, pretending to be everything that Edmond was. Rhodes was ignorant of Edmond's background, as he only knew him as Murf the Serf, coke dealer. Morley, unable to resist, looked down at Rhodes' shoes and was humorously gratified to see that two shiny pennies adorned his loafers. While it was true Stonefield Academy was a boarding school run by the Jesuits, it was hardly on the level of a proper East Coast prep school. Only about a third of the student body boarded at Stonefield, and those few, including Morley, Billy, and Leo, were mostly disciplinary cases or boys of parents who didn't want to be bothered with raising teenagers. Rhodes belonged to the two-thirds that went home every night, while Morley, Billy, and Leo were sent home on weekends. Rhodes always yearned to be one of the bad boys, to have a reputation among the girls (and some of the boys) of being dangerous. It was an obsequious drive that eventually endangered everyone around him.

LJ gave Morley her hand in such a way that he had the uncomfortable thought that her next move might be to thrust it down the front of his pants. He could feel the aggression on her skin as she liltingly pulled her hand away, stroking the tops of his fingers.

"It's so nice to finally meet the missing piece to the puzzle," she said, swinging her arm around Rhodes and kissing him on the cheek, her eyes still fixated on Morley.

"Come, sit with us, we have a table," Rhodes said, almost as an order. "The Serf can join us, too, if you'd like."

They returned to their table, Billy in tow, and Morley hesitated for a moment and turned to Edmond.

"The Serf would not like; go ahead and join them. I have some business to attend to."

"You sure?" Morley said.

"Never more certain in my life."

"I'll just go for a bit, catch up, I guess."

"Fine," Edmond said. "When you're done listening to that bullshit, maybe you can take me to make a delivery."

Morley nodded that he would.

"Emmett," Edmond said, finishing his scotch. "Be careful."

"Yeah, I have some history in that regard."

"No, with the pair of them," Edmond said. "They hunt as a pack."

Rhodes held court at the table, LJ at his side, but her eyes never wandered far from Morley, who sat at the far end with Leo and Billy and the old stripper. Between taking mean jabs at the dancer, who was too drunk to comprehend being the butt end of several jokes, Rhodes caught Morley up on the years that had transpired since their senior year. He had gone on to design and architectural school, graduated with exemplary honors and a national design award, which landed him a job at one of the big firms in town that specialized in sports arenas. He was an up-and-comer, LJ kept saying, not just here but nationally. Each time she mentioned it, Rhodes' head seemed to double in size. Rhodes talked about the projects he was working on, how he solved this problem or created another new, fantastic element to a design that would be immortalized forever in reinforced concrete, marble, or limestone. Two Bushmills later, Morley had only managed to ask one question, and that was to inquire—not that he really cared—where LJ had gone to school. Her answer explained why he had never heard of her before. She attended the Sunrise School, an institution (as the boys of Stonefield joked) for young white women of breeding. Though the school was only blocks from Morley's home, located on the north end of the Great Park, it was a universe of prim and proper Protestant money where bad Catholic boys were not welcome. That she was attached to Rhodes was a testament to his family connections as well as her desire to rebel by slumming with a fish-eater.

When the stripper asked for the time and excused herself to go to work, Morley used the opportunity to disengage himself from Rhodes' court, saying that he had promised Edmond a ride.

"Who's Edmond?" LJ asked.

Morley pointed to the end of the bar.

"Oh, the midget," she said, turning to Rhodes. "Did you get some from him?"

Rhodes shook his head, looking chagrined. LJ tilted her head toward Morley, the spark back in her eyes.

"Edmond, is it? Could you ask him?"

"Ask him what?" Morley replied, annoyed, knowing exactly what LJ was getting at.

"Oh, you know," she said, playing coy while turning up the charm. "Just a few lines."

"I don't know what you're talking about," Morley replied, as he turned his back to the table and walked away.

Morley made his way through the crowd and stood at the bar next to Edmond.

"And how was your reunion?"

"Stupid," Morley said.

"Another whiskey?"

"I think this would be a good time to leave," Morley said. "They're looking to score."

"Well, that is never going to happen," Edmond said, placing several $20 bills on the bar. "In the immortal words of Cab Calloway, 'Let's went.' At least I think it was Cab Calloway. Regardless, let's get out of here before the begging starts. I can't stand it when they beg for the stuff. It's so demeaning. Especially women."

"I never took you for a misogynist," Morley said with some surprise.

"I should qualify that," Edmond said, jumping down from the barstool. "Not all women. In my experience, most women don't like it at all. But the ones that do get hooked quickly and lose all sense of decorum and personal decency. It can be shocking."

"And you've never taken advantage of that, have you?" Morley joked.

"Of course I have, Mr. Morley, of course I have. Choosers can abide beggars, if the need arises. Let's go out the back door."

The rain ended, and with it came a cold front that chilled the air enough that you could see your breath. It took the Ninety-Eight a little longer to warm up.

"So what did you think of Little Miss Redundancy?" Edmond asked.

"What are you talking about?"

"Rhodes' girl, LJ," Edmond said.

"I don't get your meaning."

"Her name."

"What, LJ?"

"That's just her nickname," Edmond said. "Her full name is Elysium Joy."

The two of them burst out laughing until tears rolled down their faces and their sides hurt.

"God, how cruel," Morley said. "The man with two last names running around with a redundancy."

"Just think. If they married, she'd be a contradiction."

Their laughter was unabated.

"What would that make their offspring, oxymorons?" Edmond said, his small hands pressed against the door panel for support, as he tried to breathe through the hysteria of the moment.

"Cruel indeed, cruel indeed," he said.

<hr/>

It was a short drive to The Tent, Edmond's last delivery of the night, an out-of-the-way yet fashionably raucous and entertaining gay bar that featured cross-dressing cabaret entertainment. The décor was high concept Arabian Nights executed with low-tech aplomb. The Tent attracted hardcore cruisers as well as sophisticated and curious heterosexuals.

Tonight's cabaret theme was Singing Sirens, and a voluptuous Nancy Sinatra, wearing fishnets and thigh-high patent leather boots—and sporting an Adam's apple—was onstage about to belt out her hit single when Morley and Edmond entered the place. It was if the deep bass riff announced

Murf the Serf's arrival to court; and the bouncer, a body builder of extraordinary shape, waved them past without a cover charge in front of the few people waiting for a table. Immediately, the bartender recognized Edmond and shooed two young men from stools at the quieter end of the bar. He pulled a bottle of Edmond's scotch from a cabinet and poured him two fingers in one glass and filled a separate glass with ice. Without a word, he looked at Morley and waited.

"Bushmills, neat," Morley said, watching the man, dressed in an Aladdin costume, pour his drink. The bartender was emotionless, appearing tired and a little cranky in his movements. The place was packed, the clientele notoriously finicky and dramatic. The man, Morley surmised, couldn't wait for last call and tallying up the night's tips.

"Agnes has been driving me crazy all night; I'll let him know you're here," the bartender said, placing Morley's drink in front of him. In the cocktail was a lemon rind skewered by a plastic scimitar bearing the name of the bar.

"Busy night, Ronny?" Edmond asked.

"Yeah, swells and swags," the bartender replied. "Most of them are waiting for a snowstorm."

Edmond raised his glass.

"More's the power to me," he said, taking a drink. "You know the Golden Rule, Ronny. He who has the gold...rules. I'll make sure the wind blows a snowflake or two your way."

Morley observed a faint smile in the corner of Ronny's mouth before he turned to yell at one of the other bartenders to fill an order of champagne at table 10. Then he went to the middle of the bar, picked up a phone, pushed one of the plastic buttons on the bottom of the keypad, and had a brief conversation.

"Agnes said to go on up."

"Thanks, Ronny. Take care of my friend here," Edmond said, swinging a leather satchel over his shoulder. Morley knew it had three to four ounces of high-quality cocaine inside. There would be no pleading "personal use" if they were arrested. The quantity was a "go directly to jail, do not collect $200" penalty, which made Morley uncomfortable, not so much for himself but for his friend. It had been eating at Morley as he got closer to Edmond over the past few weeks. He knew Edmond had a future; he would be a doctor, and he had means. Dealing cocaine was a lark for Edmond, an amusement, but one with consequences that Morley knew better than Edmond could be with him the rest of his life.

Edmond tugged at Morley's elbow. "Don't let anyone violate you while I'm gone," he said.

Morley surveyed the crowd as a husky Carol Channing entertained them with a raspy version of "Diamonds Are A Girl's Best Friend." It was an eclectic mix of people with several tables populated by what appeared to Morley, at least, his view limited by the stage lights, attractive young women with moderately beyond middle-aged businessmen. Thursdays, as Edmond had said, were, for these men, date nights with their mistresses or girlfriends on the side. Weekends, unless other arrangements were made, were for wives and social events like patronage parties and dinners at country clubs. On Thursday nights, one could still be working late at the office or at a board meeting of some sort; even until 1:00 a.m. "Drinks with the boys," was the excuse Morley imagined was most used. Lame at best, he thought. Anyway, for most men with mistresses or girlfriends, here or anywhere, it was a charade of tolerance with their wives, an unspoken but nonetheless understood agreement between spouses that the two—wives and other women—never cross paths.

As Morley contemplated the infidelities of other men and nursed his whiskey—he still had to drive Edmond and himself home and needed to retain some of his motor skills—he realized a middle-aged businessman stood next to the empty stool next to him, and he began to concoct a polite way to brush the intruder off. The man was in his mid-fifties, dark complexion, likely of Mediterranean descent, more than likely Italian; he was balding but still retained some darkness and fullness in his hair. His suit, shirt, and tie were tailored, expensive, and impressive. He was successful, no doubt, but the overly manicured hands and the chunky gold chain bracelet on his right wrist sent an entirely different message. As did his smirk as he looked at Morley.

"Hey, Ronny, when is that champagne coming?" he demanded, in confident yet polite manner, all the while his eyes still on Morley.

Ronny turned and walked to the end of the bar with a dutiful and respectful response, indicating the man next to Morley was a regular—and a big tipper.

"It just arrived at your table, Mr. Rossini," Ronny said, contritely. "Sorry for the delay. I wanted to make sure it was chilled properly."

"Thank you, Ronny, but next time let's anticipate a little better."

"Yes, Mr. Rossini," said Ronny, who quickly went back to taking orders from a loud, flamboyant group of young men at the far end of the bar, who were singing along with Carol.

Morley was relieved by the exchange. He would not have to talk to this Rossini character. It wasn't a pickup. The man was impatient and just wanted to know what had happened to his champagne.

"Hi, my name is Fran."

Crap, Morley thought to himself; and against his better judgment, he turned to look at the man. If he confronted the situation immediately, he could diffuse it faster. Rossini had his hand out, a large mitt that was practically covered with hair. Morley had never seen knuckles with that much hair before. It was repulsive, but Morley was polite and shook hands with the man.

"I'm Emmett," he responded, and began to withdraw his handshake—but Rossini held on.

"Nice to meet you, Emmett," Rossini replied, gently yet firmly continuing to shake and possess Morley's hand, despite his obvious discomfort. "I've never seen you here before, Emmett."

"Because I've never been here before," Emmett said, his sarcasm building as a defense.

"Well, welcome, welcome. This is great place," Rossini said. "Anything goes."

"Apparently so," Morley said, looking Rossini straight in the eyes. "Fran?"

"Yes, Emmett?"

"Can I have my hand back now?"

Rossini reluctantly let go of his hand. Having parried Rossini's passive attempt at physical intimidation, Morley returned his attention to the stage and his whiskey in an attempt to show his disinterest. Rossini, however, was undeterred. He liked tall, thin, handsome young men, and Morley was not as docile as the ones he was used to picking up.

"You're a pretty confident guy," Rossini said. "Let me get straight to the point. I'm kind of freaky."

Morley did not respond.

"I'll suck yours if you suck mine."

As Morley contemplated what response to give, he figured that whether it was verbal or physical, it would involve some sort of violence, the outcome of which would not be good for anyone. Ronny materialized suddenly, as if he had been listening in on the entire conversation. Ronny saw hundreds of pickup scenarios every night. Most were consensual. What he saw playing out at the end of his bar was not. He knew Rossini was arrogant and predatory. He also knew Morley was straight. He also could see in Morley's demeanor that something disruptive was about to happen, and that of the two men, Morley had the upper hand when it came to fighting. Tending bar for so long had given Ronny the ability to size up situations and people quickly. The way Morley breathed; the dead calmness in his eyes; and the fact that his left hand was palm down on the bar, ready for leveraging his body weight, while his right hand was clenched was all the indication Ronny needed that it was time to step in.

"He's here with Murf, Mr. Rossini," Ronny said quietly, leaning into Rossini, partly to whisper and partly to put himself between the two men.

Rossini, oblivious to what might have transpired had Ronny not intervened, looked disappointed at first, then turned gregarious and oblivious to Morley. It was as if his proposal had never been spoken and time had been rewound several minutes.

"Oh, thank God Murf is here," Rossini said, and then started to do a little twist dance. "It's time to party."

He walked off, humming, "Let it snow, let it snow, let it snow."

"Murf said to watch out for you."

"Thanks, Ronny."

"Not your usual thing, is it?"

"No, just Murf's ride tonight."

Ronny pointed to Morley's glass.

"Another?" he asked.

"No. But I'll take a club soda and lime."

"Coming up," Ronny said. "Can I ask you something?"

"Sure."

"Were you in the service?"

Morley nodded, affirming Ronny's question.

"Marines?"

"Yes," Morley said, with a hint of amazement on his face.

"Thought so," Ronny said, turning to get Morley his drink. From the small scars on the young man's face, Ronny knew he needn't ask him if he had seen any action.

Morley watched Rossini back-slap and shake hands in the crowd all the way back to his table—Table 10 with the champagne—as if the man were running for office. Morley felt chagrined at his own anger. After all, he *was* sitting by himself in a gay bar. What else should he have expected? He didn't like getting that close to losing control. The adrenalin was still coursing through him as he watched Rossini sit down. It was then that he saw her, the girl in the window. *Girl*, Morley thought, *hardly*. A woman, an incredibly attractive and alluring woman with auburn hair and alabaster skin, and here she was, not only in a gay bar, but sitting with two other young, attractive women escorted by successful, paunchy, balding, middle-aged businessmen, one whom had just propositioned him.

Rossini sat down next to the woman Morley was watching—watching as if he were sighting in a target through the scope of a rifle—put his arm around her, and gave her a kiss on the top of her head. In unison, everyone at the table lifted their champagne glasses in a toast as the stage lights dimmed and the room plunged into a twilight that reduced visibility. When the stage lights erupted, announcing the musical stylings of Cher as performed by a tall, thin black man, Morley's view of the crowd, of the woman and Rossini, was reduced to dark silhouettes.

With all that had happened in the span of several minutes, Morley was feeling utterly confused and a little heartbroken as Ronny set the club soda in front of him. As he looked at the drink and thought about changing his order back to whisky, Edmond returned from the upstairs office, climbed the barstool, and motioned to Ronny.

Under his right hand, which slid across the bar toward Ronny, was a $20 bill wrapped around two small, white paper envelopes. Ronny politely nodded "Thank you" to Edmond before discreetly placing the small packages of cocaine in his trouser pocket. The $20 went to the cash register. He was an honest barkeep, which is why Agnes kept him around.

Edmond, his business done for the night, let out a deep sigh of relief. Despite his *savoir fare* and devil-may-care arrogance, carrying around that much coke weighed on a man, more so on a man like Edmond. Certainly, there was the illegality of what he was doing; a drug bust he could afford. The other price that would have to be paid was losing the opportunity to earn his medical degree. He would be thrown out of medical school. Still, it was the routine of violence that had started to worry him. *Routine* was the word that kept rolling around in his head. Thursdays were now predictable, not only to Edmond and the select few he sold to, but also to the people they sold to and those that were further down the magic powder food chain from them. There were rats and cockroaches everywhere in the world. It was only a matter of time before they infested his world, no matter how cautious he was. Morley was his friend, not his bodyguard. And though close in age, he felt he was Morley's guide, not his employer. Edmond had less than two years remaining before he could call himself a doctor, and most of that last year would be spent in clinical work that would leave him no time for his sideline hobby as Murf the Serf. Edmond, more than anything, was bored of it. He needed a new hobby, and he was about to find it.

A deep baritone voice called out behind Morley and Edmond. It was Agnes, all six-foot-seven of him dressed in a cream sequined floor-length gown, heavy makeup, and a long, curly white-blonde wig.

"Ronny, my dear, make me a Tequila Sunrise. I feel tropical tonight," Agnes said. "Now, Murf, you enjoy yourself. I have my rounds to make."

And with that, Agnes began to work the floor of his bar, covertly distributing small white packets from his matching sequined purse with one hand, while accepting folded bills with the other.

Other than to take in Agnes with a brief glance, Morley's attention did not waver from Rossini's table and the woman he was with. Edmond watched Morley watching, and a wry smile formed.

"Emmett."

There was no response.

"Emmett," he said a little louder.

Still, there was no response, so Edmond picked an ice cube from Morley's drink and threw it at the side of his head, garnering his attention.

"I called your name twice. What seems to have you so entranced?" Edmond demanded jokingly, looking in the direction of Morley's attention.

"Oh, sorry, I was distracted," said Morley.

"By what?"

"Do you know that man over there," Morley pointed at Rossini's table as Edmond strained to look above the people at the bar blocking his limited view. "Said his name was Fran. Ronny called him Rossini."

"That's Franny," Edmond said, laughing. "Did he hit on you?"

"You could say that, yes," Morley said, more at ease about what had happened.

"Franny can be pretty aggressive, almost predatory, but he's not a bad guy for being a big-shot, egomaniac, prick attorney," Edmond said. "He can actually be very entertaining and gracious when he isn't trying to get someone's dick in his mouth."

The two of them laughed. Morley hesitated for a moment, then turned to Edmond with an adolescent seriousness of getting down to business.

"Who's the woman with him?" he asked.

Edmond stood on the top rung of the barstool, craning to see over the crowd.

"Which one?"

"The one he's with," said Morley.

Edmond sat back down. Ronny had delivered a fresh scotch in the meantime, and Edmond inhaled the aroma before taking a swig.

"Henna Freer," he said.

Amid the din of the show and the crowd, Edmond could see his friend had trouble discerning the name so he said it more slowly and an octave higher.

"Henna Freer."

"His mistress?" Morley asked, expecting to be disappointed again, though he had no connection to the woman and had only just learned her name.

"His mistress beard," Edmond said, this time with more interest in Morley's reaction, which was one of confusion, if not a little frustration.

"I'll give you the short version," Edmond said. "'Franny' is Francesco Rossini, an influential corporate lawyer who works for a prominent law firm in town. He serves on a number of visible charitable and civic boards." Edmond went on to say that Rossini's wife, although a "monolithic bitch," was an even bigger social climber. They had several children and what Edmond called "a marriage of agreement." It was acceptable to be seen, occasionally, with a mistress or girlfriend. It was not, however, acceptable to be seen with young men, which was Rossini's predilection. That would end his marriage, his career, and, even in these enlightened times, his professional reputation.

"But at a gay bar?" Morley quizzed.

"But at a gay bar with a pretty young woman after a night that likely involved dinner somewhere where they were seen and his heterosexuality confirmed," Edmond said. "This is a lark, slumming, rubbing elbows with the counter-culture, even though he is here almost every Thursday night—and, I might add, rubbing more than elbows. Just not with Henna.

"Ergo, my friend, his mistress beard."

Morley ruminated on what Edmond had told him.

"So, she doesn't belong to him," Morley said awkwardly, causing Edmond to burst out laughing.

"Belong? Jesus, Emmett, this is 1980, not the Middle Ages," Edmond laughed. "Maybe you missed it, but there was this thing called Women's Lib. And Henna Freer, of all people, doesn't 'belong' to anyone. She's definitely been with almost everyone—but belong, no."

The backend of Edmond's comment left an inexplicable sting in Morley's chest that, for the moment, he chose to ignore.

"She's single?" Morley asked, coyly.

It was then that Edmond found his new hobby. Matchmaker. *How perfect*, he thought, *I even look like Cupid*. His head was full of new energy and machinations.

"She's single," Edmond replied.

"I've got to take a piss," Morley said, quickly excusing himself, though not knowing where the bathroom was, and feeling slightly exhilarated. The woman in the window had a name. She was single, and his friend knew her.

"Of course you do," Edmond chuckled. "It's down that way, to the right."

Morley moved in that direction.

"But I do warn you, keep your eyes to the wall, and try to ignore anything else going on in there," Edmond added.

Morley walked by several male couples engaged in affection or taking short snorts of coke from the cup of their hands between the thumb and forefinger. In the dimly lit bathroom, he did as he was instructed. He found an empty urinal and, keeping his eyes focused on the wall and the graphic graffiti it displayed, he relieved himself as quickly as his bladder allowed. Yet, even with Henna Freer looping in his head, it was difficult to turn off the sounds of faint moaning and an occasional slurp coming from the toilet stalls behind him. He finished his business, turning and zipping in the same motion. He would, at least this time, forgo washing his hands, and instead brushed them on the back of his pants. He looked down to avoid any possible eye contact and, to his surprise, behind the door of one of the stalls, the one emanating sounds of passion, were a pair of loafers, each with a shiny penny set in the tongue.

My God, Morley thought, as he walked back down the dark hallway, *what new and bizarre revelation will the night bring next?* He had a "gotcha" smile on his face, thinking about Rhodes' loafers and what was transpiring in the bathroom, when he turned the corner to see Edmond's equatorial grin beaming back at him. Standing at the bar next to Edmond was Henna Freer.

"Dear Henna, this is my newest and best friend ever, Emmett Morley," Edmond said. "Emmett, Henna Freer."

Upon the introduction, the first thought that entered Morley's head was that of his mother telling him to flush the toilet and wash his hands. Reluctantly, he accepted Henna's outreached hand and gave her a quick and, what he thought, rather weak greeting, followed by an awkward silence.

Her hair was not pulled back in a braid, as he had first seen her that winter day in the window. She wore it long, with a part on the left that was drawn across the right side, obscuring the upper part of her face and lending a fair amount of mystery to her look. Morley was drawn to her eyes. They were not the sapphire he remembered from that brief and distant encounter, but an opalescent turquoise that reminded him of pictures of cool pools of water fed by waterfalls.

Henna replied with a quick hello and turned toward Edmond to ask if indeed, as Edmond offered while Morley was away, she could get a ride home. It was late, and she had work in the morning, and she was bored of being part of Rossini's entourage. She had played her part for the evening, though Morley was unsure what she got in the deal other than dinner and a night out.

"Okay with you if we give Henna a lift home?" Edmond asked, rhetorically, as he knew Morley would not refuse.

"No problem. I have work as well and an early start," Morley said. "Are we ready?"

❧━❧

The trio left The Tent and walked silently, Morley leading the way, to the Ninety-Eight parked a block away. The air was still damp but surprisingly less chilly than after the thunderstorm, as the breeze had settled to a near calm. The lights of the city reflected off the low-hanging clouds.

Henna sat in the back seat, out of Morley's sight when he looked up at the rearview mirror to ask her where she lived. Her voice, more audible outside of the noise of the bar, had a slight depth to it. Not quite hoarse, yet still containing a sweet and quiet tone. His first experience with Henna was only to see her. Now he could only hear her. She lived in one of the buildings on the west edge of the Plaza commonly referred to as The Poets.

It was past midnight, and the stoplights along the boulevard flashed red in one direction and yellow in the other as Morley turned up a side street that wound around the tennis courts of the Rockhill Club before passing the Nelson-Atkins museum, its limestone façade brilliantly lit for the night. The car began to warm up, and the rise in temperature circulated a hint of gardenia from the backseat. The fragrance was more intoxicating to Morley than the whiskey he had been drinking that evening.

"You work at Herons?" Morley asked.

"Yes, how did you know?" Henna replied.

"I've seen you in the window before," he said. "You were setting up a springtime display."

"Not just window displays," Edmond interjected. "Henna is an artist. Her work is quite amazing. You got quite a bit of publicity on your Christmas windows, didn't you?"

"Yes, but not much of a raise," she said, dryly. "What is it you do?"

"Me?" Morley asked. "I observe."

"What the hell does that mean?" Henna asked, with a flash of emotion.

"I'm a journalist," he said, slightly embarrassed at his oafish attempt to be witty.

"Who do you work for?"

"A British news agency," Morley said, keeping to the facts. "I was stationed in Dublin but transferred here when…well, there was an opening for a correspondent and I had some family matters to take care of."

"Family matters," she said. "Are you married?"

"No," said Morley, taken by surprise, as he half coughed out the response, then hesitating, he continued, "My mother died."

Another awkward silence fell inside the car. Morley looked at Edmond, who rolled his eyes and shook his head slightly at his friend's poor attempts at discourse with Henna.

"I'm sorry," she said. "I wasn't trying to push you. I do that sometimes. I'm sorry."

"That's okay," he said.

Edmond could not restrain himself any longer.

"Emmett's bureau is at the Board of Trade building, just up the way from you, Henna. You two should have lunch."

At that moment, Morley felt like veering into a large oak just off the curb intersecting Main Street.

"I think I might like that," said Henna, who had thought Morley's smile warm and genuine when she first saw him emerge from the dark hallway at The Tent. She found his face handsome, rugged, and scarred, as someone who had seen the best and worst of the world early in his life. But what she found most attractive about Morley was a gentle sadness in his eyes.

Morley pulled the Ninety-Eight around the corner and in front of the entrance to Henna's apartment building. She scooted across the back seat to the right passenger door, opened it, and got out of the car. A moment later, she tapped on Edmond's window, which he opened with the switch on his door panel. Henna squatted down and dug through her purse before producing a business card.

"Call me at this number," she said. "Mondays are bad."

As she handed Edmond her card, she pulled her hair back with her right hand, her face catching the harsh light from a street lamp. Parallel to her eye and running to the middle of her temple was a large, strawberry colored birthmark that took Morley by surprise, but he showed no reaction and reached for the card.

"I'll call you Tuesday," he said, firmly.

Henna smiled.

"Then I'll hear from you Tuesday, and thank you for the ride home," she said, kissing her hand then placing it on Edmond's forehead. "Good night to you, my shining knight."

Morley waited until Henna was safely inside the building foyer, then accelerated into the main lane and steered toward Edmond's apartment. They sat quietly for several blocks.

"Have you ever seen Indian beadwork?" asked Edmond.

"That's a rather random subject," Morley replied. "Yes, I'm sure I've seen it in museums."

"Particularly Sioux bead work," Edmond said. "If you look closely, somewhere in the bead work you will find one misplaced bead. For example, you might find one red bead in a field of white."

"Okay, and what is your point?"

"It was put there intentionally by the bead worker," Edmond said. "The Sioux believed that there is no such thing as perfection, and to try and represent perfection was bad luck."

"It's a belief shared by some Eastern religions as well."

Morley, though still buzzed and high from the whiskey and scent of gardenia, got the point.

"Hemangioma," Edmond said, in rote definition. "A benign self-involuting swelling of endothelial cells."

CHAPTER 13

The events over the weekend left no doubt it was time to move out of the house. Friday night began at The Pike and ended at Morley's. He hadn't really thought of the house as his, although legally, with his mother's will out of probate and everything settled, it belonged solely to him. So did the responsibility of upkeep, maintenance, and, as he discovered around 3:00 a.m. Saturday, neighborly manners. He was, after all, living in the heart of a Midwestern, upper-middle-class dream, among people who either had children or were more settled, quiet, and conservative in their daily lives, which typically ended with a ten o'clock bedtime. What had been an enclosed and insular environment during the winter opened as the petals of the now-fading daffodils scattered around the yard, which itself was in need of a trim. Their revelry still in high function in the early hours of Saturday, the windows of the second floor open to accept fresh air and dispel the sounds of the blaring stereo and smell of cigarette and hashish mingled smoke, not to mention the laughter and loud banter between Morley, Billy, Leo, and Edmond, was interrupted by the flashing lights of a police cruiser in the driveway and a loud knock at the back door. The cop was polite and asked only, based on complaints from neighbors, that they keep it down. Morley apologized, threw in that it was just "a couple of old Marine buddies in town", and said there would be no further disturbances. The cop was

89

satisfied. There were much bigger crime issues unfolding at that hour than having to quell a loud party in a swanky neighborhood.

The next day, after sleeping in, Morley went to the bureau to work on several dispatches and feature stories, which kept him there until late in the afternoon. When he arrived home, Billy was upstairs, stoned and listening to music. He had given Billy keys to the house, which he was welcome to use anytime, and did. Between his working at helping set up the store for its opening and living with his folks, Billy had turned Morley's room into his personal opium den. It was the least Morley felt he could do for his friend. The poor guy was saving money by living with his parents and siblings until he shipped off to law school in August, and there was little privacy for a twenty-five-year-old man under those conditions. Regardless, Morley was tired and wanted to take a nap alone, and he wished Billy would burn through the last of his brick of hash and be done with the stoner routine. Morley wanted to say they were too old for that shit. The thought surprised him. Instead, he lay down on his bed as Billy nodded off in one of the chairs.

The nap didn't last long. Leo arrived (he too had a key), shook both Morley and Billy awake, and announced he would barbecue. Leo had already pulled the grill from the garage and had the coals going and a case of beer on ice. They watched baseball on the television in the living room while they ate and drank. The drinking continued on into the evening, although much quieter than the night before, until Morley was exhausted and fell asleep in one of the guest rooms.

The next morning, sometime after nine o'clock Mass, Morley estimated, the doorbell to the back door rang repeatedly. The sun was bright, the springtime air light and dry, and a symphony of lawn mowers played in the distance.

He was hung over and tired. The previous few nights of too much alcohol and too little sleep had caught up to him. As he made his way out of the front guest bedroom, Morley saw Leo passed out on the upstairs landing, his face pressed between two balusters. Morley gently stepped over Leo and used the elaborate, twisting railing to steady and navigate himself downstairs. The smell hit Morley's nostrils when he reached the bottom step. There was a large pool of drying vomit, half on the oriental and half on the marble floor of the foyer, which explained the placement of Leo's face upstairs. The doorbell continued to ring, as did Morley's head.

Thankfully, it was the ringer for the back door by the kitchen and not the front door. Morley expected to be greeted by the police when he opened the door, the bright sun forcing his eyes to blink as they adjusted to the harsh light. For a few moments, the residual booze and lack of sleep prevented him from getting a sharp focus on the figure before him.

"Oh, Christ," Morley said softly, but loud enough to be heard.

Standing in the doorway, unannounced and uninvited, was the wife of his cousin—the woman, he remembered, who had propositioned him about the house in the reception line at his mother's wake. Standing several yards behind her, looking sheepish and uncomfortable, was his cousin Tommy, along with their small brood of children, looking quizzically behind him. He didn't remember her name. He didn't care, either. Politely, he waved to Tommy, who gave a small wave back.

In a quick and rather terse tone, she explained how they were still interested in the house and would like to take a quick tour. She did this without any apology for the surprise visit or for the terms under which she would like to purchase the house, which were not advantageous to Morley's interests at all. Her demands set out, she stood, determined and unbending, waiting for Morley to reply. He focused on her face, the broad jaw and deep-set dark eyes framed by a well-coifed helmet of frosty blonde hair, the color of which came from a bottle and not her genetic makeup.

"Piss off," Morley replied, slamming the door in her face. It was the most courteous answer he was capable of at the moment.

Several hours of cleaning up Leo's vomit, the empty beer cans, glasses, ashtrays, and leftover dishes and food strewn about the house, and having shooed Billy and Leo out and opened the windows, Morley reached a decision. He called another cousin, Denton, who was the executor of his mother's estate, and who now ran the family business. They agreed to a lunch meeting the next day to set things in motion. His second call was to Edmond, who had a line on several rentals in his neighborhood and was delighted to help Morley find a new home.

Morley entered the Kansas City Club through the large brass revolving doors on the Baltimore side of the building, bounding up the marble stairs and into the ornately oak paneled lobby with its heavy furniture and strong tobacco smell. He took the elevator to the fifth floor, where the maître d' for the Old Grill Room penciled off Morley's name on the reservation list and led him to a table in the corner of the room. Denton was already present.

For a moment, Morley took in the aura of the room; its crisp, white table linens; the tiled floors and walls; elaborately carved arches; and unique chandeliers. This, Morley knew, was truly a gentlemen's club, though membership was now open to women. Their table was by the hand-painted mural depicting the lives of the "Great Heroes of Medieval Times." Morley had not been in this dining room, not even in the club, since he was a little boy and his father would occasionally bring him for a swim and lunch on Saturdays. The memory surfaced a tinge of melancholy in Morley, along with the recollection that it was Denton who was dispatched to Stonefield that fall day so many years ago to break the news of the death of Morley's father.

Despite the relatively few years that separated their ages, Denton looked older than a man in his mid-thirties. That was partly due to being the sharpest of the Morley clan and having taken the heavy reins of the family business—the company, quite successful, arranged municipal bonds in rural communities—and partly due to his tour in Vietnam with the 101st Airborne. Denton, like most of the Morley men, had graduated from Stonefield. Unlike most of the Morley men, he attended West Point, where Morley himself had planned on going until the trouble his senior year. Although it was Denton who arranged for a pass from the judge, it was also Denton who stood by Morley's decision to take the same punishment meted out to Billy and Leo, and he also helped smooth it over with Morley's mother. Denton was the only person, besides his mother, whom Morley allowed to visit him at the VA hospital during his convalescence. Denton, too, spent some time at the VA after returning from war. He was now the only real family Morley felt he still had.

Morley ordered French onion soup and a Reuben sandwich, and Denton ordered the Cobb salad. The two talked about current events, and Morley barbed Denton about Carter's mistake in using Army Special Forces for the previous week's botched attempt to rescue the American hostages in Iran instead of "Marines, who know how to do these things." Morley had some experience in that area, although his last experience off the coast of Cambodia did not end well.

"You Airborne guys are always getting lost," Morley teased. It was black humor. Eight American servicemen died in the failed rescue. Morley and Denton had seen men die in similar situations. Humor or denial—or both—was how they dealt with the scars.

Denton talked of his concerns about the troubled economy, inflation, rising interest rates, and the growing unemployment numbers. Though Morley saw those stories on the Monitor on a daily basis, he was disinterested in larger economic issues, focusing instead on the stories that were right in front of him and that could make the A-wire.

After lunch was served, Denton advised Morley on an appropriate price for the house. Interest rates were high, Denton told him; and if he wanted to sell the house quickly, he might knock 5 percent off for Tommy's wife. She had been in contact with Denton as part of her campaign to get what she wanted, which was the house and, ostensibly, everything in it except Morley. Denton could take care of the legal issues through the business, and it would only be a matter of transferring the funds from the sale into Morley's already existing trust, which would be more advantageous for tax purposes. Morley agreed to the sale, and that Denton would act as the middleman for obvious reasons, but not all of the furnishings would go to the cousin. Instead, he would put them in storage until a future date. *Serves the bitch right*, Morley thought to himself.

"How are you doing?" Denton asked.

"Good; work is good, busy," Morley said, looking at his watch to see if he had enough time to make it to the closing bell.

"No, how are *you* doing?"

"I'm okay," Morley said. "It's weird, being back here, but I think getting out of the house is a good move."

"Sweats? Dreams? Flashbacks?"

Morley took a sip of water from the goblet that had just been refilled by the waiter.

"Sometimes."

Denton pulled a card from the inside pocket of his suit coat and handed it to Morley.

"I want you to take this," he said. "It's a good program for vets. I go about once a month, more if I need to. I'm just saying, in case you feel like it."

Morley took the card from Denton, gave a faint glance at the information, and thanked his cousin.

Outside the club the two shook hands, and Denton said he would call in the next day or so to let Morley know about the house. Then he walked back to his office. As Morley waited for the parking attendant to retrieve the Ninety-Eight, he took the card Denton had given him, folded it in half, and threw it into a nearby waste bin.

CHAPTER 14

On Tuesday, Morley called Henna to arrange lunch as promised. He had been nervously looking forward to doing so ever since they had agreed on it. He was distracted by work all morning; then, thinking he had forestalled the call long enough so as not to seem overly eager, he dialed the number from her business card. The phone rang for a long time, long enough that he thought he was becoming a nuisance. He was about to hang up when someone answered. It was not Henna, but the female voice said to hang on for a minute and she would get her. Before doing so, however, the voice asked who was calling, and Morley provided his name. When he identified himself, there was a giggle at the other end of the line that made Morley feel like he was twelve years old. This was territory he had not been in for some time. The women he had been with, except for the girl in Dublin whom he met at Trinity, were not the type to be courted. And the girl in Dublin, as it turned out, was interested only in a green card. That relationship ended as quickly as it began. Morley was not in the least bit interested in marriage.

Henna, a bit breathless and distracted when she answered the phone, said work was busy but she could squeeze in an early lunch. Morley lied and said he was busy at work as well and that an early lunch would be perfect. Henna said to meet her at the French bakery on the far side of the Plaza at eleven-thirty to beat the crowd. She then hung up, leaving Morley feeling a little bruised yet still anticipating lunch.

Self-conscious and keenly aware of the butterflies in his stomach, Morley arrived at the bakery/restaurant ten minutes early. Henna, on the other hand, was fifteen minutes late when she breezily entered and sat down at the table. It was the first time he had ever seen her in direct sunlight. Her skin was like alabaster, smooth but not cold, and her eyes had a sparkle to them that complimented her auburn hair and eyebrows. She talked as much with her hands and slender fingers, which he silently admired, as she did with her mouth, which was framed by thin lips accented with a burgundy lipstick that matched her fingernails. Morley was surprised when, despite the table being directly next to the window and in full light, Henna brushed the hair back from her face, exposing her birthmark. She was comfortable with him, he thought. She need not hide from him.

Henna explained, without apology, that she only had twenty minutes for lunch and had to get back to work. She was in the middle of setting up the display windows for the summer beach collection. Morley thought this humorous, as they were in the middle of the continent and were at least a thousand miles from any beach. They ordered ham and cheese croissants, iced tea, and two pastries from the display case.

Morley did not get a word in throughout lunch. Henna busily chatted away, dominating the conversation, talking, eating, and gesturing with her hands about the creative constraints of her job, how little she was paid, and how her real passion was painting—but she didn't have the time, space, or money to pursue it at the moment. Morley drank all of it in, every word, every movement, and every vision Henna unleashed to him. He was fascinated by her and her apparent lack of boundaries. Henna had energy.

As abruptly as she had appeared, Henna stopped midsentence, took a bite from her half-eaten sandwich, looked at her watch, and said she was already late for a meeting and had to leave—now. She wrapped up what remained of the croissant and uneaten pastry and put it in her purse as she stood up to leave.

"Wait," Morley demanded in a loud tone, which stopped Henna cold. She turned and looked at him as a scolded, yet defiant, child might look at a parent.

"Don't talk to me that way," she said.

"I'm sorry, I didn't mean to be rude," Morley said, taken aback by her response and searching for what to say next. "I thought, well, I thought we'd have more time. Can I call you again?"

Henna glared down at Morley.

"Maybe," she said, before turning away and walking out the door, which triggered a little bell whenever it was opened.

Morley sat there, confused and hurt. That, he thought, did not go so well.

CHAPTER 15

There were three messages for Morley when he checked with the answering service after returning to the bureau from lunch. The first was from an editor on the sports desk in New York, asking if Morley could do a short piece on Kansas City Royals catcher Darrel Porter working out with the team after spending six weeks in a rehab center in Arizona for alcohol and drug abuse; the second was from Edmond, saying he believed he found the perfect apartment; and the third was a request to call Henna Freer at her work phone. Morley's first call was to New York.

He said he'd jump on the story just as soon as he filed the closing comments for the market, and he'd send whatever he came up with directly to New York for editing. The sports editor told Morley to request a season press pass from the team, as it looked like the Royals might be competitive; and from his end, the editor would arrange for the appropriate credentials be sent to the Royals front office for Morley.

Morley looked at the clocks on the wall and decided to call Edmond later that night, as he was likely in classes throughout the rest of the day. Morley wasn't sure if he wanted to call Henna at all. Lunch had not been pleasant. She was flighty and a little rude. Yet, he still felt drawn to her for reasons he was unable to sort through. Instead of calling her, he went to the trading floor for the closing bell.

It was a lackluster session, and the comment took less than ten minutes for him to bang out and file. Two calls to the media relations office of the baseball team provided Morley with enough information to cobble together a short dispatch for the sports desk, which he sent, and it was quickly filed to the wire.

When the phone rang, Morley picked it up, expecting to address the sports editor.

"It's Morley; did you have some follow-up questions?" he answered.

There was a momentary silence on the other end of the line.

"Yes; did you get my message?" Henna asked, catching Morley off guard.

"Oh, I'm sorry. I was expecting someone else when you called," he said.

"Oh, I'm sorry, it's just me."

"No, I mean yes, I did get your message," he said.

"You're busy, this is a bad time. I'll let you go," Henna replied.

"No, don't. This is a good time," Morley said.

"I just wanted to say I'm sorry about lunch," Henna said, trying to be soothing. "There is just a lot going on at work and I rushed, and sometimes I'm too direct."

"That's okay," Morley said, feeling lighter on his feet.

Silence ensued between them for a moment, neither sure who should speak next.

"How would you like to meet up Saturday night?" Morley asked. "Nothing formal. A group of us are going for drinks at The Pike. Do you know it?"

"On Main, right?" answered Henna.

"Yes, say about eight o'clock," Morley said, clenching his eyes shut and wishing a positive reply. "Casual. Just jeans. There will be some friends of mine there."

"Okay," Henna said. "I might be a little late, but I'll meet you there."

They hung up. Morley felt strangely accomplished and buoyant.

Leo's speech was already beyond slurred as he sat at a back table in a corner of The Pike. Above him was a large poster of a pin-up girl, holding a bottle of ketchup; it gave the illusion she was pouring it on his head.

Edmond made vain attempts to communicate with Leo from across the table. The Pike was known for being the first establishment in the city to get a liquor license after Prohibition was lifted. It was where one could find about any local Democratic politician after five o'clock on a Friday night—and where Leo banked most of his weekly paycheck. It was nine o'clock Saturday, and Leo's funds had run out, along with his wits. He was done for the night.

Soon, having come from a social event and still dressed, respectively, in tuxedo and ball gown, Rhodes and LJ had joined the group. Rhodes immediately began to dominate the conversation by discussing his newest acquisition, an antique BMW motorcycle. No doubt, Morley thought, it ran much like his antique Austin Healy, though German vehicular engineering was far more dependable than British. The image of the two of them tooling in and out of the formal event on the motorcycle was pure spectacle, an obvious and classic attention-getting maneuver by Rhodes. Nonetheless, it elicited laughter from everyone at the table, save Leo.

It was, Edmond thought, if only for this moment, a convivial group of friends enjoying each other's company, despite the obvious, if unspoken, tension between Morley and Rhodes. There were several empty pitchers of beer on the table, and lively and entertaining conversations were being exchanged among them. The moment also was rife with symbolism Edmond thought appropriate and quite precise. In a bar with walls crammed with collectible kitsch, he was amused to see, hanging on the wall abutting the ketchup-wielding blonde, a print of the Last Supper. Beneath it was a cartoon of the Three Wise Monkeys, lampooning the Japanese proverb of "see no evil, hear no evil, speak no evil." *Precisely*, Edmond thought, as he paired the cartoon with what he saw sitting across the table—and, from their perspectives, what they faced. Leo never spoke ill of Rhodes. He tolerated him with a kind of benign patience. Billy, motivated by a mixture of fear his father might lose his job and a strange need to curry favor, refused to hear anything bad about Rhodes. What remained a mystery to Edmond was why Morley was blind to Rhodes and his destructive nature. He had been burned by Rhodes before and was likely to be hurt again.

"Edmond, you need a refill," Morley said, topping off Edmond's glass with more beer.

"Indeed, I do. Fill her up."

The five of them hoisted their glasses skyward to toast.

"Back together again," Rhodes said.

"Yes, back together again," added LJ.

Morley kicked Billy's leg under the table. They said nothing.

"Here, here, you two," Edmond said. Morley and Billy smiled and nodded their heads.

"Cheers," they said in unison, and began to chug their beers.

"So, Em, what have you been working on?" Rhodes said, surprising Morley, as the attention was now focused on him and not on Rhodes.

"The markets have kept me busy lately, but on the feature side, I'm finishing a piece about jazz in Kansas City and efforts to build a museum as part of a revitalization of the 18th and Vine district," Morley said. There was little reaction from either Rhodes or LJ, which left Morley feeling like he needed to map it out for them.

"The city's jazz history is actually a pretty big deal outside of town," he explained. "A story like that gets good play in Europe. I do work for an international news service, you know."

"That's cool, I suppose," Rhodes said, in a backhanded manner. "What else?"

"Dogfights," said Morley.

That one word, as Morley expected, had the effect of electrifying the table and creating a tense and excited silence among them. LJ's face became flush, as if she were on the brink of orgasm. Blood sport did that for some women. It almost always did it for men, and the look in Rhodes' eyes, as well as Edmond's and Billy's, was confirmation.

Before Morley could elaborate, Henna walked through the front door, catching his eye. He waved to display his location. She smiled, waved back, and came over to the table, sitting in the empty chair next to Morley.

"I'm sorry I'm late," she said, as Edmond poured her a beer. "Did I interrupt anything?"

"Indeed you did," Edmond said. "Emmett was just about to tell us about dogfights."

Henna looked at Morley and wrinkled her face with disgust.

"Dogfights? Eww," she said. "What about them?"

"Yes, what about dogfights?" LJ said, enthusiastically.

"Yes, tell us more," Rhodes chimed.

"Seriously, man, what about them?" asked Billy.

Morley, enjoying this rare moment when the attention was on him, took several long sips of his beer before elaborating.

"Fuck you, asshole," Billy said. "Don't tell us."

"All right, all right," Morley laughed. "Akin to what I said about jazz, my audiences are international, mostly, European. Animal cruelty is a big deal over there. They take their pets seriously. Hell, the Germans had laws before the war that if you hurt a horse, you could go to prison. Killing Jews was okay, but just don't fuck with any animals."

"Skip the history class," said Billy.

"Yes, skip the history," Edmond said. "Get to the point."

"I am; relax," Morley replied. "A couple of weeks ago, there was an *AP* story in the *Star* about a raid on a dogfight ring in the Ozarks. It got me interested, so I started calling around.

"Turns out it's a pretty big thing around here, almost cult-like. I figured I'd get some color, history, tie in the underworld element and lack of state laws protecting the animals, and it would get good play."

"Can we go?" asked LJ.

"Sounds disgusting," said Henna.

"Could you get us in?" Rhodes asked, his eyes set on Henna. "It would be a fun group outing, don't you think?"

"It is dangerously arousing," said Edmond.

"Jesus, what a kettle of vultures you all are," Morley said. "And it's not like Pamplona. There isn't some fancy festival where you dress up in costume and run with the bulls through the streets of Dogpatch.

"They don't sell tickets or issue press passes at these things. It's a very closed and violent culture. And what happens to the dogs isn't pretty."

"But maybe, pretty please," Rhodes said, in a tone Morley found overly feminine.

"Yes, pretty please," said LJ, in a manner suggesting an invitation of entry into more than a dogfight.

Her demeanor made Morley uncomfortable, though it did not surprise him, given his coincidental discovery of Rhodes' alternative desires. That was a revelation Morley kept in confidence to himself, although the knowledge provided some satisfaction. He possessed a truth about someone he did not like, let alone trust, which could be seen by some as a flaw. Surely, he thought, LJ had physical and emotional needs that were not being met; needs that would not be met by Rhodes.

"What do you think, Billy?" asked Morley, turning to his friend and, again, kicking his leg beneath the table. "Think you could be LJ's bodyguard for the dogfights?"

"Sure thing," Billy said. The idea repulsed him at first, but then he started to see LJ in a different way.

"The whole thing sounds disgusting," Henna said.

"But maybe," Edmond said, still intrigued by the danger and the idea of experiencing something new and forbidden.

Morley could see Edmond was truly interested, as an observer.

"Maybe," Morley said, talking only to Edmond. "I'll see."

The table ordered another two pitchers of beer. Leo's snoring was barely audible over the noise of the music playing in the background.

After another hour of drinking, Rhodes and LJ sped off on his motorcycle, looking like an odd bride and groom leaving a strange wedding for their even more bizarre honeymoon. Soon after, the bartender rang the bell for last call. It was nearly one o'clock in the morning; the music died, and the lights were turned up. The sudden quiet and brightness felt like a bucket of water had been poured over the patrons, announcing the start of the next-day hangover.

"What's that on the wall?" Henna asked, pointing to a box-like container fashioned from wicker.

"It's a casket," said Morley.

"A what?" Henna said, with some shock.

"A casket, a coffin."

Henna looked quizzically at the container.

"But it's made from wicker," she said.

"Yes, it sinks easier that way," Morley said.

Henna turned to Morley and, without uttering a word out loud, said, "Explain yourself." Morley smiled. He liked that they could now communicate with looks.

"It's from the Aran Islands off the west coast of Ireland," he explained. "It's mostly rocks, so what dirt is there is fairly precious. So when you die, they put you in one of those, fill it with rocks, and bury you at sea."

"How do you know that?" she asked.

"I did a story about it once," he replied, giving her a look back that said, "It's the truth."

She believed what his face said.

"It gives me the shivers," she said.

"What, death?"

"No. Being buried at sea."

"Why is that any different than being buried in dirt?"

"It's so wet, and cold, and…well, so vast," she said. "It would be too engulfing. I think your soul would feel lost for eternity. Don't you think that by being buried in the ground, you would feel the warmth of the earth from the sunlight above?"

"I think dead is dead," Morley said, somberly. "From what I've seen, you don't feel anything anymore."

"Don't mean nothing," Billy shouted, his words now slurring. Edmond had dozed off across the table from them.

Morley turned to Billy, his right hand in the air with a clenched fist.

"Goddamned right, it don't mean nothing," Morley replied, returning the clenched fist, the gesture of camaraderie and its meaning lost on Henna.

At that moment, Leo woke up and looked around the bar. His eyes focused on an empty pitcher in front of him, which he quickly grabbed and proceeded to vomit into until he emptied his stomach and nearly filled the receptacle. Relieved, he put the pitcher back on the table and passed out.

"It's time to go," Morley said to Billy, turning to wake Edmond.

Morley and Billy, who wasn't in much better condition than Leo, wrapped Leo's arms around their shoulders and dragged him out the back entrance into the parking lot behind The Pike with Henna and Edmond in tow. The cool night air had a hint of dampness that energized Morley. They hadn't gotten ten feet from the exit when Billy's back gave out under Leo's dead weight.

"Henna, quick, grab Leo, my back," he shouted emphatically.

Henna rushed to catch the tilting Leo as Billy limped off to the side, bent over, and Edmond rushed to his attendance.

"We're just over there," Morley said to Henna, nodding toward the Ninety-Eight. "We'll lean him against the trunk, and I can throw him into the back seat."

Henna wrapped her arm around Leo's hulk and immediately felt as if all his crushing weight were on top of her. But it was his smell that caused

Henna's knees to buckle. The Old Spice, stale beer, and sweat smothered her instantly, forming a knot that moved quickly from her stomach to her throat and triggered an unexpected response.

"Stop it, stop it," she cried, in a convulsive voice, tears running down her now bright red cheeks. Her thoughts fell backward, down a deep well, and she could see herself in the distance. There was a pain between her legs, a moving pressure that seemed to rip at her. She floated away, above the room, above the pain; only the scent lingered.

To Morley's surprise, Henna peeled away almost as quickly as she had arrived, though he managed to drag Leo to the passenger side of the car and prop him up before opening the door and depositing half of his bulk into the back seat. Morley quickly swung around to the other side of the car and, hooking Leo by his armpits, hauled the rest of him into the comfort of the Ninety-Eight. Leo was inside, safe, Morley thought, where he would likely sleep for the next few hours. By the light of the parking lot floodlight above the car, Morley gazed closely at Leo's face; it was a purple and white puzzle forced together in a haphazard manner as if the pieces no longer matched. The scars, broken nose, and ruddy skin made him look like Frankenstein. Leo was a mess, Morley said to himself, looking at friend in a new and completely different way. Compassion and concern mingled in Morley's mind. It was the first time, he realized, that he had seen Leo vulnerable. Morley tried to think of ways to help Leo, but any scheme was quickly interrupted.

"Emmett, come here, quickly," Edmond said, in a tone that carried with it a tinge of fear.

Morley gently shut the door, making sure there was enough clearance for Leo's head, and walked over to Edmond, who was standing two cars away. Billy was doubled over by the back door but pointed in Edmond's direction.

"What is it?" Morley asked Edmond.

Edmond said nothing and pointed down between the two cars. Henna sat on the ground, her knees tucked up into her face and arms wrapped around her legs like a vice. She gently rocked back and forth against the rear tire of one of the cars, quietly sobbing and muttering words neither Morley nor Edmond could discern.

"What happened?" Morley asked Edmond.

"I don't know," he said. "But whatever it was, it's not good. She's practically catatonic."

106

Morley squatted in front of Henna, who flinched when he first put his hands on her shoulders but relaxed slightly when he told her who he was. Words of empathy and encouragement came from a well deep inside Morley that he previously did not know existed. For several minutes he whispered those words to Henna, stroked her hair, slowly, and she began to relax. After a moment she looked up at Morley. Her eyes, bright shining beams of blue light, emitted a pain he felt in his chest. Her face was wet and smeared from crying. She was in his heart now, fragile and sweet and delicate like his mother's perfume bottles.

"It's not my fault," Henna said repeatedly. "It's not my fault. It's not my fault."

Uncertain of what Henna thought she had done, Morley reassured her that she was not at fault, that she was safe, and not to worry. His words eventually calmed her. He found some tissues in her purse, and she began to collect herself.

Morley stood up, his hands on his hips, and surveyed the situation; he was clearly in charge of managing the evening's disastrous conclusion.

"Billy, can you drive?" he yelled. Billy waved affirmatively and limped toward Morley and Edmond, as Morley was not about to move an inch away from Henna.

"Head back to the house and leave Leo in the back seat to sleep if off," he ordered, tossing the keys to Billy. "You can crash in the guest bedroom."

He looked down at Edmond.

"I think you should come with us to get her home and settled," he said. "Once she's okay, I'll take you home. Billy can follow me in the morning to drop her car off."

"Sounds like the best plan possible," Edmond said.

As Billy pulled out of the parking lot, Morley explained to Henna what they were doing. He helped her up and into her car parked on the street. Edmond stayed close but at enough distance to make sure Henna was comfortable. No one spoke on the short drive to her apartment building.

"I'm okay," said Henna as they pulled up to the entrance; then, turning to address Edmond in the back seat, she mouthed "Thank you" to him.

Morley escorted her to the front door and removed the key to her car from her key chain. They looked at each other for a moment, a hint of embarrassment between them. Morley broke the silence, telling Henna that he would call before he brought the car back. Henna went inside the lobby and disappeared into the elevator without looking back.

"I don't know where to begin," Morley said, closing the car door.

"There's a lot we don't know," Edmond said, pausing to reflect. "In time we may understand. But there's the possibility that we may not."

CHAPTER 16

"Can't you smell the crispness of the winter air, the oils from the paint, and coffee brewing in the background?" Morley said, an animated and bouncy tone in his delivery. Stepping back, he pointed to the right lower quadrant of the canvas.

"There, see the pink balloons," he said, moving his finger slightly to the left of the string of balloons. "But mostly I love it because I have a crush on the lady in the pink dress."

"I think I'm jealous," Henna laughed, enjoying a passionate side to Morley she did not previously know existed. "Why this painting?"

"I don't know," he said, standing further back and admiring the licks of pigment dashed across the canvas. "My mother was a docent, and whenever she would bring me here, I always gravitated to this one.

"I also like its history and its location. Paris. It was done from No. 35, the apartment of Felix Nadar. That was the pseudonym Gaspard-Felix Tournachon used for his photography."

"Yes, go on," Henna encouraged him.

"He was quite a fellow," Morley said. "He did a lot of famous portrait work, dabbled in erotica, and was a balloonist."

"Is that why there are pink balloons on the street in the middle of winter?" Henna teased.

"Don't know," Morley said. "You'd have to ask Claude. Strangely, Nadar is best known for inventing crowd control barriers. They still call them Nadar barriers in Belgium."

"Trip your trigger, and you're just a fount of information, aren't you?" Henna said, her attention now on the Pissarro hanging opposite the large "Water Lilies." Her shoes made soft tapping noises as she walked across the parquet floor of the Impressionists' Room.

They had spoken over the phone, but the trip to the museum for lunch was the first time they had been together since the night at The Pike. Morley wished to tread lightly with Henna, as he was still uncertain what had happened in the parking lot. She studied the pointillist dots on the canvas as he moved next to her.

"It reminds me of your work," he said. "The hundreds of small slips of paper and colors that made up the grass of your spring window."

"It pisses my manager off," Henna said, eyes intently focused on the painting.

"Why? It's so good—it's art what you do," replied Morley.

"Because it takes too much time; and, as he reminds me daily, it's retail, not art," she said. "He's selling clothes. I'm selling feelings."

Morley didn't know what to say in response. He had never thought of it that way, though he could see the manager's practical point of view.

They went through the food line and chose a table beneath one of the columns in Rozzelle Court that was out of the sun, hidden under the second-floor walkway that circled the enclosed courtyard.

They had some light conversation, during which he found out Henna was an only child from a small town in western Kansas. Her mother ran a beauty shop. Suddenly, Henna put her fork down in a declaratory manner. Morley stiffened, as if a punch were about to be thrown.

"I can't tell you what happened," she said. "I'm sorry, it just happened. Your friend."

"Leo."

"Yes. It wasn't him…I mean…well, it's hard to explain."

"Like a flashback."

"Kind of, yes," she hesitated for a moment and took a sip of her iced tea. "We really don't know each other very well. Not in a close way. Not in that way."

"In what way?" he asked, thinking sexually.

"I didn't mean biblically," she laughed, reading Morley's mind. "In a soulful way, like feeling like we're inside each other's skin."

"I see," Morley said, a little embarrassed and ignorant to her meaning. "You're right. We don't know each other that well."

"I'm not saying that it's not possible," she said, almost apologetically.

Henna saw Morley was deflated by her words, which was not her intent. Still, the result was obvious. She was afraid of what she had started to feel for him, yet compelled to pursue what was foreign to her.

"I like spending time with you," she said. "I'd like to spend more time. But…"

"Ah, there it is," Morley said. "Yes, but…?"

"You're putting words in my mouth. Stop," she said. "Friends. I want to be friends with you. Good friends, I hope."

The boundary was established between them. Morley thought for a moment and, though wounded, agreed to it. He was intrigued by Henna, and he was willing to be with her under any terms.

"Okay," he said.

Henna stood up and held out her hand.

"I'm Henna Freer," she said.

Morley stood up, reached across the patio table and shook her hand.

"I'm Emmett Morley."

"Friends, Morley?"

"Friends, Freer."

CHAPTER 17

The bell on the service message wire rang intermittently throughout the day. It had gotten to the point that Morley was able to block out the single and double rings, paying attention only to the triple ring. The number of rings determined the priority of the message directed to the manager or correspondent in the bureau. Three and four rings were practically forbidden on the message wire. In fact, sending a message with four rings required a protocol involving superiors. However, threes and fours were more common on the general news wire, harkening assassinations, declarations of war, or the unlikely alien invasion, which had actually been filed by a Far Eastern bureau. Subsequently several things had been killed: the flash, the story, and the sender's career. When Mount St. Helens blew up several days earlier, shearing 1,300 feet off the previously dormant volcano, killing more than twenty-four people and leveling 150 square miles of forest, the headline went out as a snap on the Monitor and three bells on the machine. Marshal Tito's death, however, got a four-bell flash. The bell to the commodities wire had rung so incessantly that Morley had it turned off within a month of reopening the bureau.

Covering the wheat market soon became tedious and boring for Morley, but the market routine allowed him to focus on investigative stories and news situationers, stories that supplemented breaking news stories and contained background, interviews, and interpretations more suitable to feature pages in newspapers.

Soon, though, the three separate wires with their incessant appetite for rolls and rolls of paper would become obsolete in the bureau, as more information was being processed across the Monitor. Morley already was talking in real-time computer messages to the Chicago commodities desk through the computer screen. Quick, one-line comments would magically appear on the top of the green, monochrome landscape of the Monitor. Technology, Morley thought, was moving much quicker than he had ever anticipated. That had become even more evident earlier in the week when a large box arrived containing a Texas Instruments Silent 700 remote word processor. The 700, about the size of a typewriter and encased in a yellow plastic body, would allow him to write and file stories remotely. All he needed was a touch-tone phone. The handset fit into the cups in the back of the 700. As advanced as it was, Morley found the thermal-electric paper and codes to overwrite typos or entire sentences cumbersome. He knew he would, with enough practice, eventually master the machine, and that would allow him more freedom to write from the field. That meant more travel. Although the 700 had originally been issued to him through approval by the New York sports desk, allowing him to file directly from the press box at Royals Stadium, Morley quickly saw the value of it for the upcoming Kansas wheat tour and other remote stories he had on his list of story proposals.

Morley leaned back in his chair, feet on his desk, scanning through a stack of newspapers that had accumulated as he drank a cup of coffee. An item about a former Kansas City television news anchor who had been fired from a station in San Francisco caught his eye. Morley remembered the anchor's loquacious and obsequious delivery when he had been at the Kansas City station. The San Francisco station claimed the co-anchor made little impression on Bay area audiences. No doubt, Morley thought; the guy was an obnoxious hick with a voice better suited for radio commercials. In the story, the co-anchor countered that he quit due to questionable news and ethical practices at the San Francisco station. Morley laughed. *What*, he thought sarcastically, *television news unethical? No way!* Morley hated what he called "television fucks." The on-camera talent was, from his field experience, just acting. The real journalists in television were behind the camera. They were the ones who took the risks and got the stories.

Morley finished the story and said, off-handedly and to no one in particular (as there was no one else in the bureau), that he pitied the city where this guy landed, if he ever landed back in the news business at all.

Morley was pouring himself another cup of coffee when the phone rang. It was the call he had been waiting for over a week. It was Kenny Dyce, the unofficial local chapter president of organized dog fighting. The call was short but clear. Dyce would meet with Morley, off the record, to "check him out" before providing any background or entry to a fight. They agreed to meet at a bar north of the river, known to be a biker hangout and fairly rough place. The call left Morley excited. It was real investigative journalism. Finally, he smiled.

The phone rang again. This time it was Denton. The closing date was set on the house, which Morley had anticipated; he had already arranged for pickup and delivery of items he would move to the new apartment. Other possessions of his mother's would be placed into storage. As it turned out, when he inventoried the contents of the home, there was very little Morley wanted for the apartment, and only a little more—mostly artwork and mementos—that he would relegate to storage. The bulk of the furniture he agreed to leave for his cousin and his bitchy wife, and he did so without asking for additional money. That gesture bought Morley privacy from unannounced visits. By the weekend he would be out; the house would have new sounds, new experiences, and new dramas that were not his. The history of his father and mother, his childhood, would only be random thoughts and memories. He was relieved to be getting out.

CHAPTER 18

The buzzer in the apartment was steady, long and jarring as Morley looked for the glassware box amid several dozen boxes the movers had left in the apartment. Unsure of how he wanted to setup his new domicile, Morley released the movers from unpacking. Now, the boxes' labels identified their contents only in a generic manner—if they were labeled at all. That did not aid in locating the stemware. Undaunted, he scrambled to open all the boxes.

The apartment Edmond found for Morley was the third floor of a large mansion off Warwick, just around the corner from Edmond's own condominium. The house had been divided into apartments years before; the largest was the third-floor space that had originally served as a ballroom, back when the house was built by some lumber baron over a century ago. Calling it a ballroom was deceiving, however, Morley thought. Either people were quite small a hundred years ago, or the homeowners hosted very intimate dances. Still, the space was large, bright, and airy enough for Morley. There was a separate bedroom that faced the street. Outside the louvered doors of the bedroom was the main living area, flanked by a long bank of open bookshelves that hid the stairs leading up from the second floor. Behind the bookshelves, hovering over the stairwell, was a set of windows; Morley figured it would become a warmth issue come winter. On the opposite side of the room, taking up almost half the length of the ballroom, was a studio where a small kitchen had been installed, containing a midsized refrigerator, a four-burner gas stove, a sink, and several open cupboards. It was more than functional for Morley's needs. The studio space was encased in a glass sunroom built out as a dormer from the roof to take advantage of the southern exposure and light. Although the main area of the ballroom was carpeted, the studio remained uncovered hardwood flooring, stained with hundreds of pools and drip lines from various colored paint, giving the impression of a work by Jackson Pollack. Luckily, Morley thought, all the windows in the studio space opened, which would relieve the buildup of heat.

Along the same side of the room, behind the wall of the kitchen, was a small bathroom with a large, claw-foot bathtub, which could be converted into a shower by attaching a hose affixed to a showerhead. There were shower curtain rings attached precariously to the wall. Morley targeted that arrangement as his first project in the apartment, once he was settled in. The second project would be to install a window air-conditioning unit in the bedroom and buy a few extra fans for air circulation. The cable television installers were scheduled to arrive the following week.

At the far end of the ballroom were two large windows that framed a glass-paneled door leading out to a small roofed porch, facing west. It had a view of the hospital and treetops of large pin oaks and maples, and there was enough space for two comfortable patio chairs that belonged to his mother.

The buzzer sounded again, more impatiently, it seemed. It was his first visitors. Edmond had phoned to say he and Henna were coming over with a bottle of champagne to christen the *SS Morley*, as Edmond called the space, throwing in a line about how his friend had finally launched himself from home.

Morley abandoned his search for the champagne goblets. He rushed down the stairs, through the second floor hallway that led to the other apartments, and onto the top landing of the staircase. This was large and elaborately carved from oak, descending from the twenty-foot-high ceiling of the first-floor entry area. Reaching the landing in a near sprint, Morley saw Henna and Edmond just inside the door below. Each wore big smiles. Henna held a bouquet of Gerber daisies, and Edmond hoisted a bottle of Veuve Clicquot with its bright orange label.

What Morley did not see was a small puddle of water one of the other tenants had failed to wipe up after spilling a glass of water. In an instant, Morley slipped and was careening down the stairs in every bodily contortion possible, trying to maintain his balance and keep from falling. In such moments of panic, time is slowed, and there are flashes of clarity despite the anticipation of imminent disaster. Although he was flailing wildly, Morley felt as if he were floating, and everything moved in slow motion. He could see the look of shock on Edmond's face and the Gerber daisies splayed across the floor, as Henna ran in an attempt to catch him when he landed at the bottom of the stairs.

It was the look on Henna's face that both amazed and calmed Morley as he fell. Her jaw was set with a determination he had not seen before, yet what struck him, what would haunt him for the rest of his life, was her expression as she attempted, in a clearly sacrificial way, to save him. Morley had never seen courage and compassion expressed with such brilliance. That it was directed at Morley turned his heart.

Henna's effort was in vain. Morley kept his balance and arrived at the bottom step intact and upright.

"Ta da," Morley yelled with false bravado in an effort to suppress his embarrassment. "And for my next act, ladies and gentlemen, I will juggle three chainsaws."

Seeing Morley safe, Henna expressed fear with anger and half-heartedly punched and pushed him backward, averting her eyes because they had begun to fill with tears.

"You scared me," she said, retrieving the broken arrangement of flowers from the floor.

CHAPTER 19

"Morley?"

"What is it, Freer?"

"Can I go through your closet?"

"Don't know what you're looking for, but help yourself."

"Thanks."

It was Memorial Day, and the seasonal humidity began creeping through the city like an uncontrolled vine intent on choking the life out of whatever its tendrils came upon. The summer heat wasn't far behind, lurking just behind the humidity, but today Morley sat on his rooftop porch, enjoying a nice breeze from the north. The extra fans he had bought lent a comfort to the apartment by circulating the air, and the large windows in the studio were now almost always open—which, they soon discovered, also allowed the free movement of bugs in and out of the apartment. To alleviate the invasion, Morley rigged temporary screens in the louvered openings.

In a few short weeks, Morley and Henna had settled into a domesticity that was comfortable to them, yet appeared unconventional and curious to their friends. They were not lovers, but they were more than friends. They believed they had developed an ability to communicate intimately without the tension that accompanies sexual discourse between man and woman. Opening himself up to Henna was new for Morley. He had never been as honest with a woman or so eager to sacrifice himself for one. He would do anything for Henna, including suppressing his passion in hopes that, in time, they would be intimate. If he loved her on her terms, he thought, loved her with everything he had, she in turn would love him, want to be with only him forever, and they would be happy. The agreement made between them that day at the museum was to be friends; and as just friends, and as if they were of the same gender, they now only referred to each other by last name. Henna had even gone as far as to correct Morley once when he slipped. The boundaries of their relationship had been set almost exclusively by Henna, passively, silently, and without open discourse between them. Morley, the soldier, acquiesced for the moment, seeing her boundaries as borders to be invaded at the right time and with the right force. His was a strategy of appeasement, patience, and agreement.

Henna had her own set of keys to Morley's apartment, as did Billy—though, uncertain of the depth of their relationship and respectful of Morley's privacy, he called first before dropping by. Henna used the studio for her art and had settled into a routine of coming by the apartment after work several days a week to paint. She was there most weekends as well. She had brought all of her art supplies, which took up the entire studio area, leaving a small pathway directly in front of the kitchen to allow for food preparation. This usually consisted of Morley arriving with takeout.

Morley had begun spending more time at the bureau and on the road. Sometimes, he would arrive home late and find Henna asleep, dabbled with paint, on one of the comfortable chairs. Usually he would wake her, and she would go back to her own apartment, as all of her clothes, makeup, and jewelry were there. On two occasions, recently, it had past midnight, and he carried her into his bed and they slept together—she silently and deeply, he restlessly, both platonically.

Morley flipped through his reporter's notebook, transcribing haphazard notes taken the previous week. He knew they would be undecipherable in another week if he didn't go back over and make them legible. The exercise also helped him fill in blanks in stories and formulate additional questions and research needs. He retrieved an open beer from a small plastic cooler next to his chair and guzzled two long draws from the bottle; the cold water dripped on his bare chest before rolling to pool in his belly button.

"How about a Memorial Day fashion show?" Henna said.

"Sure," Morley said. "Want a beer?"

"Yes."

Morley pulled a cold bottle from the cooler, opened it, and held it in the air for Henna to retrieve.

"What do you think, soldier?"

Henna walked through the porch door and stood at attention, saluting Morley. In her archeological dig through his closet, she found his Marine Corps dress blues uniform. She wore the jacket, without the white belt, all of his medals dangling as she laughed. Underneath the dress jacket she wore one of Morley's white tank top t-shirts and the khaki shorts she always wore for painting. Morley, despite his best effort, felt the blood start to pool in his groin, so he crossed his legs for propriety.

"I don't think I've ever seen the uniform so disrespected and looking so good at the same time," Morley replied, handing Henna her beer, which she took as she flopped down in the chair next to him.

"What are all these for?" she asked, fingering each medal.

"Just shit," he said, trying to steer his thoughts away from his crotch.

"Seriously, Morley, what are they for?"

"You really want to know," he said.

"I asked, didn't I?"

"Okay," he said, turning his chair slightly toward her. He reached across and, touching each of the commendations for the first time in years, relived how each was earned. The pressure between his legs abated.

"This is for being a sharpshooter. These are all kind of redundant. They are for serving in Southeast Asia, the Philippines, Cambodia, and Vietnam, all part of different operations."

"What about this ribbon?" she asked.

"Embassy duty."

"And this one," she said, holding the pointy bronze medal up toward him.

"Bronze Star."

"What's that for?"

"Being in the wrong place at the right time."

"No, really."

"Bravery, I guess," Morley said, pulling away from Henna and taking a long pull from his beer.

Henna was silent and let Morley be quiet for a moment. She took a sip from her bottle and gazed at the shirtless Morley. For no particular reason, she silently counted the small scars that peppered his chest and arms before fixing her gaze on the tattoo on his left shoulder.

"Do you all have them?" she asked, reaching across and stroking her finger across his inked skin.

"All Marines?" he answered, looking across at the treetops, and enjoying her touch. "No."

"You and Leo and Billy?"

"Yes."

"Tell me about it."

"It was our first leave from boot camp, and we were drunk."

"What does it mean, G.H.M.F.?"

Morley opened another bottle of beer and looked up, smiling.

"Give Henna More…"

"Stop. Really."

"Leo's dad was a Marine in the South Pacific, and they had them." Morley said. "They were some bad-ass Jap-killing motherfuckers. They called themselves Gung Ho Mother Fuckers. We thought it was cool, at the time."

"But Rhodes doesn't have one?"

"Oh, hell, no," Morley said, indignantly.

"What's the story with all of you?"

"You really want to know?"

"Yes," she said.

"I'll give you the short version," Morley said. "We stole a car in high school and got caught. The judge said we had two choices: go to jail, or go into the Marines."

"So Rhodes went to jail?"

"No," Morley said. He finished his beer and let out a sigh. "Rhodes got a third option. Cry like a bitch and use your family to get you out of it. He never even had to stand in front of the judge."

"And you didn't get that option?"

"Leo and Billy didn't get that option," Morley said, turning toward Henna, his eyes focused directly on hers with an intensity and seriousness she had not seen before. "And I sure as hell wasn't going to…well, somebody had to watch out for those two fuck-ups."

Henna sat back in her chair and watched the horizon with Morley, drank her beer, and thought about a young Morley and his trouble, and Rhodes. Why, she wondered to herself, did he tolerate Rhodes and, if even in a remote way, let him still be part of the group? She had pushed too far, she thought, and the buzz in her head from the beer distracted her.

"What's this one for?" she asked, her finger rubbing the purple ribbon and the cameo of George Washington.

"Purple Heart," Morley said. He reached over and touched the heart-shaped medal, brushing his finger across hers by accident.

"Come with me," she said, grabbing his hand and standing up.

Morley followed Henna into the main room. He was nervous and uncertain what would happen next. She sat him down in one of the big chairs and directed him to remain upright.

"What are we doing?" he asked.

"I want to see you," she said, disappearing into the studio.

Morley heard her rooting around on the big art table she had set up. A minute later she returned with a large box of red strips of paper she used for her window collages and a roll of tape. She tore a piece of tape from the roll, attached it to a strip and stuck it on one of Morley's scars.

"What are you doing?" he asked.

She shushed him with a finger to her mouth.

"I told you," she said, in a whisper. "I want to see you."

The room went silent, and Morley sat erect, as ordered. He moved only his eyes to watch Henna at work on him. Each time she affixed a strip to another scar he felt a tingle and pressure as if stitches were being removed from his skin. He could hear and feel her soft breathing as she searched his body for the nicks and cuts caused by shrapnel. The scent of gardenia mingled with a faint smell of sweat.

It took more than a half hour for Henna to map Morley's wounds with the strips of paper. Satisfied all had been found and marked, she rocked back on her heels then sat cross-legged on the floor before him. Morley was covered with hundreds of small slips of red paper from his stomach to his forehead, and up and down the length of his arms.

Morley was, for Henna, in context. She understood him now. He fit into her world, which was made up of shreds of cut and torn paper held together with only thin, invisible patches of adhesive. He was shredded, like her, and damaged. The strips covering Morley had begun to darken as they absorbed his perspiration, giving the appearance he was bleeding. He was both vulnerable and frightening to her.

Morley watched Henna study him, intently. As he did, the corners of her mouth began to turn down and her lower lip trembled. The normally bright blueness of her eyes darkened with moisture. Large tears soon rolled down her face, dropping onto the jacket and staining the ribbons and medals arrayed on the breast of the uniform.

CHAPTER 20

Trancelike, Morley tapped away at the keyboard, not thinking so much about wheat as about his friends, his routine, the stories he had written and was working on, the last few months, and Henna. He stopped typing midsentence, having forgotten the price difference between the old-crop, new-crop contracts, and ruminating on how much his global view had shrunk since February. Stuck, he thought, in the American desert, as an editor in New York called the geography west of the Hudson River.

The bell on the message wire rang four times, startling Morley from his daydream. Somebody fucked up, he thought, and sent the wrong priority. He swiveled his chair around and, without rising, launched himself and the chair across the office to capture the message. It read as follows:

MORLEY-KC (EX-CHI)
REGRET TO INFORM YOU. MAJ T. COLLINS-BROWN AMONG KILLED IN PUB BOMBING PRO BELFAST 1748 GMT. SORRY MATE. KEEP YOUR POWDER DRY. MISS YOU THIS SIDE OF POND. DIGGER.

CHAPTER 21

A wailing harmonica greeted Morley as he made his way up the stairs to his apartment. The times were most definitely a-changing, he mused to himself. The air in the stairwell was fetid and still until he reached the main room, where the fans and open windows allowed a cross breeze and a fresh, if warm, breath of air. Despite the late hour, he had expected to find Henna slumped half-asleep in one of the big chairs, work on her current canvas completed for the day. The room was empty, the lights off, and a raspy Dylan played softly on the stereo. A faint light on the porch glowed briefly, then disappeared as quickly as a summer firefly would. The familiar hint of perfumed smoke curled into the main room, taken inside by a warm breeze. Billy sat outside, smoking hashish. Morley deposited his valise by the desk in the corner of the room and sat down in the chair next to him. Neither spoke for several minutes as they stared at the darkness before them, listening to the traffic on Main Street two blocks away.

"This is a somber moment," said Billy.

"Why is that?" replied Morley.

Billy held up a plastic sandwich bag. Morley squinted in the darkness and made out a square of mustard-colored hashish about the size of a quarter resting in the corner of the bag.

"The end of an era," said Billy.

Morley laughed in disbelief.

"No, really," Billy said. "I'm actually sick of this shit. My time is done."

"Sure," Morley said. "We'll see."

"I'm out of here in less than two months, my friend," Billy said. "I've fucked off and been fucked up long enough. It gets to a point where we're too old, I think. And I busted my ass to get into law school. I don't want to fuck that up."

Another breeze swept across the porch and they sat, reflective and silent again for a few moments. Billy softly stoned and Morley tired, hungry, and feeling empty and disappointed Henna wasn't there.

"Yeah, I'm starting to see what you mean," said Morley, thinking about himself and Henna and where, if anywhere, they might be in the future—if there was a future for them.

Billy passed a small slip of paper to Morley. Henna was always leaving them around the apartment for Morley. She once left one on the cardboard tube of an empty roll of toilet paper, instructing him to replace it with a new roll, which had been placed by her on the bathroom floor underneath the dispenser. There was too little light to make out her diminutive handwriting. Morley gestured for Billy's lighter and thumbed the flame alive.

The note read: *No see you before you leave. Boo-hoo. Miss you already. You're OK Morley. Freer.*

Her notes to him always ended with "You're OK Morley." He wasn't sure if she was trying to convey comfort or reassurance—comfort in her feelings for him, or reassuring him that he was, indeed, okay. He never asked her about it, not wanting to jinx the sentiment.

"She taped that to my forehead when I got here so I wouldn't forget," Billy said. "She's something else."

Yes, she is, Morley silently agreed.

"So what's your MOS?" asked Billy.

"What?"

"Where are you off to, and when are you leaving?"

"Tomorrow morning," Morley said. "Chicago for a week, then I fly into Wichita for the wheat tour, and I'll end up back here the week after next."

"What the hell is a wheat tour?" Billy asked. "It sounds awful."

"Part of the job, my friend," Morley said. "I get to drive all over Kansas with a bunch of millers, traders, and agriculture guys, estimating the condition and size of crops. Walk the fields during the day and get drunk at night, is what I've been told."

"Well, half awful."

"And I get to do it again at the end of July in North Dakota, except at the end of that, you and I meet up in Denver."

"Excellent," Billy shot back, filling the pipe with a section of the square of hash.

It had been arranged. Morley would fly from Fargo to Minneapolis and then take a plane to Denver at the end of the North Dakota spring wheat crop tour, which straddled late July and early August. Billy would drive the Ninety-Eight across I-70 and pick Morley up at Stapleton, and they would fish for a week. The area they had chosen was known as the Dream Stream, situated along a stretch of river between two reservoirs on the eastern slope of the Continental Divide. There were cheap cabins and plenty of local bars nearby. It was to be Billy's send-off before he left for Berkley and three years of hunkered-down memorization. The idea of mindless hours spent studying gave Morley the hives, but he knew Billy was well suited for it. He also knew Billy would be a good lawyer, because he was such a lousy writer.

Billy exhaled a big toke from the pipe, giving the impression that most of his soul had departed his body. He slumped back in his chair, once again reflective and stoned, and offered the pipe to Morley.

"Well, if it's the last for you, then it can be the last for me," Morley said, taking the pipe and the lighter.

He held the hot metal pipe and lit the bowl; the edges of the piece of hash glowed beneath a layer of ash. Morley took in a deep breath and held it in his lungs, which burned sweetly until they felt like they would explode. He released the pressure, and the dreaminess of the hash bathed his head.

"Shit," Morley said, coughing and handing the pipe back to Billy. "I'm definitely done."

Billy laughed and took another toke before stuffing the last remaining hashish pieces into the pipe. Morley went into the kitchen to get a beer for himself and a fresh one for Billy, who kept smoking away. They drank their beers and reminisced about pranks they pulled in high school. Billy recounted the time they stole bowling balls from the Plaza Bowl and waited until late at night to roll them down the hill at the top of Wornall Road. The first ball hit a bump next to the Alameda Plaza Hotel, which sent the black orb bouncing as high as sixty feet before shattering on the pavement. The second bounced and lodged in the branches of a tree along one of the small parkways. The third, and last, rolled by Leo, went through the windshield of a parked car, which was, thankfully, unoccupied.

"Jesus, I can't believe we didn't go to jail for some of the shit we pulled," Morley laughed.

"No, dumbass, we went to the Marines," Billy said, which had the effect of dampening the moment, and they sat quietly again. Their mood, set by the high, fell into a still reality.

"I'm worried about Leo," said Billy.

"He does drink a lot," said Morley. "A lot more than I remembered."

"Too much." Billy said. "I've been called to come get him from The Pike a couple of times. He's got two DUIs as it is."

"I didn't know that."

"He's in a bad place."

"I'll keep an eye on him when you're gone," Morley said.

"It's not your job, Em," Billy said.

"Sure it is, Billy," Morley replied. "You've been looking after him; now it's my turn."

"That's not what I'm saying."

"Well, what is it you're saying?"

"We've got to start being responsible for ourselves," Billy said, hoping Morley would get the point. "We can't be the Terrible Trio for the rest of our lives."

"Fuck, you're stoned," Morley replied.

"Yeah, but no," Billy said. Morley detected a serious, sincere tone in his voice.

"Don't mean nothing," Morley blurted out.

Billy let it drop. He took the last hit of hashish from the pipe and tapped out the ash on the armrest of the chair. An ambulance, its siren screaming, sped down Main Street. In the distance, they watched a helicopter circle, its spotlight illuminating the ground below before heading off in a new direction. The discomfort about Leo passed, and Billy tentatively broached a new subject, likely more sensitive to Morley than Leo.

"I like Henna," Billy said. "She's different."

"Yeah, Freer's okay," Morley said.

"So what's with you two?" Billy said, hoping to probe deeper.

"What do you mean?"

"Well, are you two..."

"Fucking? Is that what you're asking?"

Billy's silence and the expression on his face answered Morley's question.

"No, we're just friends," Morley said. "It's intricate."

"Hey man, I'm not trying to get into your business," Billy said. "It's just that...."

"It's just that, what?" Morley asked, pressing Billy.

"It's just that Henna's been, well, well-traveled," Billy said. "Not that there's anything wrong with that, believe me."

"Why are you being such an asshole?" Morley asked. "Are you trying to tell me you and Henna...?"

"No, no, not at all," Billy said, effusively. "I know you, Em. I've known you your whole life, and I've never seen you like this before."

"Like what?" Morley asked.

"Wake the fuck up, man. You're in love."

Billy's observation left Morley speechless. He had not allowed himself ever to think it, and now Billy put it on the table for Morley to see for himself.

"For all your distance and hardassness, you've always been a big pussy when it comes to that," Billy said. "I just don't want you to get hurt."

CHAPTER 22

During Morley's week in the Chicago bureau, a high-pressure ridge began to form over the central and southern United States, causing temperatures to soar above 90 degrees almost every day until September. The heat was intermittently mixed with high humidity levels. The system effectively put a lid on the development of thunderstorms, exacerbating already dry conditions for the hard red winter wheat crop and causing general misery for everyone living in the region.

When he landed in Wichita to meet up with the wheat tour, Morley felt like an overcooked piece of meatloaf, walking through the covered metal gangway that connected the plane to the terminal. The terminal itself, despite its industrial air-conditioning, was warm and swampy, but it offered far better comfort than the furnace blast that greeted him when the glass doors leading to the parking garage and rental car lots opened. It was so hot it took Morley's breath away. His eyeballs seemed to shrink into his skull, and sweat quickly beaded on his face. He hadn't taken twenty steps across the sun-softened asphalt before the armpits of his shirt were drenched from perspiration.

"Just another beautiful day in Saigon," Morley muttered to himself.

For the next three days, he tromped through somewhere between nine and fifteen Kansas wheat fields a day, assessing the quality of the harvest by a formula that took into account plants per foot, the number of spikelets on each head, and the number of kernels. In the previous year, the state produced 410.4 million bushels of the golden grain, a record harvest. This year, however, though likely still a big number, the early dry conditions put forecasts at 385 million bushels. More optimistic forecasters were calling for a harvest of between 400 and 405 million bushels.

Another accounting of the heat wave, conducted by a very different reaper and assessed at the end of the harvest season, tallied 1,700 weather-related deaths. When one threw in $20 billion in agricultural damage, the summer's weather was one of the worst natural disasters in U.S. history.

It was, in the words of one of the farmers they talked to, "hotter than a whore's ass on payday."

Morley, who diligently filed quick updates to the Chicago office at every pay phone he could find along the routes, could not have cared less. It was hot. It was awful hot. It was goddamned awful hot. His forearms, the tops of his hands, and the back of his neck were sunburned from walking the fields. It had been a long stretch. He was tired, and he missed Henna.

In the week and a half he had been gone, they had exchanged messages through the answering service. She never picked up the phone at his apartment or hers. On the last day of the tour, before they headed back to Kansas City and the Board of Trade to release their final estimates and finish up, Morley got Henna a souvenir: a yellow and green seed cap from one of the grain elevator operators they visited. He was pleased with himself, thinking it kitsch and, perhaps, a reminder of home. Henna had only spoken once of her home to Morley, and in very little detail. She was from Grainfield, Kansas, which was a small farming community on the western edge of the state. The only memory she shared with Morley about the place was of her sitting in class in high school, which overlooked I-70, and daydreaming about getting on the highway and never coming back.

The tour over, his round-up filed with Chicago, Morley checked his messages with the answering service. There were several from public relations folks trying to pitch stories to him, of which he had no interest; one from Henna, telling him she would probably get off early on Friday, which was today; and one from Kenny Dyce, whom he had met with before leaving for Chicago. Kenny's message was an invitation to a Fourth of July party. Morley was to call him for more details. It was code. They were in for the dogfight.

It was late afternoon when he closed down the bureau for the weekend. Morley was hot and anxious to see Henna. He stopped by the grocery store to pick up a few things, some food and beer and a bag of ice he hoped wouldn't melt before he got to the apartment.

Walking up the stairs to the apartment reminded Morley of deplaning in Wichita; only here, there was a dank smell of plaster and dry wood as the house baked in the heat. Once he was in the great room, still hot even with all the windows open and fans churning the air, the smell of gardenia greeted him. A soft melody played on the stereo. The bank of windows in the studio had been covered over with tinfoil to thwart the piercing sun. It lent a calm darkness to the room.

"Freer, you here?" he called.

Morley heard the subtle movement of water.

"In the tub, trying to cool down," Henna said.

Morley put the food and ice away in the refrigerator.

"They're telling old people to lie in a cool bath if they don't have air-conditioning," she said, shouting above the noise of the fans.

Morley laughed. He could hear the window air-conditioning unit in the bedroom whirring away behind the closed door.

"We have air conditioning, you know," Morley said.

"I wanted to take a bath."

"Do you want a beer?" he asked.

"Yes," she said. "Did you buy any ice?"

"Yes."

"Bring in the whole bag."

The request seemed odd to Morley, but he opened two beers and carried the bag into the bathroom.

Henna lay in the bathtub. The opaque water, made cloudy by a gardenia-scented bath milk, hid most of her body, yet revealed her trim form, including the roundness of her breasts and shape of her nipples. When she moved slightly, there was only a light shadow between her hips. Morley had never seen Henna entirely naked before, although she had changed in front of him and exposed her breasts. What soaked in the tub below him was, in his eyes, perfection. There was not a single blemish on her body, from what he could make out below the waterline, irrespective of the birthmark on her face. Not a mole or a scar. She was, he thought, made from pure marble.

He handed her a beer and sat down on the toilet, averting his eyes from her breasts as she reached for the bottle.

"What do you want me to do with this?" Morley asked, holding up the dripping bag of ice.

"Dump it in."

"Really? The whole bag?"

"Yes."

Morley pulled open the top of the plastic bag, then poured its contents into the water as if he were spreading a bag of fertilizer. The ice slid into the water and quickly began to melt.

"Oh, God, that feels perfect," Henna purred, her eyes closed and her face relaxed.

Morley felt a twinge between his legs and held the cold bottle to his face to fend off any building pressure.

"How was the trip?" Henna asked.

"Long, hot, glad to be home," he answered.

"Home," Henna said. "You've never called this place home before. You must have heatstroke."

He drank half his beer, sat back against the tank of the toilet, and exhaled.

"You poor thing," she said.

Remembering the souvenir, Morley bolted up to retrieve it from his suitcase.

"I almost forgot, I got you something," he said.

As quickly as he left, he returned and placed the cap on Henna's head.

"What's this?" she asked.

"A seed cap," he answered. "I thought you'd get a kick out of it."

"Oh, great, just what every girl wants," she said, mockingly.

"I think it looks great," he said. "You look sexy."

Too much, Henna thought. As much as she desired Morley, she remained confused about him, about them, whatever it was they were. Henna had been with many men. The seed cap reminded her of the boy who worked at McDonald's back home, her first consensual encounter. Then there were the boys in college. Then there was the string of men after she graduated, young and old. But never was there any feeling. They could be on top of her, in her, but she felt nothing. There was only the power she felt she had over them before sex. Afterward, though, she was empty. The men would be drained, and with them went any power she had.

There was none of that with Morley. No desire for her to be in control in that way. He was as wounded as she. They were friends, after all. He made her feel safe and protected, and she didn't want that to disappear. Sex would change that, she knew. It had changed everything for her a long time ago. Losing Morley frightened her. Morley's caring frightened her as well. Still, she had stopped seeing other men after that night in the parking lot behind the bar. She stopped taking the pill, which she hated anyway because it made her nauseous. She stopped wanting to have power over men.

Morley hovered over Henna, his weight supported by his arms that held onto the curved edges of the bathtub as if he were about to do a pushup. The green and yellow of the cap complimented the redness of her hair, dark and wet from the water. Her eyes stared through Morley, he thought, but where were they focused? He wanted, badly, to bend his elbows and kiss her, finally. He had never been as frightened in his life as he was at that moment. It was the biggest risk he had ever taken.

Henna dipped lower into the bathwater, away from Morley as his arms began to move. Just then, the phone rang.

"You better get it," Henna said, relieved.

Morley, frustrated and unsure what had just happened—or hadn't happened—pushed himself up and off of the bathtub. He answered the phone on the third ring.

"Fuck," Morley said, hanging up the phone.

Henna had quickly dried off and slipped on shorts and a t-shirt and was toweling her hair. The seed cap lay on the bathroom floor behind the tub.

"What is it?" she asked, coming out of the bathroom.

"New York," he said. "A train carrying toxic chemicals derailed in Iowa. A bunch of people dead, and some shit-hole town is being evacuated. The networks all have it. Fuck."

"So?"

"I've got to go back into the office and chase it from there," he said, rummaging through his desk for fresh notebooks. "They want something on the wire in the next half hour. I'll be back later."

"Okay," she said.

"Will you be here?" Morley asked, without looking up to notice Henna had already made her way into the bedroom and closed the louvered doors to keep the cool air from escaping.

Later that night, Morley returned from the bureau. The apartment was dark. The only sound came from the fans circulating air and the whirring of the window unit in the bedroom. He pulled off his shirt and kicked off his shoes before going into the bedroom. Henna, to his surprise, lay asleep on the bed. Exhausted, and not wishing to wake her, Morley put on a pair of boxers and fell asleep next to her. The next morning, when he awoke, he rolled over to find Henna gone. A small slip of red paper was taped to the pillow next to him.

It read: *Early errands. You're OK Morley. Freer.*

CHAPTER 23

The open-door warning chimed anxiously on the Ninety-Eight as Morley and Leo paced about the parking lot next to the car. The engine was running and the air-conditioner turned to high. Edmond and Henna sat in the car, talking. Finally annoyed by the dinging chime and the torpid air, Edmond crawled across the front seat and slammed the door shut.

Morley was distracted and oblivious to his lack of consideration for Edmond and Henna. He looked at his watch.

"I'll give them another fifteen minutes, and we're out of here," he said to Leo, who nodded back in agreement.

A week earlier, Kenny Dyce had agreed to extend an invitation to Morley for the Fourth of July Convention, which was one of the big dogfights of the year. There would be eight scheduled matches—"scheduled" being a loose term, as some dog men showed up and others didn't for unexplained reasons, usually involving the law. The main fight was to be between a grand champion named Caesar and an up-and-coming champion named March Madness. Grand champions were undefeated dogs with five wins. Champions had at least three fights, all victories, and were known for having great tenacity and a strong willingness to battle to the death. That earned a dog the accolade of having gameness.

Kenny was not warm to the idea of Morley bringing people with him. Unknowns were unknown, and Kenny Dyce didn't like what wasn't known, because it meant he had to rely on luck. He didn't believe in luck. There was a greater power that decided fate, and Kenny preferred to control fate as much as he could in this world. He liked Morley. He didn't trust him, but he liked him, if only because they shared the Corps. Morley didn't just talk the talk, he walked the walk; and like Kenny, who had picked up a facial tick and a limp at Khe Sahn, Morley had "been in the shit" and wasn't the same when he crawled out.

Morley had told Dyce there would be three extras, but Billy, drunk at The Pike earlier in the week, let it slip in front of Rhodes, who relentlessly lobbied Morley to be included. Morley regretted saying yes as soon as the word slipped out of his mouth.

Waiting in the parking lot of a nearly vacant strip mall on the eastside of the city, Morley said a silent prayer that Rhodes didn't show up, or that if he did, it would be long after they had left.

The brutality of the day's heat still radiated up from the asphalt of the parking lot. It was late twilight, and the western brim of the sky was a bright but quickly fading orange. Though the sky was clear, the high humidity levels created a suffocating haze over the city. The summer had barely started, and already the greenness of the landscape started to look more like early fall. The grass crunched when you walked on it, and watering plants was futile.

Morley grew more anxious with each sweep of the second hand on his watch. *To hell with fifteen minutes*, he thought, *we'll just go now*. As he grabbed the door handle and motioned to Leo to get in the car, a small pair of lighted eyeballs swiveled off the street and headed toward them with reckless abandon, blinking and swaying to avoid the decaying speed bumps and potholes in the parking lot.

Rhodes screeched to a stop inches from Morley, the squeal of the Austin Healy's tires accentuated by the warm pavement.

Morley was immediately pissed. Sitting in the passenger seat was LJ, who had not been invited. On top of that, they were dressed like they had just come from a "Great Gatsby" costume party. Rhodes wore a salmon-colored linen suite with white bucks and a blue-and-white striped shirt that was unbuttoned to the middle of his hairless chest. LJ was decked out in a floral print sundress that had more colors than a toucan. From her lap she produced a large, floppy summer hat, which she immediately stuck on top of her head and tried to smile innocently at Morley.

They were both drunk and too talkative. Morley didn't listen; he simply told LJ to put the hat in the trunk because she sure as hell wasn't going to wear it into the dogfight. He looked at Rhodes, who aped a stupid smile back at Morley as if to communicate his innocence in bringing LJ and their appearance. They piled into the Ninety-Eight, and Morley pulled out of the parking lot and headed toward the agreed rendezvous with Kenny Dyce, whom they would follow to the secret site of the dogfight festivities.

"I told you we needed to blend in, and you show up looking like a Puerto Rican ice cream man," Morley said, getting no response from the backseat. Edmond, sitting between Morley and Leo in the front seat, smiled broadly.

A half hour later, they arrived at the meeting spot. It was on the edge of an industrial area along the Blue River that still retained a rural feel, with blocks of weed-filled empty lots and large trees. Occasionally there would be a small, run-down manufacturing building or an old bungalow home. All of the structures were long past their prime and looked like a strong wind could topple them. The six of them sat in the car, lights off but engine running to feed the air-conditioning, which was barely cool as it competed with the body heat they generated. Within a few minutes, an older-model pickup truck pulled alongside them. They heard the truck door slam, and the outline of a man came to the driver's side of the car and knocked on the window, which Morley lowered electronically.

A scruffy, bearded man in his mid-twenties, his hair tied back in a ponytail, poked his head through the window and counted out loud. The man was not Kenny Dyce.

"Kenny said there'd be four of you," the man said. Morley reacted quickly.

"Kenny said bitches don't count," he said. "So we're good, right?"

The man looked puzzled for a moment, then grinned, showing a big gap in his teeth.

"But they pay," he said, almost whistling through his teeth. "Six hundred now and an extra hundred for them's that don't count."

Kenny had told Morley to bring plenty of cash. There would be the cover for the fight, plus any incidentals they might want like food, booze, or drugs. It was also expected that they would lay bets on each fight, of which the house, meaning Kenny, got a percentage. Morley took a roll of bills from his sock that could stop up a toilet. The extra people—and especially Rhodes and LJ, dressed like clowns—were all the trouble he wanted. If he spread enough cash around, and they did their best to blend in, there wouldn't be any trouble. *Hell*, Morley thought, *it still might be fun.* He peeled off $800 and palmed the cash through the window.

"There's an extra c-note for your trouble coming to get us," Morley said.

The man nodded his thanks and pocketed the cash.

"Follow me," he said. "It's just down the road, but stay close."

After a few miles of what seemed to become darker and darker territory, the sun having set for the night, they pulled down a gravel road that led to a medium-sized cinder block building that had once been a furniture factory. There were lights strung up outside, the smell of barbecue smoke, and the sound of Lynyrd Skynyrd blaring from speakers hanging on brackets from the roof of the building. Morley figured there were over one hundred cars and trucks parked in the grass field next to the building. An arm waved to them from the pickup truck in front of them, directing them to park in the grass. Morley instinctively parked at the edge of the field closest to the road, away from where most of the vehicles were parked.

"Expecting the need for a quick getaway?" Edmond asked jokingly, as everyone piled out of the car.

"Always have an exit strategy," replied Morley.

Morley walked over to Henna and LJ, who were standing at the back of the car.

"I'm sorry about the 'bitches' comment," he said.

"You were just thinking on your feet Em," LJ said. "I kind of like that I'm one of the bitches tonight. This is just so…well, risky. I love it."

"Hey, bitch, let's go," Rhodes said, grabbing LJ's hand and walking toward the festivities.

Henna rolled her eyes at the pair of them, then turned and frowned at Morley.

"Well, we're here; let's go," she said, sternly.

The six of them wove their way around the picnic tables set up outside the building, taking in the crowd and the haphazard stands where one could buy grilled hamburgers, hot dogs, and ribs. Henna stared in horror, tugged on Morley's arm, and pointed to an open fire pit behind the food stand. On the spit were three evil-looking animals, roasting slowly over the coals.

"Possum," Morley said. "You want some?"

Henna's face twisted in revulsion, and they walked on.

The convention had a carnival atmosphere. The crowd was mostly white—mostly bikers, with some rural folk thrown in—and ranged from blue-collar workers to the unemployed living on welfare and food stamps. All, however, were excitedly anticipating the upcoming fights. There was plenty of drinking; some couples danced wildly by the make-shift speakers, and others ate and boasted loudly about their dogs or the dogs they had come to see. Everybody was sweating in the humidity. Occasionally, the sound of barking could be heard from inside the building. Morley's eyes darted around, checking out everything that was happening around them. "Situational awareness" was what fighter pilots called it. Morley was on edge. He wanted to know the lay of the place, the people, what they were doing, and what the general feel of the environment was. He was less concerned about color for a story than about basic survival skills. He looked over at Leo, whose head was jerking around like it was on a swivel. Their eyes met, and they both communicated the same message without saying a word: stay alert for any trouble. It was Edmond, Henna, Rhodes, and LJ who relaxed a little and absorbed the experience.

Rhodes held up a mason jar filled with clear liquid.

"Check it out," he said. The six of them gathered around an empty table. "Moonshine. Come on, let's all try it."

They sat down, and Rhodes passed the jar around the table. Morley declined and handed the jar to Henna.

"Take a small sip," he told her. "Swallow it fast."

Henna's lips began to burn as soon as they touched the edge of the jar. She took a big gulp, trying to impress as well as defy Morley. It was an act of bravado she immediately regretted. She began coughing and wheezing violently. Her eyes filled with tears, and her throat felt as if she had run sandpaper up and down her esophagus for several days. Henna tried to talk but couldn't. Morley put his hand on her back and told her to bend over and breathe slowly.

"Leo, go get a pop," Morley said. Leo jumped up and headed over to a large aluminum livestock-watering tub where ice-cold beer and cans of soda were being sold.

Henna sipped the cool drink, her throat still on fire.

"Holy shit, Morley," she finally said. "What the hell was that, gasoline?"

"White lightning," he said, chuckling. "I warned you, Freer."

Rhodes and LJ took small sips from the jar and chased them with beer. After seeing Henna's reaction, Edmond took a cautious swig. His eyes lit up like a pinball machine, and he began sucking in air while reaching for LJ's beer.

"God, that's terrible," he said between deep breaths.

Leo took the jar and a long pull from it. His eyes lit up like Edmond's. Then he stood up and crowed like a rooster, flapping one of his arms about to the enjoyment of a group of bikers at the picnic table next to them.

"Yeah, man, you on that corn liquor now?" one of the bikers yelled to Leo, who smiled back. Morley began to laugh, as did the rest of them.

"Y'all having a good time?" drawled a man now standing behind Morley, looking at them with disapproval.

The man was short, with wiry blond hair pulled back in a ponytail. He wore faded, torn jeans and big black boots. Over his torso he wore only a black leather vest, which exposed his powerful arms. A large skeleton tattoo covered his right shoulder. On his left shoulder was the tattoo of a snarling pit bull framed top and bottom by the words "Cajun Rules." A silver-plated, snub-nosed .38 protruded from his belt.

The man was Kenny Dyce.

"Let's us talk," he said to Morley. The two of them walked over to a door leading inside to the factory building. A few minutes later, and a couple of hundred dollars shorter, Morley returned to the table.

"Everything all right?" Edmond asked, tentatively.

"Yeah, we're cool," Morley said, looking at Rhodes and LJ. "He wasn't too thrilled about the extras, especially Ken and Barbie over there."

"Fights are getting ready to start up. Let's get a few beers and head inside to find some seats."

"So, Em, what's with you and Henna?" Rhodes asked, jabbing Morley in the ribs.

It was the last thing Morley wanted to hear from Rhodes, and he paid the question little attention.

"We're friends," Morley replied, not giving either interest or eye contact to Rhodes.

"Friends, friends, or *friends?*" Rhodes asked, putting emphasis on the last "friends" to imply an intimate, though perhaps casual, relationship between Morley and Henna.

"Just friends," Morley said, not grasping Rhodes' interest.

"Got it, good to know," Rhodes said, looking over at Henna, who sat on the makeshift bench seats between Edmond and Leo. Rhodes had always been intrigued by Henna. He thought she'd make a good one-timer.

"Let's place some bets," Rhodes said, slapping Morley on the back. "And see who the winner is."

The extra money Morley shelled out to Kenny also bought them some of the best seats for the show. They sat on the fourth row of benches overlooking the ring. Another set of stadium-style benches were across the ring from them. For the rest of the crowd that had started to gather inside the factory, it was standing room only. The ring was made of wood and stood about three feet tall to keep the contestants from jumping and bolting into the crowd, and anyone in the crowd from doing the same if their dog was losing. It was a twenty-x-twenty-foot square, and there was a layer of sawdust to absorb the blood. The first thing that struck Henna when they entered the building was the smell of feces and urine. Then there was the sound of wild barking coming from the keep at the back of the factory floor, where the dogs brought in for tonight's fights were caged. Their handlers poked and teased the animals with sticks to get them riled and agitated before a fight.

Kenny entered the ring, raised his arms for quiet, and proceeded to go over the rules for the night. The fights were held under Cajun rules, which Morley briefly described to Henna and Edmond as Kenny spoke. There were, Morley explained, nineteen rules of dog fighting that, according to the story, were established in the 1950s by a Louisiana police chief.

The first two dogs were brought into the ring. They were prospects, young and aggressive, and it was their first fight. Each dog and his handler were placed behind their scratch line by a referee assigned by Kenny. Shouts of encouragement for the respective dogs erupted from the crowd, which also started to cheer.

"Face your dogs," the referee shouted, and the trainers turned their dogs toward each other, their hands holding the release clip on the animals' collars.

"Watch for the first dog that scratches the floor," Morley shouted to Henna so she could hear over the now-screaming crowd. "That dog is called the down dog."

The brown-spotted dog on the far end scratched first.

"Let go," the referee shouted, and the down dog charged at its opponent in a bolt.

The opponent, which had an almost pure white coat, reared back on its haunches, and just as the down dog came within several feet of its attack, the dog sprang forward in a blur, launching itself slightly above and to the side of the charging animal. The white dog's jaws caught the down dog just above and below its ear and rolled in midair, using its momentum to spin its opponent into the side of the ring with a tremendous thud. The white dog's unexpected and acrobatic attack move sent the crowd into a frenzy of amazement. Everyone leaped in the air, arms waving, betting slips and money, screaming and thrashing wildly for the next move in the action. It reminded Morley of the trading room floor right before the closing bell.

The white dog turned and charged the dazed spotted dog, sinking its powerful jaws deep into the neck of the cowered beast. Using its powerful shoulders, the white dog shook its prey back and forth with such violence that blood from the wounded animal sprayed into the crowd, further elevating the excitement of the onlookers. This went on for several minutes until the white dog's upper body was nearly covered in blood, giving it the appearance of having been dipped in dye. The spotted dog, though still alive, was spent and lay whimpering under the strength of its opponent. The referee called the fight. A small cheer came from the crowd, which quieted down quickly to settle all bets. The white dog's handler approached the heaving heap of blood and animals and clipped a chain leash to the collar of his winning dog. He then pulled a stick from his back pocket that resembled the handle to a hammer and placed it into his dog's mouth.

"What's he doing?" Henna asked.

"It's a break stick," Morley said. "The dog's jaws are locked down, and he has to pry them back open. Sometimes they have to break their jaws to get them off."

Henna winced as, with a jerk of the stick, the white dog released its death grip on the wounded animal and was led away by its trainer.

As soon as the winner was out of the ring, the owner of the losing animal walked up, cursed, and pulled a small revolver from the band of his belt. He fired two quick reports into the head of the animal, which yelped once before slumping quietly into the blood-soaked sawdust.

His retribution was so swift, it took all of them by surprise. Henna's mouth dropped open in shock, and Edmond grabbed her arm, more to console himself than her.

"There's no poetry in this, no art," Edmond said disapprovingly to Morley. "It's base violence."

The smell of the gunpowder lingered in Morley's nostrils, and he could sense the metallic flavor of blood. The room was much hotter than it had been, and he could hear the beating of rotor blades and the grittiness of wet sand in his clothes. He clenched his jaw and fixed his eyes around the room, measuring distances and elevations in his head.

Henna looked at Morley, who was in a trance. He had not heard what Edmond said. He did not react when she asked him if he was okay. His eyes were somewhere else, she thought, somewhere very far away and very frightening. The color had gone out of his face. She shook him until he slowly turned his head toward her. His eyes, she thought, were blank and fixed. He looked at her with the same expression the owner of the down dog wore right before he pulled the trigger. Edmond saw the look in Morley's eyes as well and pulled Henna slightly away from him. Just then, Leo stepped between them, grabbed Morley by the shoulders, and shook him once.

"Yeah, yeah, I'm good," Morley said to Leo. "Don't mean nothing."

The two of them pounded their fists on top of each other, and Morley was back in the moment.

Henna and Edmond weren't sure what to make of what just happened. Morley was back with them, but where had he been? Had something snapped in him? Henna wondered. Edmond thought about triggers. He also was growing concerned about some of the looks they had gotten from the crowd. There was nothing discreet about a midget, an auburn-haired beauty, and a guy in a salmon-colored suit at a dogfight. Not to this mob. A ball of fear had started to form in Edmond's stomach.

The crowd rose into another frenzied, emphatic crescendo as the second dogfight began. They stood like one mad body, waving and weaving in unison, cheering their dogs on as each animal took vicious swipes at the other with their powerful jaws. The fight was stopped at one point, and the dogs separated. One had fanged itself, and its trainer was tending the wound, while the other combatant was held taut on a chain, pulling and writhing to get free and attack again.

Morley began to look away from the blood sport, as did Henna. Her face, almost always a bright alabaster, except for the birthmark, was now a pale, chalky white. Her eyes darted about, mostly looking at the bench below her, just never looking in the direction of the ring. Leo, who was nervous and agitated, jumped down from the bench to the factory floor, but remained within an arm-reach of Morley, Henna, and Edmond.

There was the sense in the four of them that a high-voltage power line had fallen to the ground and was whipping around the factory indiscriminately. The electricity fed the action, but it also held the deadly risk of direct contact. The loose end of the wire seemed to spark past Morley; his instinct was charged with the reality that coming here, coming with his friends, was a mistake. He wanted to leave with all of them, and he wanted to leave soon.

Rhodes relished the violence, much like a child discovering chocolate for the first time. LJ stood in the shadow of his pleasure, eating the crumbs Rhodes dropped behind him. Not satisfied with the view from the bench seats, he had moved closer to the action, LJ in tow. He stood right up to the edge of the ring. Darkening streaks and splatters of blood from the dogs now complimented his salmon suit. He waved his betting slips and cash in his fist and yelled with the onlookers at each snap, jerk, and growl in the ring.

To the disappointment of the crowd, the fight ended in a draw, each dog too exhausted to go on, despite the exhortations and prodding of their trainers. Morley could see Henna and Edmond had seen enough. Their faces were both drawn and exhausted, as if they themselves were whimpering in the blood-soaked sawdust. Morley crouched down and grabbed Leo on his shoulder.

"We're out of here," he shouted. Leo looked up and shook his head in agreement. "Get Rhodes and LJ."

Morley turned to Henna and Edmond and motioned with his head that it was time for them to leave, which was met with looks of relief.

There was a lull between fights, and the pack, not satisfied with the outcome of the last match and fueled by a long evening of booze and violence, was unconsciously looking for something to boost the gathering to its next high. Helping Henna down from the top of the bench seats was a gesture that would receive no attention. But as Morley helped Edmond down, one of the now bored and impatient men within the mob caught site of the strange event.

"Look, a fucking dwarf," he yelled, pointing in Edmond's direction as that section of the crowd directed its attention toward the bench.

Morley heard the shout, saw the faces turn toward him and Edmond. The flailing electrical line touched him, and he could feel the voltage shoot through his body.

"Hey, let's fight the dwarf," another man shouted, laughing and drinking from a mason jar.

"Yeah, let's fight the dwarf," came from another voice.

"Fight the dwarf, fight the dwarf," a small group began to chant.

Morley scanned the interior of the building for all the visible exits, chastening himself for not having mapped out an exit strategy when they first entered. His mind reeled back in time, and he wished he could call in a dust-off or supporting fire, but he only had his wits and however fast Henna and Edmond could move. Remembering how she reacted when he slipped down the stairs at the apartment, he knew Henna could stay up with him. Edmond, however, was at an obvious disadvantage. The chant, though not loud, continued to build as more of the mob, as if caught up in the current of a fast river, began to join, not really aware of what was going on around them. Morley looked down at Edmond and instantly saw the fear he had seen in other men's eyes, one of submission and resignation to impending death.

Out of the crowd, a man reached down and grabbed Edmond. Morley cocked his arm back, clenched his right fist, and landed a punch in the man's jaw, sending him backward toward the factory floor. Morley felt pressure on the left side of his face and a stinging sensation as he absorbed a blow to himself. He recovered quickly and prepared to retaliate, but as he was about to release, the eyes of his opponent rolled back, and he fell to the floor in a loose pile. Leo stood next to the fallen man, the scars on his face red and purple and threatening with each pulse of blood. He had another man by his neck and shook him into submission as the crowd that gathered around them shrank back.

"We're out of here, now," Morley said emphatically, grabbing Henna's arm and moving swiftly to the nearest exit. Leo, still holding onto the man's throat, unceremoniously picked Edmond up and tucked him under his left arm. He held the man's throat hostage, dragging him several feet before releasing his grip and picking up speed. In his peripheral vision, Morley made out a salmon-colored object followed by a rainbow of flowing colors he figured were Rhodes and LJ.

Fireworks exploded in the sky outside as they exited the building. Large bursts of red and blue stars shot through the thick air, then gently floated toward the earth. They stopped at a picnic table to regroup. Leo put Edmond down and stood back from the light of the doorway to see if they were being chased. The mob had lost interest quickly, as their fight was over and the next fight in the ring had begun.

They were all there, out of breath, but out safe. Also there, standing on the bench of one of the picnic tables, was Kenny Dyce. Two other men stood on either side of the table. Morley, who was in front of Kenny, took a deep breath and waited for him to speak.

"Y'all gone," Kenny said. "You's outta here now."

Morley was about to nod in agreement but was interrupted by Rhodes.

"Bullshit," he said. "You owe me money. I still have bets on the fights that haven't been paid off."

Kenny Dyce opened his mouth in a wide grin, exposing several gold-capped teeth. He pulled his silver—plated revolver from his waistband and held it to Morley's head, silencing Rhodes and garnering the attention of all of them. Leo moved a step forward, but Morley waved him off. Henna sidled up next to Edmond, who was shaking. Undaunted by the circumstances, Morley looked straight at Kenny and, with an ease of resolve, stepped closer to the short barrel of the gun pointed at his forehead.

"Don't mean nothing," Morley said, his eyes locked on Kenny. They were both in the moment, the two of them, together, but they were thousands of miles away in another hot country.

"Pull it," Morley implored.

Kenny Dyce laughed.

"Yeah, dat what you want," he said, still holding the gun to Morley's forehead. "I git it. Sometime dat what I want, too."

He lowered the gun and laughed again, then scowled down at Morley.

"Git the fuck outta here now," he hissed. "Don't never call me again."

<hr/>

They drove in silence a mile or so down the road, the flashes of what had just happened snapping through their memories, burning into them forever. The cool air from the air-conditioner soothed their skin but not their stomachs.

"Pull over," said Edmond, who was wedged between Morley and Leo in the front seat.

He trembled from the cold air coming from the vent and from the shock of their escape. Morley pulled the Ninety-Eight off the road onto a grassy patch, wet with midnight dew, and got out to let Edmond out on the driver's side of the car. Edmond, half stumbling, put his right arm on the front of the car for support and began retching uncontrollably. Morley stood by him, giving silent comfort.

"Jesus, what a pussy," Rhodes said, a distinct tone of mocking judgment in his voice.

Leo, furious and fed up after years of restraint, reeled around toward the backseat, reached over, grabbed Rhodes by the lapel of his stained suit coat, pulled him closer, and, with the back of his hand, slapped him as hard as he could, leaving a large red welt on his face. LJ sat stunned, aware for the first time that Rhodes did not have the close bond he claimed to have with this group of classmates.

"Enough!" Henna shouted, exiting the car to avoid the conflict and to see if she could help Edmond, who remained bent over but recovering.

Morley walked over to where she was standing at the back of the car. The dark silhouettes of the trees on either side of the two-lane road towered over them, almost blocking out the hazy night sky. In the distance, they could hear the popping reports of fireworks. He put an arm on her shoulder.

"Are you okay?" he asked.

She turned around and saw the small rivulet of blood that had formed on the corner of his mouth, where he had been hit. She ran a finger across the blood, now starting to dry; put her arms around his neck, drawing his face closer to hers; and kissed him deeply but briefly. The sound of fireworks in the distance stopped. There was only the briny taste of blood in their mouths.

"You're okay, Morley," she said.

BOOK IV

"White Christmas" playing on the radio. Good, as long as we hear that we're okay. Nobody's pulled the fuck out and left us, yet. I'm real worried about that, getting fucking left behind. We're all fucking worried about that. It's all anybody is fucking worried about. That and getting our asses shot off. "Hey, man, let's get the fuck out of here." "Yeah, man, ARVN's fucking flakey, and Charlie's going to be here any fucking minute; let's didi." I turn around to tell the squad to shut the fuck up. It's Billy. Billy? What the fuck are you doing here? Back up the street, Leo's firing off rounds into a Citroen that's burning underneath a tree. What the fuck is he doing? We're so scared, every other word out of our mouths is "fuck." Because we're fucked. The heat is blowing the leaves off the branches. Leo? No way, Leo's not supposed to be here either. This is weird shit. "There it is! There it is!" And there it is. A Sea Stallion is thumping its way through the thick air, throwing debris and shit all over the place as it sets down in a park at the end of the street. A park in Saigon? Why the fuck is there a park here? There are kids swinging on a swing set Billy's father bought at Sears. Leo's yelling over the rotor wash. "Billy's hit. Billy's hit." Oh, shit, Billy's bleeding. It's his leg, where I shot him with a BB gun in the fourth grade. His mom's going to be pissed. I turn back to the helicopter, and the engineer is on the ramp, waving for us to hurry. The kids on the swings are running up the ramp. There are hundreds of people lined up. They're screaming and fighting to get on the ramp. Ah, fuck! I've never seen this kind of shit before. Mothers are throwing their babies into the back of the helicopter. The engineer is kicking them back and waving at us to hurry up. Christ, we've got to get on that bird now*! It's the last one out. There are bodies all up and down the street. The car is on fire. Shops are on fire. People are looting. The place is a mess. I grab Leo. Where's Rhodes? Rhodes was in the car with us. It was his idea. Where is he, Leo? Leo is looking at me, deadpan. "Rhodes isn't here. He has connections." All of a sudden it's quiet. I can see the fires, the helicopter, and the crowds, but I don't hear them. I don't get it. Leo is smoking a cigarette and he says, "Rhodes got off, remember?" Oh yeah, Rhodes didn't get the deal we got stuck with. Now I remember. Leo is gone. I look down, and Billy is gone. It's Dee-nay. His leg is shot bad, and the medic is fixing him up. We roll him over to get him ready to lift, and he throws up. Corn for breakfast. Out of a doorway, an old gook grandma in black pajamas scurries out on her hands and knees and starts to eat the kernels from the puke puddle. She looks up at me with black stained teeth and smiles like it's the best meal she's had in days. I'm losing it. I don't want to hang here anymore. The medic and I are hauling Dee-nay to the helicopter. More Marines are on the ramp, firing over the heads of the crowd pushing toward the aircraft. The guys freak out and start firing into the crowd. Some people fall, and the*

others scatter. We're almost there. Hang in there. We're almost there. I feel the heat of the concussion first, then hear it; I'm flying through the air. "Wake up, son." Feel stupid. Sleeping on the floor in the front hall of the Chancery building. It's my shift. Sergeant has his hand on my shoulder. Says crowds are building but to keep it cool. Sarge is cool. Wall duty. Checking IDs and papers. Lifting people over the wall. Throwing others back like fish. Look at my wrist. Got about two hours of rack since we came from the airport. Sky is overcast but slip on the Black Panther Ray Bans I lifted from Jackson. Can't see my eyes. Better that way. Walk outside to the noise and smell of chlorine. There are people everywhere inside the compound. Bits of burned paper and money cover the ground. A fistful of charred $20s in the bushes. The water in the pool looks inviting. It's humid but not boiling hot. Heavy clouds. Heavy with rain, maybe. This place needs a shower. A bath. A cleansing. Still, in the still, it is sticky. We're pulling out. Unwinding perimeters. Thank God they are keeping the pool water safe. The water looks good. Could do some laps. The blueness of the bottom of the pool is serene. The black lane lines are comforting. It's calm. It's order. But a cardboard box floats in the second lane with someone's shirt. Get winked at by a fat Aussie drinking whiskey in a deck chair. Really, asshole? Get on a chopper and get the fuck out of here. There is cutting and sawing. The tamarind trees and shrubs are coming down. Make way for a new LZ. Still feel asleep. Sleep walking through history. Don't notice the thumping helicopters anymore. On the wall it clicks. Outside there is an ocean of people with stupid looks of hope on their faces. Hits like when you feed a cigarette machine, and the last coin clinks, and you pull the knob and get that satisfaction of knowing the pack is coming your way. I get it. They don't. They are feeding the machine, but it's sold out. Empty. The whole place is empty, except for the fear. An ARVN soldier points his rifle at us then targets the sky and fires. Another shoots at us with his finger then gives us the finger. They know. They get it. No more cigarettes. Almost fall off the wall but get grabbed by another Marine. "Hang in there. It don't mean nothing." Time passes, and it's dark-thirty, and a major orders us to form a semicircle around the main entrance to the Chancery. This is it. Baker Charlie. B.C., as in we are history. Be cool. Be calm. Do your job, Marines. The semicircle retreats into the building. The light goes on in the crowd. The cigarette machine is empty. Panic. A rush. The Main Gate crashes. Get the doors bolted, then bolt our asses up the stairwell. Pass and lock each grill gate. Elevators are shut down. Hear the crowd. Big crash. There's a water truck in the lobby. The crowd pours in, flooding the stairwells. They bleat like sheep. Can feel a whoosh of air come up with the crowd through the stairwell. Is this what it's like on a sinking ship? Feel like a rat again. Hear some shots. Hope it ain't rat season. On the roof and start *stacking lockers with reactionary gear and fire extinguishers on wheels against the doors. Now what? The choppers stop. The world stops. Just sit there and watch my dog tags swing. Memorize my blood type and religion like I forgot. Shit. I don't hear "White Christmas" anymore. No way they are leaving us. Hear some thumping in the distance. "The temperature in Saigon is 112 degrees and rising." Start laughing and pass a cigarette around. Climb up one of the red ladders to the top of the roof and into the chopper. Flick the cigarette out the door. Peace with honor, my ass.*

CHAPTER 24

Henna sat at her desk, repeatedly clicking the ball-point pen in her hand, imagining the click to be the sound the trigger of a revolver might make, wondering if Kenny Dyce's silver-plated gun would have made the same clicking sound if he had pulled the trigger. Deep in a trance, she was a little girl again and heard the clicking of the lock on her bedroom door. She winced and dropped the pen from her hand. There was pressure on her chest, and her breathing was labored. She took in a deep breath, held it in her stomach, and slowly cleared the air from her lungs. The old thoughts went away, but Morley was still in her head.

He was what she desired and feared the most. He wanted to be saved. He wanted to be loved. He was willing to give himself over, to lose himself in her. She looked at the shelf across from her desk with the rows of different-colored and -sized boxes, each wrapped with a distinct ribbon or bow. She imagined putting Morley in one of the boxes. *Just which one?* she wondered.

She rationalized the relationship with Morley, with her life, with what she was capable and not capable of doing. Morley wanted to make love, she thought. But there was no such thing. It was just screwing. It was what people did in the moment to feel better. Then they move on, hoping to feel better with someone else, someone different. No real attachment. It was easy to pass them on. In time, they become too mean, too demanding, too jealous, too dishonest, too old, too fat; or not rich enough, funny enough, good enough, photogenic enough. It was easy for Henna to find something wrong with all of them. Morley was too much for her. He was too nice, too patient, too helpful, too willing.

Tears formed in the corners of Henna's eyes. She was broken, she said to herself. She was not worthy of love, to be loved. Sitting in her small back office, surrounded by her shreds of paper and glue and tape and display clothes and fancy boxes, she was as she had felt for most of her life—empty and alone.

She wiped the tears away with the back of her hand. Looking up at the largest and prettiest box on the shelf, she untied the gold ribbon in her head, opened the box, and put Morley in it. She gently put the lid back on, retied the bow, and placed the package back in its spot on the shelf.

She breathed easier. She felt more in control of herself. Everything was as it should be, where it should be.

Good, that's settled, she thought, just as the phone rang. It was Rhodes. He had a project on the Plaza, he said. Could he buy her lunch? Sure, she replied. Why not?

Not once over lunch did Rhodes mention the weekend and what happened at the dogfight. He acted as if nothing happened. *I can do that*, Henna said to herself. *I can act like nothing happened*. It was familiar, comfortable territory for her. In Morley's own words, she remembered, it don't mean nothing.

⋈

A pair of expensive, matching suitcases lay on the floor of Edmond's apartment as he scurried about packing for his trip. Morley, sitting on the couch, sipped iced tea from a tall glass, his gaze fixed on Edmond's monogram printed in gold on the suitcases.

"So you haven't heard from her at all, then," Edmond said, neatly stacking a half-dozen laundered shirts, folded and wrapped in plastic.

"Not since I dropped her off at her place after," Morley said, hesitating at the thought of what transpired at the dogfight.

Edmond froze, recalling the night that was just days ago, though it felt as if it happened a decade earlier. He looked at his friend Morley, his face low and almost beaten, like one of the losing dogs at the fights.

"Look at me, Emmett," Edmond said. "It wasn't your fault."

"How's that?" Morley replied, without looking up.

"We pressured you to go," Edmond said. "Especially me. I was titil-lated by the idea. It was illegal, taboo, and dangerous, and I, and the rest of us, I think, craved that. It was a new kind of lust for us.

"I think we all thought it would make us better. In some way we'd be more experienced in life, and oh, so much better and wiser for it. And we were oh, so very wrong."

Morley was gloomy and unmoved, feeling responsible for what hap-pened and for whatever could have happened, even though it didn't. *But it still might have*, he thought agitatedly. The possibilities played out again and again in his mind. He had not been able to stop the myriad scenarios his imagination spun out. Still, what looped through his head more than the other projections was the gun pointed at him. It wasn't the gun that disturbed him; it was an urge he felt was woven into the very fabric of his soul—he *wanted* Kenny to pull the trigger. That, and Kenny knew he wanted him to pull the trigger, but he didn't. Instead, he chose to disap-point Morley in the end. Kenny understood Morley better than anyone. Better than Morley did himself.

"Fuck, it don't mean…"

"No, Morley, it *does* mean something," Edmond said in a commanding voice, capturing Morley's attention. "It means everything."

Edmond walked over to the couch in his waddling way and stood in front of Morley, his hands on his hips.

"It meant everything to me," Edmond said in a controlled and reflec-tive tone. "I've been afraid my entire life. Afraid of being hurt because of who I am, what I am. I was ashamed of myself. Being the cool drug dealer was a way to manipulate people into liking me. As if having good coke would make me a good person."

Morley lifted his head from his chest, the look on his face softening as he listened intently to Edmond.

"It was all bullshit, my friend. They wanted the drugs, not me. Did you know, when I quit making deliveries, my phone stopped ringing? So did the invitations. But what didn't stop was my fear. I didn't understand that until I saw it in the face of that asshole that wanted to throw me into the ring."

Edmond took a sip from Morley's glass of iced tea. He sighed and looked up at the ceiling with a reserved calmness.

"I had to bottom out before I could get some perspective," Edmond said, smiling. "And, holy shit, did I bottom out that night. But when I looked up, what I saw were two friends willing to sacrifice themselves for me."

"You're welcome," Morley said, smiling back.

"I'm not thanking you," Edmond retorted. "When something like friendship, or love, is unconditional, sacrifice is unspoken."

Taking the glass back from Edmond's hand, Morley nodded understanding to his friend, raised it in a silent toast, and drank. The two of them fell into a comfortable conversation for the next half hour as Edmond packed. His flight was scheduled to leave early that evening, and Morley had volunteered to take him to the airport. Edmond had a three-week break in July and, after the long semester and everything else that had happened, had decided to spend time with his family at their beach house on Martha's Vineyard. It would, he felt, be the best place to rededicate and reenergize himself to return in August, fully focused on completing his medical degree and ramped up for the competition of landing a prestigious residency. And now, he felt, he was sure of what field of medicine he would follow. A shrunken man, Edmond joked with himself, is best suited for shrinking heads.

The summer heat wave had intensified, bearing down on the city with temperatures that had soared over 100 degrees each day since the Fourth of July. High humidity levels only drove the misery index higher. The heat also made Morley's apartment unlivable. An air-conditioning unit can only do so much. Edmond offered, and Morley accepted, the use of Edmond's apartment while he was gone. Among the few things he moved over to Edmond's—clothes, typewriter, and notebooks—were several of Henna's paintings. The heat in the apartment had softened the pigment, which Morley was afraid would start to run down the canvases and ruin her work. He had phoned her several times to tell her of his plan to move the paintings and where he could be found. In response, there was a message from her left at the answering service that said only, "Freer says okay."

"So what do you think about Henna?" Morley asked Edmond, as he clipped shut the locks on the last suitcase.

Edmond cautiously mulled over his reply before responding.

"Think about her in what way?" he asked.

"What do you think is going on with her?" Morley said, slightly annoyed at having his question answered with another question.

"It's obvious she's hiding, Emmett," Edmond said. "What from, I don't know. We, you, may never know. Probably, like me, from fear. You'll hear from her when she's ready, I guess. Maybe you never will."

Morley frowned. He had hoped Edmond would have been more encouraging; he wanted to hear something hopeful. Edmond could see his answer was not what had been expected.

"My friend," Edmond said. "You and Leo were responsible to me at the fight. But you didn't save me. I have to save me. I think it's the same with Henna. You can't force something to happen in someone."

"I'm not sure I follow."

"Stop following," Edmond said. "Find your own way."

Edmond looked at his watch and slapped his hands together.

"But right now, it's time to find your way to the airport and get me the hell out of this godforsaken place before I melt," Edmond said. "Don't take this personally, this being your hometown and everything, but after graduation, I'm never coming back here again. The weather is dreadful."

For the first time since February, Morley thought about leaving, too, and never coming back. The weather truly was dreadful.

CHAPTER 25

By the third week of July, rain had become as scarce as Henna and Leo. Less than an inch had fallen in the city, and with the brutal heat wave blamed for at least a dozen deaths in the metropolitan area, authorities expected the number to go even higher. The normal routine of the summer season also suffered. The scent of rotting fish from a large die-off in Swope Park Lagoon filtered through the park, causing the public pool, one of the few places inner-city kids could cool down, to close because of the over-whelming stench. The zoo, generally a bit aromatic anyway, also saw a drop in visitors. Patio restaurants like Putsch's Sidewalk Café and The Prospect in Westport had almost ceased to operate in the sweltering weather, as cus-tomers avoided the outdoors as much as possible. Sidewalks were empty by midday throughout most of the city.

Morley felt he, too, was being abandoned. He had called Henna dozens of times over the previous weeks and even left messages with her co-work-ers. He received no response other than the last cryptic message regarding the relocation of her paintings. He checked his stifling hot apartment each day to see if she had been by, but each time he walked away dejected, as there was no sign she had been by the place. Toward the end of July, he felt he had done all he could to reach out to her, though what wrong he might have caused baffled him. If only, he hoped, they could just talk and get whatever it was out in the open and move on, in whichever direction they decided to go. Morley felt a void in his soul, and he responded by burying himself in his work as a distraction. Still, there was an attendant anxiety hiding in the corners of his stomach that sometimes gushed up through his neck and exploded in his head. "Screw it," he would think when it surfaced, usually without warning, "I'm not weak; we weren't even lovers." But the emotional attachment to Henna was there, despite his denials. He attempted to shrug it off, thinking it didn't "mean nothing," but Edmond's words haunted him—it did mean something.

Concurrent with Henna's evaporation amid the heat, Leo had dropped out of sight, almost the day after the dogfight. Morley was consumed with Henna, and Billy was consumed with the Brooks Brothers opening and preparations to move to Berkley and begin law school in August. Neither of them gave much thought to Leo's absence until Billy got a phone call from the bartender at The Pike. He expected to be told to come collect Leo from the bar. Instead, the instructions were for him and Morley to retrieve a letter Leo had left for them. It was late afternoon; Billy called Morley right away, and they agreed to meet up at The Pike in a half hour.

The Pike was quiet when Morley arrived, except for the loud air conditioner above the front door, laboring to cool the air. One other customer sat in the corner by the front window. Billy came in the back door within minutes of Morley. They motioned to Tony, the bartender, who, without asking, pulled two draws of beer and two shots of whiskey. He brought them over to Morley and Billy and produced an envelope from the cash register. He handed it to Billy.

"The drinks are on Leo," Tony said. "He said to toast to him first, then open the envelope."

"Fuck that, Tony. What the hell is going on?" Billy demanded, fearful of what Leo might have done to himself.

Tony stepped back, holding his hands up as if he was being robbed at gunpoint.

"Hey, man, I'm clean," Tony said. "I'm just doing what he told me to do. And I know damn well you don't want to fuck with Leo."

"When did he give you this?" Billy asked sternly.

"A week ago," Tony said, retreating toward the far end of the bar.

"And you're just now fucking giving it to us!" Billy barked back.

"Just doing what I was told, Billy," Tony said.

166

As Morley put his hand on Billy's shoulder to calm him, he recalled how he felt when the priest put his hand on Morley's shoulder right before he was told his father was dead.

"Let it go," Morley said. "What is, is."

"Fuck," Billy said as they raised their shot glasses.

"G-H-M-F," Billy said, sadly.

"G-H-M-F," Morley replied, both of them quickly downing their shots and chasing them with the beer.

"Open it up," Morley said, with morbidity in his voice, glancing quickly at the wicker casket hanging on the wall behind him.

Billy tore through the envelope and pulled out a single, hand-written letter and read it aloud.

"*Commilitones in bello Fratres*, I've been in the same water too long. It's like rereading a book or going back with an old girlfriend, I know what's at the end. It was time to get clean, and this was the best I could come up with. I managed to land a job through a buddy from Pearl. It's on the North Slope, working on the oil field at Prudhoe Bay. The weather during the winter is extremely cold, but they pay very, very well, and you have no expenses while you're up there. It's two weeks on and two weeks off. Work is twelve hours a day for the entire time, and you can make about $1,500 to $2,500 per week, depending on the shift. I think I could do that for a while just to say I've been there, and was part of it. My buddy went up there and worked twenty-six weeks straight and made $58,000 after taxes, but he said it nearly killed him mentally. What don't kill you makes you stronger, right? After that, he took off for Europe for six months and blew it all. I figure I can dry out up in the cold. That might work for me. I paid for two rounds, so don't let Tony screw you out of them. I'll drop you a line if I get a chance. Stay fearless. Leo."

They looked at each other and began laughing out loud. Always the dramatic one of the three, Leo had played them again. Tears rolling down his face, Billy raised two fingers to Tony for the second round.

"That fucker," Morley chuckled.

"God, he scared the shit out of me," Billy said.

Tony delivered the next round, and they toasted Leo and Alaska and hoped he got raped by polar bears while he was up there. They laughed some more and ordered another round.

"Might as well keep going," Billy said.

"Might as well," Morley said, the first big smile on his face Billy had seen in some time.

"That must have been some night," Billy said, hoping not to stir up too much in Morley.

"Oh yeah," Morley said.

They downed the third round of shots and had a chugging contest with the beers. With the buzz from the alcohol settling in, Morley and Billy rested on the comfort of their friendship, now minus one.

"Did he really slap Rhodes?" Billy asked.

"Like a bitch."

Billy took a swig from his mug.

"God, I love Leo," he said.

CHAPTER 26

The water geysers in the outfield fountains, flanking the giant crown-topped scoreboard, danced to the organ music in a ballet of spray and novelty that excited fans already feverish from their team's play this season. Coming into the weekend series against the Yankees, the Royals topped the Texas Rangers by 10½ games in the American League West Division; and the three-game home stand was, fans hoped, a prelude to post-season play. Having toughed out the worst of the heat wave, which had begun to dissipate in the last week, and a recession that saw local manufacturing jobs evaporate along with the scant rains of July, hope for an October afterlife for their baseball team had begun to germinate. Kansas City's nemesis had long been New York, which had historically seen Kansas City as a farm club. In recent history, New York had thwarted all attempts by the Royals to get past the playoffs and into the World Series.

The unnaturally green Astroturf stretched below Morley's prime front-row spot in the press box and out toward the fountains that, during slower innings, caused him to be lulled into a half sleep and miss key plays when they happened. If not for his press box neighbor, Tug Drecker, Morley would be, in locker room parlance, left sitting there with his dick in his hand. Tug, originally from Oklahoma, worked for the *Associated Press* as the Kansas City bureau's sports reporter. Had it not been for Tug taking Morley under his tutelage early on in the season, Morley surely would have wandered around the press box with his hands affixed to his crotch. Because Morley worked for a "foreign" newswire—Tug and the *United Press International* sports reporter battled constantly for deadlines, quotes, exclusives, and parking spots—Tug did not generally see him as competition. He liked the affable and eager Morley, who would shag quotes from the visitor's locker room after the game in exchange for an accurate box score.

Morley liked going to the stadium. Though not a sports fanatic, and having only covered a handful of Irish football games in Dublin, he fondly remembered his father taking him to Kansas City Athletics games at the old Municipal Stadium and attempting to show him how to score a game while he peeled away at peanut shells. Good memories, but Morley was always more excited in the fall for hunting season than he was for baseball or football.

"Big Timer, or Jock Sniffer?" Tug asked in his loud Okie drawl, waking Morley from his trance.

"What?" Morley replied.

Tug pointing toward an announcer in the broadcast booths where the television and radio guys were housed separate from the print media. There was no love between the two mediums, and even less respect.

"Jock Sniffer, without a doubt," Morley laughed.

Tug, short and squat, stood up from his padded press box chair and yelled out, "Score one for Morley." The newspaper beat reporters all snickered in agreement with Morley's choice, and the *UPI* reporter, without looking up from his notes, raised one finger in silent approval for the vote as well.

They were a good half hour away from the first pitch, and the press box was electrified—as was the nearly sell-out crowd in the stadium—with how well the team was playing, the Yankees being in town, and the streams of off-color commentary about a story that had broken earlier in the day.

Heat aid workers had been called to a three-story building on the east side of town earlier in the day, where they found a twenty-five-year-old man caged in a filthy, vermin-infested room. The man, who lay on the floor in fetal position and did not speak or respond, was dressed only in underwear. The windows in the room had been shuttered by plywood, and the two padlocked doorways to the room were covered with wood and chicken wire. Authorities found grooves on the wooden frames of the doors, where the man had tried to claw his way out with his fingernails.

It was fodder for the press box, where no subject was taboo. The black humor and raunchy language appealed to Morley. It was a man's world, just as the squad bay in basic training had been, only they served booze in the press cafeteria after the seventh inning.

"Fucking sounds like a dream date to me," a red-haired reporter from the *Topeka Capital Journal* yelled out after the story in the newspaper was read aloud.

"Let's see your fingernails, because I think you're the date," the *Wichita Eagle Beacon* reporter yelled back. The place erupted with laughter.

"Big Timer, or Jock Sniffer?" Tug offered to all the scribes.

"Jock Sniffer," was the unanimous vote yelled by all, eliciting more laughter.

Amid the sea of guffaws, Joe McGuff, sports columnist for the *Kansas City Star* walked into the press box and descended the stairs to take his seat in the front row, his face alight from the banter. Tug turned to Morley.

"Big Timer," he whispered. "One of the last of 'em."

Big Timers where, according to Tug, guys who knew how to report and how to write in short, concise language. They called it as they saw it, based on facts, with no agenda and no desire to idealize the players. Jock Sniffers collected autographs and made heroes of the players who would let them hang out after a game. Drunks, drug addicts, sex fiends, and habitual gamblers—if they played well on the field and threw some crumbs to the Jock Sniffers, they were made into gods in print and on video. Tug hated Jock Sniffers.

Morley was working on a situationer on Royals outfielder Willie Wilson. Going into the weekend series, Wilson was batting .338 and leading the league in hits, runs, and triples. On top of those accomplishments, Wilson ranked in the top five in total bases and stolen bases in the league, and he had only missed two games this season. But he, like the Royals themselves, had been overlooked in the American League All-Star voting. He had not even been named as a reserve.

Morley thought Wilson a bit prickly and wearing a chip on his shoulder in his interview earlier in the day. He acted, Morley thought, as if it was the media's fault he was not getting the attention he felt he deserved. It was always the same in the locker room, Tug advised. "If they aren't getting what they feel they deserve, it's our fault," he said.

Whining athletes get more attention, he told Morley. And a story like that will get good play back East. Especially, he said, with the Yankees in town this weekend.

Tug was right. Morley's piece made the New York papers on Saturday, after the Royals downed the Yankees 6–1. New York bounced back the next day, to win 5–3 off a Reggie Jackson homer in the eighth. On Sunday, the Royals blanked the Yankees 8–0, and that victory spawned a confidence within the players that an October playoff was doable for them. The entire city began to believe. It was, everyone hoped, the start of a new era.

The success of the team and Morley's reporting, which was unique for his agency in the Americas, also meant he'd be spending more time at the stadium. That was good, he thought. It distracted him from thinking too much about Henna. But, as he told the New York sports desk when he filed his story after the Sunday game, not until after the Spring Wheat Tour in North Dakota and a week's vacation fishing in Colorado.

He packed up his notes and the Silent 700 and told Tug he'd see him in two weeks. Morley's flight for Minneapolis left at 6:00 a.m. the next day. From there, he'd fly into Fargo.

"Hey, Morley," Tug called out, as he walked down the aisle behind the beat reporters busily banging out their stories and sidebars for the evening newspapers. Morley stopped, and Tug threw him a Snickers bar. Morley laughed. It was the third food group of a sportswriter's diet: a Coke, a hot dog, and a Snickers bar.

CHAPTER 27

The sizzling and popping of bacon and eggs woke Morley from a deep sleep. He still wore his clothes from the day before and had only managed to throw a wool blanket over himself for warmth. He could smell the grease in the air and the strong coffee percolating on the primitive gas stove in the small galley area of the cabin. The front door was open, and a cool breeze filtered its way through the screen door. He and Billy had arrived at the cabin late the night before, though Morley had little recollection of it. He had fallen asleep in the car almost as soon as Billy pulled out of the parking garage at Stapleton International Airport. Morley's plane from North Dakota did not land until late in the evening, as the sun dipped below the eastern range of the Rocky Mountains, painting them in different shades of purple and blue. The North Dakota Spring Wheat Tour had been five grueling days of early mornings and late nights that took the group in a large circle of the state, starting in Fargo, going on to Bismarck, up to Devil's Lake, across to Grand Forks, and back down to Fargo for the last day. Morley filed over six dispatches a day, along with a roundup of the day's field and crop observations and estimates, from his motel room late each night. He was, like the spring wheat crop itself, exhausted, parched, and spent.

Morley got up and poured a cup of coffee into one of the mismatched mugs on the shelf above the stove. He pushed open the screen door, which opened with a metallic screech that announced a relaxed familiarity. Billy was sitting on the small covered porch of the rustic cabin, his feet kicked up on the pole railing and a steaming cup of coffee warming his hands. Morley peeked out from beneath the low-hanging porch roof to a perfectly clear, Wedgewood blue Colorado sky. The air was dry and carried with it the faint scent of pine and dirt. He took a deep breath, closed his eyes, and enjoyed the warmth of the sun on his face.

The cabin was one of a dozen small cabins that made up a small fishing resort camp in Spinney Mountain State Park. Morley figured they had been built in the early 1950s and hadn't seen much renovation since then. However, the resort was more than adequate in accommodations and price for them.

Billy had unpacked the car the night before and put away the groceries and coolers he had bought in Denver before picking Morley up at the airport. On the drive down to Colorado Springs, he told Morley—before he nodded off—that the trip across Kansas had gone fine. Billy's only complaint was about the about the price of gas being $1.24 along the interstate, versus the $1.14 back home. Billy also had made a stop at the Sports Castle to pick up some new hip waders, flies, leaders, and tippets. As a surprise going-away gift for Billy, Morley had called ahead and paid for a new graphite rod and reel.

Morley's fishing rig was already complete. He had picked up fly fishing in Ireland, borrowing Digger's car on occasional weekends and venturing into the countryside to try out different streams and rivers. His favorite place was the upper reaches of the Kenmare River. While sorting and packing everything in the house before it was sold, Morley found his father's split bamboo fly rod. The reel of the setup lay on the wood plank deck next to Billy, who had put on a new line.

Growing up in such a large family had taught Billy a number of self-reliant skills that Morley admired. The hot coffee in his hands and the smell of breakfast were what he appreciated most at the moment. The ease with which Billy could be domesticated made Morley feel good. Billy was going to be all right in San Francisco.

A loud pop in the skillet made Billy jump in alarm that the food was burning, and he raced inside the cabin, pushing Morley aside and spilling some of his coffee on the deck.

"You're going to make someone a great wife," Morley teased.

A few minutes later, Billy produced a plate of bacon, eggs, and toast. Morley sat in the other chair on the porch and began to eat as Billy came back with the pot of coffee and warmed up Morley's mug.

"When you're done here, can you turn down the bed and run a bath for me?" said Morley, still teasing Billy.

Billy responded with a grunt, paying little attention to Morley's efforts to goad him.

"We need to go into Hartsel to get licenses," Billy said. "There's a package liquor store there, too, so we'll be able to stock up on supplies."

"Sounds good," Morley said, lifting up his coffee mug. "Thanks for breakfast, my friend."

Billy nodded back to acknowledge the appreciation.

—⸙—

Big cotton-ball clouds filled the sky by early afternoon as they fished the waters between the Spinney and Eleven Mile reservoirs. They were part of a series of dams built along the headwaters of the South Platte River, which fed water to the front range of the Rockies. The stretch where Morley and Billy had been casting for the past few hours, their lines gently whipping back and forth in undulant rhythms like the second hand on a watch, was known locally as the Dream Stream. For Morley, it was more of a nightmare. His casting was off, and he had had to stop at least a half dozen times to untangle his line and replace flies that had ripped off his leader from a combination of overly aggressive casting and poorly tied knots. Frustrated, Morley waded through the cool water and sat at the bank, watching Billy, upstream, gently pull his rod back and forth, easily timing his back cast before initiating his forward arm movement and placing the fly right where he wanted.

It wasn't genius or poetry, it was just clean fishing; and watching Billy took some of the sting out of Morley's poor performance. He hadn't caught a thing and didn't feel like he was going to land much his first day on the water. Morley rested the bamboo rod in the dry grass next to him and lay back, staring at the clouds slowly flowing above him, changing shape as they were pushed around the heavens like leaves in the stream. He closed his eyes and felt the sun beat down on his skin. He lay there for some time, quietly breathing and listening to the sounds of insects and moving water.

175

He knew he would get his cast back within a few days. He would be back in rhythm. The scent of gardenia came to him, making him think of Henna. He wondered what she was doing and why she had disappeared. It had troubled him for weeks. The silence and distance between them had created a kind of chaos inside of him that ate at him constantly. Conversely, the cut-off made him want to push her out of his thoughts as much as it made him feel he wanted to draw her closer. The more he thought of it, the more the anxiety began to build within him. His arms would tense and begin to feel scaly and itchy as he obsessed on those thoughts. He took in a deep breath through his nose, filling his lungs and working the air back up into his chest before slowly breathing out. He repeated the process several times. Morley was so focused on his breathing that he didn't hear Billy slosh his way up to the bank.

"You having a heart attack or something?" Billy asked.

Startled, Morley propped himself up on his elbows and squinted at Billy.

"Just spacing out," Morley replied, cupping his hand over his forehead to shade his view of Billy. "Get anything?"

Billy held up a string of four medium-sized trout.

"Got a greenback cutthroat but had to release him, because they're endangered," he said. "We're eating tonight."

"Food sounds good," Morley said. "How about a late lunch? I'm not hitting squat anyway."

"What are you throwing?" Billy asked, as he put the fish in the grass and unloaded his gear on the bank.

"Nymphs."

"Well, that's your problem. They're hitting on brown woolly buggers."

Billy removed a black metal fly box from his fishing vest, flipped through the case like he was skimming a paperback, and pulled two brown woolly buggers from storage. He put them in Morley's outreached hand before wading back upstream to retrieve the sack that contained their lunch and the six-pack of Coors longnecks he had placed in a small rock-rimmed hole in the stream.

They lunched on sandwiches they had made from an Italian loaf, hard salami, Jarlsberg cheese, and French mustard. Billy had also thrown some Colorado peaches into a canvas rucksack. The peach season on the western slope of the Rockies had not been affected by the heat wave, and the fruit was juicy and sweet. Morley liked the contrast between the sweetness of the peach and the cold bitterness of the beer.

That night, Billy pan-fried the four trout with a little butter and oil and some sage he had picked outside the cabin. He served them with new potatoes that he first parboiled, and then seared in the drippings from the fish. They sat on the front porch of the cabin and ate, washing the delicate meat and heavy potatoes down with more beer.

For the next five days, they fished the waters between the two reservoirs. They also worked their way upstream, past Hartsel and toward the Antero Reservoir. Morley got his cast back and felt harmonious and peaceful every time he threw a line in the water. They spoke very little, either on the river or back at the cabin. There was nothing they could say that their surroundings hadn't already said. In the mountains, words were meaningless. The elements were their own language. Any conversation the two men might have would only interrupt what the earth was saying. The landscape was bigger than them. Time was bigger than them. There were no desires or fears that weighed more than the alluvial world around them. For the first time in his life, Morley felt perishable. He had protected himself by being the observer; now, he felt he was the observed: watched and judged by the rocks and trees, not for what he did, but for what he had not done. *What difference have I made?* Morley thought. Everyone he had been close to since coming back home had evolved except for him. Even Henna's distance was a change. *What about me?* he asked himself. *What do I do?*

"What did you say?" Billy asked, pouring a finger of Jack Daniels into a coffee mug as they sat on the porch and watched the last light over the western peaks fade into darkness.

"Nothing," Morley said. "Nothing."

⬛⬛➤✕⬛⬛

Billy was asleep in the back seat of the Ninety-Eight when Morley pulled off the interstate onto the exit ramp. The green reflective highway sign on the shoulder provided the number of the exit, indicating it was for the town of Grainfield. The adjustment in speed woke Billy from his nap, and he sat up, somewhat foggy.

"What's up, stopping for gas?" he asked.

"That, and I need to run a quick errand," Morley replied.

"In the middle of fucking nowhere, Kansas?"

"Yup," Morley said. "In the middle of fucking nowhere, Kansas."

The town of Grainfield was about a mile off the highway and had one main street. It took Morley less than ten minutes after leaving the interstate to find what he was looking for, Pearl's Beauty Salon. Morley had planned the stop months before, but without telling anyone, especially Henna. The salon was owned and operated by Pearl Freer, Henna's mother.

"Mind if I stay in the car and sleep?" Billy asked, not interested in Morley's errand.

"That works just fine," Morley said, pulling up in front of the shop.

A small bell attached to the jamb jingled when he opened the door to the shop. The faces of five women—three of them customers sitting in pink salon chairs, all of them over the age of fifty—turned in unison to admire the handsome young man who walked through the door. Morley picked Pearl out right away. Though older, shorter, and plumper than Henna, she had the same alabaster skin and translucent fingernails. The shop itself was, as Morley would expect, farmland chic. It was clean and neat; and, while on the whole not un-chic, it was in need of some decorative modernization.

Morley apologized for interrupting, and introduced himself to Pearl as a friend of Henna's who was passing through on his way back to Kansas City and just wanted to stop by and say hello.

A wide smile reached across Pearl's face as she fixed her hair and turned to another woman standing nearby, who apparently was her assistant.

"Alma, honey, watch Mrs. Foley's time under the dryer and do this rinse on Mrs. Federmann for me while I visit with Henna's friend," she said, ushering Morley into a small room in the back of the shop that served as both an office and storage space. There was a small table and several chairs. Pearl was almost breathless with excitement with Morley's appearance and fluttered about the small room, picking up magazines and straightening up as if a date had shown up unexpectedly.

She offered Morley a cup of coffee from the worn Mr. Coffee machine that sat on top of a small refrigerator. Guessing the coffee to be at least half a day old, Morley accepted her hospitality, and she poured the luke-warm liquid into a Styrofoam cup. She also offered a slice of "fresh" lemon meringue pie that had had been brought in by one of her customers earlier in the day. Morley thanked her, saying he'd have just a small slice. She produced the pie from the refrigerator, cut him a slice, and placed it on a paper plate while she looked around the office for a plastic fork. The utensil found, she handed it and the pie to Morley. He took a bite of the creamy, tart pie. It was, as Pearl claimed, fresh and very good, if perhaps a bit too sweet for his taste.

"Henna's never had a friend drop by before," Pearl said, her eyes still shining and smile beaming. "How is she? I haven't talked to her in a long time."

"How long has it been?" Morley said, cautiously switching into his reporter mode.

"Oh, Henna's never been one who's big on calling home," Pearl replied, looking away from Morley. "She's just so busy. I know she doesn't have time, and it's easy to forget. I know what that's like."

"She's good," Morley said, telling the first of many lies that would be told over the course of the conversation. "I was just with her a week or so back. She said to say hello."

"Oh, you're lying," said Pearl, blushing and throwing herself into believing what she had just been told.

"No really, Mrs. Freer," Morley said. "That's why I stopped off. To say hello for her."

"It's Mr. Morley?" she asked.

"Please call me Emmett," he said.

"If you don't mind my asking, Emmett, I know it's forward and I don't want to be rude..." she began.

"Yes?"

"Are you a boyfriend of Henna's?"

"I'm a good friend, Mrs. Freer," Morley said. "There's a group of us who hang out together, and I have a studio in my apartment I let her use for her painting."

A brief look of sadness swept across Pearl's face when Morley answered, but it passed as she blinked, and she perked up again.

"She's really good, isn't she?" she asked.

"Very talented," he said. "Her windows at the department store get a lot of attention, and I really admire her paintings."

"She was such a talented little girl. It used to worry me that she would spend so much time alone, buried in her drawings and making collages. She would sit right in here while I was working and spend hour after hour without saying a word. Such a determined soul."

179

Morley took another bite of the pie and looked around the office. He found it curious that there wasn't any sign of Henna on the walls. There was none of her childhood artwork on display, something he thought most parents would be proud to display. But then, nothing he ever produced in grade school art class was ever displayed in his mother's house, or in his father's office either.

"Tell me more about Henna as a little girl," Morley gently pushed. "She doesn't talk much about growing up."

Pearl began to ramble almost nonstop about how hard it was at first for Henna, because her father died when she was two; and her birthmark made her self-conscious at school, even though the kids didn't tease her about it, not that much, at least. She said she named Henna after the plant because of the color of her hair, and that Henna would spend hours going through the fashion magazines at the salon. Henna would talk about growing up and moving to Paris or Milan and becoming a famous fashion designer.

"She was full of spark and energy," Pearl said, then trailed off. "Well, then...."

"What, then?" Morley asked, almost in a whisper, hoping Pearl would sense that whatever she said would be kept in strict confidence. It was Morley's "off-the-record" voice.

"Well, I remarried when Henna was eleven," Pearl said, looking through the open door of the office to see if anyone were listening. "His name was Lloyd Evers, and he and Henna didn't get along. And it was her preteen years and everything, and you know how girls can get."

"Not really, I was an only child," Morley said, trying to imply embarrassment in his tone as a way to disarm her.

"The hormones start, and everything else starts, and Henna was earlier than most of her classmates, and they just get moody and sassy," Pearl said. "Lloyd didn't care for the way she would talk back to him, and they fought a lot."

"She talked about Lloyd," Morley lied, hoping to draw more from Bette, who shot back a look of immediate and stern disbelief at him.

"Henna never talked about him, not after," Pearl said sternly, then stopped herself midsentence.

"No, you're right, not by name," Morley said, scrambling to regain his momentum. "She just mentioned once that she didn't like her stepfather, is all. I'm sorry, Mrs. Freer."

Morley paused to let the strained conversation settle, hoping the silence would work to his advantage for one last question.

"If you don't mind my asking, why Mrs. Freer and not Mrs. Evers?"

"I changed my name back after he went to prison," she said, looking Morley squarely in the eyes. "It was the least I could do for Henna."

Morley looked back at her and nodded, trying not to register his surprise at her candid answer. Now he began to understand without having to be told all the facts and details. He could find those easily enough when he got back to the office. As a reporter, a few quick calls to the courts and prison administration would give him the complete story. He took another bite of pie and asked Pearl if there was anything she wanted him to do for her before he left.

"Take care of my Henna, will you?" she said.

"I'll do that, Mrs. Freer."

Standing in front of the Ninety-Eight, Billy sound asleep in the back seat with the windows rolled down, a strong gust of wind created a mini-dust storm around the car. Morley recalled Henna's breakdown at The Pike; her sexual reputation; her emotional distance, which had become physical distance after the dogfight; and Edmond's vague diagnosis of everyone's past being the basis of their fears.

Even though he questioned and uncovered sordid details and the back-story of people's lives for a living, Morley felt uneasy about the conversation that had just happened. It was as if he had peeked at someone's diary and found out things about himself that hurt him more than it did them. He had invaded Henna's privacy without her knowing. If given the chance, he wasn't sure he'd even let her know what he knew.

Morley rubbed the grit from the dust between his fingers. He felt dirty. They were at least eight hours from home, but he wanted to get back to the apartment as quickly as possible and take a shower.

CHAPTER 28

Having been away for two weeks, it took Morley several days to dig out from the mess of accumulated mail, messages, and newspapers at the bureau. He had become a victim of his own success. Morley's reputation as an industrious, talented, accurate reporter had gained him profile with senior editors at the agency. It had also generated increasing demands from editors on the commodities, sports, general news, and political desks. The Chicago commodities desk was screaming for feature stories in addition to the daily market comments he filed. Corn and soybean harvest time was quickly approaching, and those futures markets were wildly gyrating in reaction to forecasts of a poor harvest due to the heat wave. The commodities desk wanted him in the field while also covering the market. It was an impossible request, as he told them, because he couldn't be in two places at once. At the same time, the New York sports desk increased its demands for updates on the Royals—and George Brett's hitting streak. As they headed into a series with the Cleveland Indians that week, Brett was batting .406. He was consistently hitting at, near, and above .400 throughout the month, which created a national buzz in the sports media. New York wanted Morley as their man in Kansas City to stay on top of the buzz.

That was okay with Morley. He could file his daily comments, produce a crop feature or two each week, and still make the night games at the stadium. He began to catch up on his baseball.

Ted Williams' record average of .406, reached with the Boston Red Sox in 1941, looked breakable to Morley. This, he thought, was history people wanted to read about. Rifling through the dozens of newspapers that had piled up during his absence from the bureau, Morley pored over the sports pages, focusing on a *New York Times* column by Red Smith—a Big Timer for sure, in Tug's view—which quoted Williams on Brett's streak.

"From now on it's going to get tougher for him," Williams said in the article. "At least, I found September the hardest time for hitters for several reasons. The weather's a little colder then, and I was never at my best in chilly weather. The sunlight gets lower, and the shadows grow longer, and the prevailing winds don't prevail the way they did all summer."

Williams went on to say that he didn't realize at the time the importance of hitting .400. It had happened only eleven years before, when Bill Terry hit for .401 with the New York Giants.

"I was young and thought maybe I'd hit .400 another time or two before I was through," Williams said. "Now it's the thing I'm remembered for, but it didn't seem so great at the time."

The quote stuck to Morley for reasons he didn't fully understand. He thought the notion of being remembered for something that didn't seem like a big deal at the time was strange.

Morley flipped through more sports pages and stopped on a story about Charlie Finley selling the A's to the chairman of the board of Levi Strauss and Co. for $12.7 million. Fed up with the direction the game was taking, Finley said he had to get out because he couldn't keep up financially. He cited the, "idiotic, astronomical, unjustified salaries of today."

The story brought back the memory of the A's in Kansas City, along with his father—and the peanuts. Then the phone rang. It was the Washington political desk. While not outright asking for a story, they wanted Morley to tag on to any campaigns that might swing through his "patch" when the political season heated up after Labor Day, running on into the general presidential election in early November. He told them they'd have to clear it with the Chicago desk first, but that he would try to help them out. He hung up the phone, thinking the editor on the other end was not really satisfied after talking to Morley.

Both the Republican and Democratic conventions had been held earlier in the summer, and Morley had paid no attention to either one. In late July, in Detroit, the Republicans had nominated Reagan, as was expected despite the controversy over his age and the behavior of some of his aides. By the middle of August, in a very contentious convention in New York, the Democrats stuck with their incumbent, President Jimmy Carter. John Anderson, in a new twist for modern American politics, decided to run as an Independent.

Of all the beats he could cover, only politics ranked lower than commodities to Morley. He had begun to miss Belfast. He forced himself to read into the political articles a little before he started to lose interest. Reagan was promising a balanced budget, economic health through something he called "supply-side" policies, a strong military, and a 30 percent reduction in taxes over the next three years.

"A recession," Reagan was quoted as saying, "is when your neighbor loses his job. A depression is when you lose yours. And a recovery is when Jimmy Carter loses his."

Morley yawned and threw the newspaper to the office floor. How, he thought, can he minimize his role in covering the presidential election?

Then he remembered he had not yet checked his messages for the day. He picked up the phone and dialed the service. There was one message. It was from a Henna Freer, asking if she could meet Morley at his apartment that evening.

CHAPTER 29

There was an unsettled queasiness in the bottom of Morley's stomach the rest of the day. He vacillated between dreading the meeting—conjuring up only the worst scenarios—one minute, and fantasizing about the pretty possibilities the next. The day moved slowly, and he drank too much coffee, which made him even edgier and quick to temper. The starter or the battery on the Ninety-Eight (he wasn't sure which) had been acting up ever since the trip to Colorado. It gave him a fit when it took three cranks to turn the engine over. Morley wasn't late to meet Henna, but he wanted to get there before she arrived.

When he pulled into the driveway, Henna's car was already there. Fumbling with the mail from his box and the key to the apartment, Morley made his way up the stairs cautiously so as not to slip, and also to ease his nerves.

The scent of Henna's gardenia perfume made him giddy and elevated his hopes as he bounded up the last step and entered the big central room of the apartment. Henna sat in one of the large overstuffed chairs. Anything hopeful escaped from Morley like a slow-leaking balloon when she looked up at him, her cheeks red and her eyes puffy and teary. A small pile of balled up tissues littered the carpet around her feet. Deflated, but undaunted and still glad to see her after over a month of distance, Morley put on his best compassionate front and sat down in the chair across from Henna. He was silent, not sure who should speak first, but it was clear Henna waited for his cue. Morley wanted her to explain where she had been since early July, why she had not responded to him, but he quelled that brief spark of anger. It was clear to him that there was a more immediate hurt to address.

"What's wrong?" he asked, in a comforting tone.

"Emmett, I'm not sure where to start," she said, as the tears started to flow again, dabbing at her face with a new tissue. That she called him Emmett sent a shock of fear through Morley.

"Tell me what's going on," he said, with as little emotion as he could, trying to steady himself for her answer.

"I'm in trouble," she said.

Morley pondered her reply, not grasping what she meant, and leaned forward cupping his hands together as if in prayer.

"How are you in trouble?" he asked. "Do you need money?"

There was a long pause, and Morley sensed the air in the room had become heavier; it was harder to breathe.

"I'm pregnant," she blurted out, now openly sobbing as the tears ran from her eyes.

Morley shot back in his chair as if a hole had been opened in his stomach and every organ inside ripped out and thrown on the floor. He felt hurt, angry, and, mostly, betrayed.

"Well, how the hell did that happen?" Morley demanded, knowing immediately how ridiculous the question was.

"How do you think it happened?" she replied.

Morley felt like the chair was swallowing the weight of his body. With some effort, he jumped up to walk around the room, startling Henna.

"You were on the pill."

"I went off it last spring," she said. "It made me sick to my stomach, and I was with you, so there was no need. I stopped seeing people after I met you. There was nobody else and we, well, we were different."

"Well, what the fuck, Henna?" Morley said, his anger rising. His emotions were raw and untethered; he wanted answers, and he wanted them from her right now. "Obviously there was someone else. So is that the reason for the disappearing act? Found someone better? Huh? Answer me!"

Henna began to shake and sob loudly. She looked up at Morley with eyes that spoke love, but her words had struck like daggers in his chest.

"No, no, no, no," she pleaded. "Not like that. Not like that. It wasn't like that."

"Then like *what?*" Morley asked, taking a deep breath in an effort to regain his composure.

"It was one time, it was an accident," she said. "I was drunk, and I don't even remember it. I didn't even know until the next day."

"That makes no sense to me," he said.

"I got sick and passed out. I wasn't sure what happened until the next day."

"I still don't get it," he said. "Other than turning up pregnant, how did you know what happened?"

"From the sheets, that's how," she said, falling into silence.

He felt like a thousand fire ants covered his body, and with each pinch there was a sharp sting and then numbness, as if their venom carried an anesthetic that left him with no feeling on his skin.

Morley was still furious and hurt, but the exchange with Henna, that look of love and need in her eyes that he had never seen before, triggered a compassion inside of him that he did not know he had. She came to him for help. Morley, despite the crushing news that had been delivered, had reached the point that he could admit to himself that he was in love with Henna, no matter what. As he promised to her mother, he would take care of her Henna, and without any conditions.

He sat down on the arm of Henna's chair and cradled her close to him as she wept.

"Why come to me?" he asked.

"Because you care," she said. "Because you are my friend. Because... I know you love me, even though I don't deserve it, even though it scares me. That's why I ran away. I'm sorry, Emmett. I'm sorry I'm so broken."

"I'm sorry, Henna," he said, soothing her.

They stayed that way for what seemed like hours, until Morley got her a glass of water and some more tissues. She sipped the water, and he sat down in the chair across from her. He looked out the door leading to the patio, at the evening shadows the big trees made that reminded him of the foothills of the Rockies. He wished this was all over, and he and Henna could be in the cabin, away from everything. They could sit and listen to the trees and streams talk to the peaks.

Henna let out a deep sigh and sat back in the chair. She was tired, Morley could see, and very fragile, most of the emotion inside of her spilled out through tears and words.

"What do you want to do?" he asked.

"I have an appointment the Friday after Labor Day," she said, without having to elaborate any further on what that meant.

"Then I'll go with you," he said.

"You don't have to."

Again, Morley wasn't sure what her answer meant, and Henna could see it on his face.

"No, I want you to; I just don't want you to feel obligated," she said.

"There was no other volunteer?" he probed.

"No," she said.

"Have you told him?"

"Yes."

"And?"

"He offered to pay for it, but my insurance covers the procedure," she said.

"And beyond that?" Morley pushed her.

"Nothing, Emmett," she said, her tears welling up again. "I didn't want anything to do with him in the first place, and he sure doesn't want anything to do with something like this."

"Who is it?" Morley demanded.

"Why do you need to know?"

"Because I do," he said. "Because it's important to me."

"Because you want to hurt him?"

"Maybe."

"Maybe you'll be the one hurt," she said.

Morley didn't respond.

"Fine, I'll tell you if it's so important," Henna said. "But you have to promise me. I swear. You have to promise right now that you won't do anything. That you will never say anything, to anybody."

"Okay, I promise."

"I mean it," she said. "You promise to me right now."

"I promise to you right now I won't do or say anything, ever."

Henna sipped the last of her water. She dabbed her eyes then wiped her nose before leaning toward Morley's and folding her hands together. The sharpness of her blue eyes locked in on him in a way that emphasized the weight his promise to her carried.

"It was Rhodes."

CHAPTER 30

President Carter kicked off his run for reelection on the traditional Labor Day start of the presidential campaign. He did what all good Democrat politicians do. He made a pilgrimage to Independence, Missouri, the home of Harry S. Truman, and wallowed in as much of the former president's down-home, "Give Them Hell, Harry" political celebrity as he could. At the request of the Washington political desk, and with the approval of the Chicago bureau, Morley traveled in the motorcade with the pool of reporters that had assembled to cover Carter for the next two months. Morley was glad to be a day-tripper on the bus. There was a stop at the Truman Library and the prerequisite visit with Truman's wife, Bess, at her home.

Not satisfied with the cloak of Truman wrapped around him, Carter had arranged that Brett would make an appearance at the Downtown Airport with him, following a town hall meeting held at Truman High School. The day before, in the Royals 4-3 win over the Texas Rangers, Brett went 0-3, dropping his batting average to .403. The Royals' magic number to clinch the West Division title was 12. Now Brett was standing next to the president of the United States, who smiled his big smile and held a bumper sticker that said "George Brett for President." Brett, wearing a modest grin, held another that said "Elect Carter President."

It was a memorable moment in on one of the most forgettable days in Morley's life. He had other things on his mind.

CHAPTER 31

The hospital elevator bell dinged, and the large stainless steel doors opened. A black orderly wheeled out an empty gurney and proceeded down the hallway through a set of swinging double doors. Morley, sitting in the small waiting area outside the outpatient section of the Jewish Hospital, was both anxious and bored. Since Henna had to check in for her appointment by 6:00 a.m. and fast for twelve hours before, they decided it made more sense if she spent the night at his apartment. To show solidarity with Henna, Morley fasted with her, and now the four cups of weak coffee he bought from the machine down the hall was curdling inside his stomach. Henna had walked through the frosted glass doors next to the waiting room about an hour earlier. In that time, Morley had read through the paucity of women's and celebrity magazines, most a good six months old, strewn on the table next to the hard, cold chairs in the waiting room. Jazzed by the coffee, his body grumbling, Morley's thoughts and emotions pinballed inside his head. His main concern was Henna. Every time the heavyset black nurse's aide passed through the frosted doors, Morley would nearly jump up to find out how Henna was doing. And each time the dark, round woman would smile and say she was fine, and there was nothing for him to worry about. Later, Henna told Morley that the woman said, "Dat boy surely must loves you, 'cause he axe 'bout you every time I sees him."

There was what he thought about Henna, and how he hadn't really said, in words, what he felt for her. That he loved her. It was the one word he hadn't said aloud to her. The time, now, wasn't right. They would get through this episode first, and then they could start over.

Then there was what he thought about Rhodes. Morley felt duped. Rhodes had taken advantage of him again, and again Morley was the one standing up to take responsibility and suffer the consequences for Rhodes' reckless indifference to people and things. He wanted Rhodes in his sights. He wanted to hunt him down and pull the trigger. No, Morley thought, a bullet wasn't good enough. That would be too honorable a death. He wanted Rhodes to suffer. He wanted to feel his flesh in his hands while he pummeled him into a bloody mess. He wanted Rhodes to feel the pain he had to feel, that he still felt. He wanted Rhodes to have the scars that he, Billy, and Leo carried—and now Henna would carry scars, too.

Morley sat there, obsessing over Rhodes, until he felt a hand on his shoulder. It was the nurse's aide.

"She be out in a minute," the woman said, smiling at Morley. "She going to be just fine. Now you take good care of her."

"I will," Morley said, smiling back. "I will. Thank you."

Henna looked frail and tired, and older, sitting in the wheelchair. She was drowsy from the muscle relaxant and didn't make eye contact with Morley. He could tell she wanted to get away from there as quickly as possible. He did, too. A middle-aged attendant wheeled her out. She clutched her paperwork, a large plastic bag filled with antibiotics, and big blue-and-white absorbent pads in her lap. The door to the elevator dinged, and the three of them rode up to the main lobby. Morley bent over and told Henna he would be just a minute to bring the car around, and the attendant would wait with her. He didn't want her sitting by herself. The attendant politely said he would wait with her. She nodded without speaking, and Morley walked quickly to the garage structure.

"Why don't you sit in the back? You can lie down if you want," Morley said, opening the back door of the Ninety-Eight.

Henna didn't speak, instead shaking her head in agreement. The attendant and Morley helped her get up from the wheelchair and navigate into the back seat. Morley gently shut the door and thanked the attendant.

It would be best, Morley had told Henna the night before, if she stayed with him for a few days after her appointment so she could recover with his help. He had arranged to have Friday off. If any news broke over the weekend, he could work from the apartment and still cater to her needs.

Henna took her time getting up the three flights of stairs to the apartment, Morley supporting her all the way. She changed into a nightgown and lay down on the bed to rest. Morley went over the post-procedure instructions she had been given, noting the dosages and intervals at which she should take her medications. He put them on the nightstand, and placed the bag of drainage padding on the floor next to the bed. Morley sat on the edge of the bed and stroked Henna's hair. He ran his fingers over her birthmark and down the side of her face. Her color had started to return.

"You doing okay?" he asked.

Henna nodded with a faint smile.

"You must be starving," Morley said. "I know I am. How about I make us grilled cheese and some tomato soup? I have Coke and 7-Up. And I bought some cookies from the French Bakery. How's that?"

Henna's smile widened. As Morley got up from the bed, she grabbed his arm and held him there for a minute.

"You're okay, Morley," she said.

"You're okay too, Freer," Morley answered, turning back to bend over and kiss her on her forehead.

"Thank you," she said.

They ate the lunch Morley made. Later, Henna went to the bathroom, then took her medications and an afternoon nap. Morley opened the windows and the patio door to let an early fall breeze circulate fresh air into the apartment. He sat in one of the big chairs and read the newspaper, looking up every few minutes through the open bedroom door to see if Henna was still sleeping. He slipped back into his thoughts, staring at the newsprint but not focusing on it. It was the first time he had thought of the appointment and what it meant, or didn't mean, to him. He had been raised Catholic, and the church's view on abortion was sacrosanct. He conjured up a vision of his high school religion teacher lecturing him on his complicity in the matter. *Sure*, he thought the priest would say, *it wasn't your child, but you are just as guilty as the guy driving the getaway car in a bank robbery.* The fantasy amused Morley. How ridiculous that kind of thinking was. But what would Grace Morley say? He pondered on what his mother's stance might be. He believed she would say he was being a good friend to Henna. Even if Grace Morley didn't believe in abortion, and even if it wounded her to think her son was involved in any way, she had raised him to be responsible. He had taken responsibility once before, and it hurt her deeply. Now he was taking responsibility again. But this time it was for love. Besides, Morley said to himself, it was 1980. It was legal. Women can make choices about their own bodies. It wasn't a man's decision, anyway. And for all intents and purposes, Rhodes had raped Henna.

He started to agitate again on Rhodes and decided to stop himself by splashing some water on his face. He stood over the bathroom sink, drying the cold water from his hands. When he turned to put the towel on the rack, he looked down. In the wicker waste bin was a bloodstained blue-and-white pad.

CHAPTER 32

By the middle of September, the Royals had clinched the West Division championship. Brett's hitting streak hit its apex September 19 when he went two for four against the Oakland A's, raising his batting average to .3995, which was rounded up to .400. By the September 27, still hampered by an injury to his right hand, Brett dropped to .387, and he was refusing to talk to the media.

That same weekend, Henna and Morley went to the Plaza Fine Arts Fair. It felt to them like a first date. The windows at Herons were done up for the winter clothing line. Henna had created a masterpiece paper-strip snowstorm effect, which was a hit with fairgoers. A picture of an admiring crowd ran in the Sunday *Star*. Henna was already planning out the Christmas window scenes she hoped would be bigger and more elaborate than what she did the previous year.

The two of them had settled into a domestic routine. A slow trickle of Henna's clothes, shoes, makeup and other belongings began to fill the apartment. It had happened without much discourse between them, feeling like the natural course of their relationship. She was still tender from the procedure and had told Morley that the doctor said to give herself at least thirty days to heal before any activity. They joked about the word "activity." Henna apologized for the wait, but Morley said he understood and that she was worth abstinence.

They never talked about the missing month of July, or the reasons behind Henna's withdrawal from him after the dogfight. Morley never told her about his visit to Grainfield, or that he ferreted out her stepfather's conviction for felony sexual abuse of a minor. Morley figured there was time for that in the future. They also didn't talk about Rhodes and avoided most places where he might turn up. Morley kept his promise to her. He wouldn't say or do anything about what happened.

Edmond had been persuaded to emerge from his medical school cocoon to join them at least once a week for dinner. The three of them took turns planning and cooking the meal. Edmond's, of course, was always better done and more extravagant.

There was back-channel chatter in the Chicago bureau that London had its eye on Morley for several openings overseas. Unless or until that happened, he wouldn't say anything to Henna, though he knew he would ask that she go with him, under whatever terms or commitments she wanted. He was sure she would go, and he fantasized about being stationed in Paris or Rome and the opportunities that would open up for her.

It was all going to be great, Morley wrote down in one of his reporter's notebooks.

CHAPTER 33

The call came before noon Monday, October, 6, just as Morley was about to leave the bureau for the stadium to work up a story on the upcoming American League Championship, a best-of-five series. The Royals would face the Yankees, who were in town working out before the start of the first game scheduled for Wednesday afternoon.

The Chicago bureau reluctantly agreed to pick up commodities coverage for the week, as Morley would be busy with the playoffs. After the second game on Thursday, the venue—and Morley—would travel to New York.

Morley answered the phone. It was a brief conversation with the senior international editor in London. The bureau chief in Riyadh was being rotated to Johannesburg, and would Morley be interested in filling the position? His commodities experience in Kansas City and his field reporting, both in Kansas City and in Ireland, suited him well to cover the oil market and the tensions in the region. Morley also had been given a high recommendation by his Dublin bureau chief. The editor told Morley he could have a few days to think it over.

He put the receiver back in the cradle and sat down to think. It wasn't Paris or Rome, but it was the next step to get to one of those cities. It was an expatriate covered position, which meant living in housing subsidized by the agency. Transportation, utilities, schools, and servants were also subsidized, as was the agency way. Henna would have plenty of time to paint. And they would be able to travel. Morley could offer her the world, and they would be able to see it together. Still, the customs and traditions of Saudi Arabia would require they be married. It was the same for the agency. The thought appealed to Morley. He would think the offer over and talk to her when he returned from New York on Saturday.

Until then, he would keep the offer a secret. *Oh, hell,* he thought. Full of excitement and anticipation, he had to tell someone. That afternoon, during batting practice and after a brief interview with Reggie Jackson, Morley mentioned the promotion to Tug, who told him he would be an idiot not to take them up on the offer.

It made sense, Morley said to himself, as he typed away at the keyboard of the Silent 700, the green expanse of the field spread out before him. Leo and Billy were gone. Edmond would graduate and leave for a residency in the spring. All that was left for him in Kansas City was Henna, and she had no ties here other than him. And there would be no Rhodes. Everything that had happened could be neatly packaged up and put away in storage.

CHAPTER 34

A joyous optimism came over the city. Heads were held a little higher. People walked a little faster. Everyone was polite, helpful, and hopeful. The Royals' 7-2 trouncing of the Yankees in Game 1 of the playoffs was an elixir the longsuffering fans had not felt since the Kansas City Chiefs won the Super Bowl more than a decade earlier.

Both Henna and Edmond, who had no previous interest in the game of baseball, got swept up in the fever. Morley was also giddy after the victory, though showing any such emotion—let alone verbalizing it in the press box—was strictly forbidden. Big Timers covered games, win or lose. They could report on the excitement of others, but they couldn't feel it. Anyone in the press box who did admit to feeling it was a Homer, which was a Jock Sniffer rooting for his own team. That meant a double dose of disrespect from the rest of the press box. And the Royals press box was packed with sports reporters from newspapers and journals from across the country.

After the first game's victory, Morley bought Henna and Edmond KC baseball caps to wear while they watched the Thursday night game. It was Henna's idea that Edmond would come over to the apartment for the 7:15 p.m. first pitch, and they would watch the game on the Sony, perhaps even spot Morley in the press box. She would boil hotdogs, and they would eat peanuts and Cracker Jacks. Her enthusiasm generated more excitement in Morley than the Royals had the night before. So that he could feel included in their newfound fan status, Morley said he would call from the press box during the seventh-inning stretch, and they could sing "Take Me Out to the Ballgame" to him over the phone. He, of course, would not be joining in on the singing.

Game 2 proved to be much closer and nerve-wracking than expected. Morley called during the stretch, but neither Henna nor Edmond knew all the words to the song and their voices faded into laughter after the first stanza. That, and their nerves were frayed, as the Royals were struggling to hold on to a 3-2 lead. Morley hung up when play resumed after the short break, and the Yankees began threatening the Royals' slim lead.

Willie Randolph made base on a single, and with two outs, Bob Watson came to the plate. The crowd jeered and yelled to distract Watson, who responded by ripping a straight shot deep into left field. Then, as Tug would say later, things got weird. New York's third-base coach, relying on Randolph's explosive speed on the bases, waved his player home. The Royals' Wilson, playing in left, fielded Watson's hit, but overthrew his cutoff man, U. L. Washington. Brett, whose field skills tended to be overlooked because of his hitting prowess, had positioned himself to back up Washington. In a move worthy of the Bolshoi Ballet Academy, Brett gloved the overthrown ball, executed a Major League pirouette and threw Randolph out at home plate. The play was stunning and sent Yankees owner George Steinbrenner into a fit—and Royals fans into ecstasy.

"Look at him, look at him," Tug said, pulling at Morley's shirt for him to look at Steinbrenner on the press box monitor above them. "He's apoplectic."

"Can you even spell that?" Morley replied.

"I guess they'll be looking for a new third-base coach after tonight," Tug said. "And yes, I can spell."

Morley didn't get back to the apartment until late. He was greeted by the smell of boiled hotdogs and Henna fast asleep. He had an early morning flight to New York and had already packed for the trip. Four hours later, the alarm went off. Henna didn't budge. Morley took a quick shower, dressed, and kissed the slumbering Henna on her cheek.

The plan was to arrive at La Guardia Airport by midmorning, take a cab to the agency offices off of Times Square, and meet with the Americas editor to discuss the Riyadh job in more detail. Then Morley could check into the hotel before heading to the Bronx for Game 3, which, if the Royals won, would send them to the World Series for the first time in franchise history. Morley would get all the specifics of the Riyadh posting, then talk to Henna once the series with the Yankees was over. It sounded like a solid plan to him. They would have time to transition from Kansas City to the overseas posting. There might even be time to travel in Europe some before taking up a new life together in the Middle East.

He called Henna at work during her lunch hour and—miraculously, he thought—she answered. He had arrived safe, and he gave her the name of the hotel and the number where he could be reached. Morley told her he'd call from the press box with that number, but Henna said not to bother. Still feeling the excitement sparked by the two victories by the Royals, she and Edmond wanted to watch the game with other fans. They had decided to go to The Pike and have wings and cheer for the team. She promised they would both wear the ball caps he bought them.

"This is going to be great," she said.

"Yes, it will," Morley said, thinking about Riyadh and the two of them going together. "I'll see you either tomorrow, Sunday, or Monday."

"Whenever it is, it will be great," she said.

Henna hung up the phone before Morley could toss in the words he felt for her. He would call in the morning.

Game 3 was a snoozer up until the seventh inning. The Royals were down 2-1. Yankees Manager Dick Howser brought in hard-throwing Goose Gossage to strike out Brett. Instead, Brett silenced the horridly loud and vicious New York crowd by slamming a three-run homer into the upper deck of Yankee Stadium. Morley swore he heard trumpets when Brett's bat hit the ball. It was pure brilliance. Brett's swing sent the Royals into the World Series and Kansas City fans into a mad delirium. It also sent Morley back to Henna earlier. By the end of the game, Morley had booked an early Saturday morning flight back to Kansas City.

⋙✕⋘

Grabbing his bag from the carousel at the airport, Morley found the Ninety-Eight in the circle parking lot outside the terminal. It was a long drive from the airport, which was located practically in Omaha, he often joked. The roads were quiet. There was a tired joy that hung in the fall air. The city was clearly hung over from last night's wild celebrations.

Morley pulled into the driveway and parked behind Henna's car. Great, he thought, she's home and probably still in bed. They could go out for breakfast and he could break the news about the Riyadh posting.

Morley bounced up the stairs behind the bookshelf as if he were being carried on air. The odor of gardenia filled his nostrils more strongly than ever before. It was good to be home, he thought, making the turn at the top of the steps that deposited him in the main room of the apartment.

Edmond, his head down, sat in the overstuffed chair Henna preferred. When he looked up, Morley could see Edmond had not shaved that morning; his face was rough, his eyes bloodshot and swollen. It made Morley smile, thinking they must have really tied one on last night after the game. The door to the bedroom was open, and Morley could see that Henna was not there. The bed was still made. Likely, he thought, she went out for coffee and croissants to help Edmond's recovery.

"You should sit down, Morley," Edmond said.

Edmond's words had the effect of a fire alarm going off in Morley's head, and that he had called him by his last name made the prospect of eminent catastrophe more real.

"No, no, I think not Edmond," Morley said, his voice carrying panic. He avoided eye contact with Edmond. "And since when did you start calling me Morley?"

"Please, Emmett, you should," Edmond quietly pleaded.

Morley let loose his grip on the overnight bag, which dropped to the floor with a thump. It didn't make him feel any lighter, and now the room seemed to be closing in on him. The light began to dim, and shadows crept into his peripheral vision. Morley walked over to the desk across from Edmond and fidgeted with the papers and pencils, still not looking at Edmond.

"No reason to sit," Morley said, taking in a deep breath. "Where's Henna?"

Edmond began to weep.

"I said, where's Henna, Edmond?" Morley demanded as he stiffened and, gaining his courage, looked straight down at Edmond.

Wiping the tears from his face, Edmond composed himself.

"Henna's dead, Emmett."

The shrapnel tore through Morley's body. He could feel every hot piece of metal piercing his flesh and branding him forever. The concussion made his ears ring. The blood in his mouth turned to iron and mingled with the acrid flavor of spent gunpowder. Morley tried to call for a medic, but no words came out of his mouth. He was looking down at himself, his shredded body lying in a sand pit on the beach, his rifle off to the side. He watched himself bleeding until he couldn't watch anymore.

"This is crap," Morley said, holding his hands up in the air in surrender. "Where's Henna?"

Edmond looked up from the chair at his friend. He couldn't say the words again. Unable to deliver more hurt to Morley, Edmond began to sob uncontrollably.

Morley shoved the typewriter off the top of the desk, and it landed on the floor with a loud crash that dinged the carriage return bell. In his frantic search, pencils, pens, reporter's notebooks, and typing paper were flung onto the floor. Morley violently opened the top desk drawer and rummaged through its contents before finding what he was after. He pulled out a crumpled pack of menthol cigarettes. A book of matches from a pub in Belfast was stuck inside the cellophane wrapper of the pack.

Morley half sat against the desk and lit the cigarette. He felt the burning coolness of the smoke coat his throat and work its way down into his lungs as he gazed out the windows to the tops of the large trees that had reminded him of the mountains, their leaves now brown and dying in the seasonal change.

BOOK V

Jesusfuck! Hydraulic fluid is spewing all over the place, and there's a big fucking hole where there used to be a fuselage. Fingers of light are shooting through thick black smoke, and we're getting tossed around like we're riding the Rock-O-Plane at the carnival. The goddamned sky is lit up like Christmas, with strings of light bulbs all headed our way. Bang, bang, bang, bang. We're getting hammered. Goddamned Zoomie fucks can't fly worth shit. Get us the hell on the motherfucking beach and off this dying bitch. Boom. Splash. Knife 31 is down. Dive through the hole and dog paddle. Swallow salt water. Zing. Crack. Splash. Zing. Crack. Splash. Taking heavy fire. Swear they are throwing cans of Budweiser at us. Get some footing, grab somebody in the water next to me, and look for shore. Where the fuck is shore? No bearings. He's dead. Let him go. Cough up some more salt water. Hear screaming. More rotors overhead. Rally point. Mortar fire. Splashes and smoke in the water, just like the movies. The downed helicopter is a bullet magnet. Front half of the cockpit is missing. Fire. Good. Keep shooting at that and not me. Help, Mr. Wizard! Knife 23 rolls in. Boom. Hu-waaang. An RPG takes out its tail. Flops down on the beach. Marines pour out its broken ass. The water is warm. Sun is starting to come up. Maybe I'll just stay in the water. Order a Piña Colada. Maybe not. Get racked by machine gun fire. Head toward the assless bird on the beach. Hey, don't shoot. Don't shoot. Marine pops up out of the sand and fires off a clip into the palm trees. "Fuck you." Shoot, but just don't shoot me. He doesn't shoot me. Head for the good guys. Get on the beach. Fucking sand sticks to me like flies to shit. Look like a big turd. I'm in the guy's hole. The sunrise sky is so pretty. "You going to take a nap or use that thing?" Take the Dragon out of its cover. Fuck. It's a mess. Field clean in a firefight. Nice. Fuck. Get my shit back together. Take a position. Slow it down. Look for muzzle flash in the tree line. Flash. There. The Dragon breathes fire. A 7.62 x 51 mm going downrange. Watch. No more flash from there. Lots of others. Looks like fireflies. Squeeze off a few more. "Hey, Morley, is that you?" Fucking A. It's Jackson. Best damn news I've had all day. Duck and roll my way over to him, closer to the tree line. "Hey, man, this is some shit, huh?" "You got my sunglasses, asshole?" "Fuck you." "Can I borrow some suntan lotion?" Pissed off lasts about two seconds. "Nice beach, don't you think?" "Yeah, it's really beautiful here." Crack. Zing. Return fire. "Too many bugs, though." This shit goes on for a while. One of the grounded pilots is calling in air support on an emergency radio. Spooky rolls in and tears the jungle to shreds as a Jolly Green plops down a hundred meters away. All the monkeys in the zoo are throwing shit at it. Not running to them. No fucking way. We stay put, and they peel away. Ass wipes couldn't get closer? Shit goes on some more, and we dig a little deeper. Coordinate the perimeter. Check ammo. Work on our tans. Forenoon, three more choppers roll in and get the shit kicked out of them. Things get quiet after that. Guess the morning vol- leyball match was too much for the slopes, and they take a siesta. Time passes. Pair of choppers moves in and ends naptime for another attempt to get us the hell off the East Beach LZ. The West Beach LZ is getting all the action, and we're just kind of sitting here with our dicks in our hands. It doesn't work. They peel off, leaving us there, again. Time passes. We work on our tans. Three more choppers get lit up down the beach from a half-sunk fishing boat and abort. Motherfucker. We ever going to get out of here? We take shots at the half-sunk boat. Big guns from the ship offshore blow what is left of it to shit. Time trickles by. The afternoon heat builds. Can't take the flak jacket anymore and take it off. Just lying there in the litter box like cat turds. You absorb everything. The smell of urine and cordite permeates the perimeter. Can't hold it forever. No breeze. Everything just stagnates there. Whoosh. But no bang. Weird. Get the worst headache I've ever had. Bells ringing. Figure Jackson really is pissed about the sunglasses and decided to start kicking my head. Can't be. Open my eyes. Jackson's face right in front of me. Can't kick my head that way. His hands are wet. Start flailing to get up and figure this shit out. Weird. Jackson pins me down. All I hear are church bells. Start to talk, and smoke comes out of my mouth. I remember when Billy handed me the firecracker without telling me it was lit and I wasn't paying attention. Damn near blew my fingers off. Lights and buzzers go off. Fuck. I've been hit. What the fuck? A whoosh, and I'm the bang. The handsome medic is over me. Why are they always so handsome? Who cares? He's my fucking guardian angel right now. Turns me all over the place. Compliant. Do whatever he says. My blouse is in shreds. He's checking me all over. Spends a lot of time on my neck, then starts talking to me. Him I'll listen to. Fuck Jackson. "Follow my finger." I follow his finger. "How many fingers?" One hand looks like it has about a dozen fingers. He starts laughing. Jackson starts laughing. "You got chewed up, but you'll live. Concussion. Fix you up when we get back to the ship. Soon." He splits. Compose myself. I'm shredded. Look like a bloody stool covered in sand. "Superficial" keeps running through my head. Still have a screaming head- ache. Jackson holds up his broken Ray Bans fished out from my blouse pocket. "You owe me a new pair." Sun is sitting low, and they finally come to extract us. Drag our sorry asses over to the Jolly Green. Can't land on the beach because of the chopper wreckage, so we have to time jumping on the ramp as it seesaws up and down and back and forth. Can't manage it. Jackson and some other guys throw me up and onto the ramp. Decide then I hate helicopters. Decide then I hate sand. I hate beaches. G.H.M.F. Get Home Mother Fucker.

CHAPTER 35

The small clock on the walnut desk in the study in Denton's home chimed that it was late afternoon. The china coffee cup chattered against the saucer resting in Morley's left hand when he lifted it to take a sip. It was noticeable enough to cause Denton to look up from his telephone discussion with the funeral home director. Denton, dressed in old khakis and a red plaid lumberjack shirt, had put aside his Sunday yard work to help his cousin make burial arrangements. That it was for a stranger and that she would be buried among the family was irrelevant to Denton. It was important to Morley, which made it important to Denton. Thanking the funeral director for his help, Denton hung up the phone. He took a sip of coffee from the china cup on his desk, then picked it and the saucer up very delicately and rounded the desk to sit in the large leather armchair next to Morley. They sat quietly; only the ticking sound of the desk clock disturbed the solemnity.

"The funeral home will arrange everything with the cemetery," Denton said. "There are plenty of spaces available in our section, and according to the deed, you are entitled to six plots."

"At the top of the hill, where it's in the sun all day, and there's a big pine tree not far," Morley said, somewhat disjointedly. "There, right?"

"Yes, it's all taken care of," Denton said.

Denton got up and sat on the armrest of Morley's chair, putting his hand on his shoulder in consolation. He was remembering his cousin much younger, and the priest walking the boy into the principal's office with his arm around his shoulder, and the anticipation of fear and pain in his eyes. Denton remembered the cemetery a week later. Morley had just turned sixteen and stood alone on the same spot, the one where a woman named Henna would now be buried. It was fall then, too, and Denton recalled the weak autumnal light of that afternoon, and how strong yet frail Morley had looked standing in the sun.

"I'm covering everything, remember," Morley said, his hand still trembling.

"Yes, it's all taken care of," Denton reassured him. "It's all handled."

Denton was unsure what to say next, just as he was unsure what to say when he broke the news to Morley about his father. What Denton knew about his cousin was that it wasn't the words spoken that mattered as much to Morley as it was the actions taken. This woman, Henna, whom Denton had never heard of until the call from Morley the night before, meant more to his cousin than words. That Morley wanted her buried among the Morleys was all he had to say.

"I would like her," Denton said, rubbing Morley's shoulder.

"You would have loved her," Morley said, his head bowed almost into his lap. Denton could see small dark circles form on Morley's trousers.

The clock ticked on the desk, announcing the quarter hour. Denton could see Morley had composed himself, and he returned to his own chair.

"Being home has never been easy for you," Denton said.

"I'm not sure what that is," Morley replied.

"What what is?" Denton asked.

"Home and easy."

Denton smiled, fully understanding the meaning.

"It took me a long time to adjust," Denton said. "There are days I don't think I have. But you just have to plow through them. Well, at least for me."

Morley looked around Denton's study as if he were taking in the entire house and Denton's complete life.

"There's nothing left here for me to adjust to," Morley said.

Denton smiled, took a sip of coffee, then spit it back into the cup.

"I hate drinking coffee from a china cup," he said. "It gets cold too fast.

"You should take the posting in Riyadh. It's where the action is. It's where the action always will be."

"Yes," said Morley.

"Kansas City will always be here, it never changes," Denton said, rising up from the chair. "There will always be a place for you."

Fearful how his friend might react, Edmond did not leave Morley alone very often in the days leading up to Henna's funeral. He was able to cover his medical school absence with the excuse of a death in the family. It gave him the week to be with Morley. And there were the arrangements to be made, which provided some distraction from their grief. But it was Morley's possible reaction and retaliation over how Henna had died that concerned Edmond the most.

Once the reality of her death settled in on Morley, the initial shock and denial having passed fairly quickly, the facts came out. As planned, Edmond and Henna had gone to The Pike to watch the game and cheer on the home team. What had not been planned, what Henna had not expected, and what Edmond was unaware of was Rhodes, who arrived at the bar with LJ in tow. Henna seemed nervous and fidgeted when the pair walked in and sat down at their table, Edmond told Morley. But Henna rolled with it, though paying little attention to Rhodes as he jabbered away and ordered more pitchers of beer for the table. Henna, Edmond said, had very little to drink. Edmond, however, caught up in the excitement of the game and revelry of the fans in the bar, drank liberally; and when the game ended and the place erupted, he thought nothing of encouraging Henna to take a celebratory "hooting and hollering" ride around the block on the back of Rhodes' motorcycle. Though apprehensive, with Rhodes' insistence and the encouragement of both Edmond and LJ, who was going to ride next, Henna reluctantly agreed. Three blocks away, going at high speed, Rhodes lost control of the bike. If only he had known, Edmond cried to Morley, of what had happened between Henna and Rhodes, he would have backhanded Rhodes and left the bar with Henna. The exchange of the truth now put Morley in the role of consoler. Edmond's guilt hung around his neck like a weight of stones.

215

On Monday, Morley obtained a copy of the police report taken by the officer at the accident scene. Though not an official autopsy, Henna had died from a broken neck. She had not been wearing a helmet. Rhodes, however, had worn a helmet, and suffered only minor scrapes and bruises, apparently landing in a nearby patch of grass. For all of his upbringing, polite airs, and proper etiquette, Rhodes did not have the manners to offer Henna his helmet. Then again, Rhodes didn't have the decency to respect her or her body that night in July, or stand up to the consequences of his actions. There was nothing decent about Rhodes. There never had been, and there never would be, Morley knew. The difference now was that Rhodes had graduated from breaking things to breaking people. Eventually, Morley believed—he hoped—there had to be a cost to Rhodes. Though he wanted desperately to search him out, to make him accountable in some way, Morley knew he would keep his promise to Henna as a way to honor her. As much as he wanted to taste retribution, to feel, see, and hear fear in Rhodes, he would leave it to fate or God.

❦

It had been agreed with Pearl Freer that Morley would make all the arrangements for the funeral. He and Edmond would pick her up at the downtown bus station on Monday, and she would stay at Henna's apartment. The funeral was set for Tuesday afternoon. Morley insisted she not worry about any costs; lying, he said they were all covered by her work insurance, and if it were all right with her, he would pick out a plot at the cemetery where his family was buried. Pearl thanked Morley and said whatever he decided for Henna would be fine.

He and Edmond chose a walnut casket. The finish was warm, and the grain carried a nice color. The inside was white satin and thickly padded. Morley thought it gave the illusion of warmth, and that made him feel a little better for the moment. He picked out the outfit Henna wore the first time he saw her in the store window. He also gave instructions to the funeral director that even though it would be a closed casket, they were to arrange her hair to cover her birthmark. Taking the trinity knot charm from his coat pocket, Morley asked the director to have it placed in her right hand. A faint but respectful smile eased across the director's face.

"If I might say, Mr. Morley," he said.

"Yes?" Morley replied, giving the director permission to speak.

"She has the most beautiful hands."

"Yes," Morley said. "She does."

It was a sunny, cloudless fall afternoon, and the sky was an azure blue that reminded Morley of Henna's eyes. The grass at the cemetery was dry and made a soft swishing sound as the small party of mourners made their way to the green tent that sheltered Henna's casket. Each brush of his polished shoes against the grass felt like an earthly caress. Morley and Edmond walked behind Pearl. There were a half dozen of Henna's co-workers, along with her boss, who had followed in the small motorcade for the graveside service. A bright floral arrangement sat atop the casket, and several other floral arrangements from people Morley did not know were placed at the back of the tent. Not that he expected it, nor did he wish it, but there was nothing from Rhodes, or even LJ for that matter. No flowers, no note, and certainly no attendance.

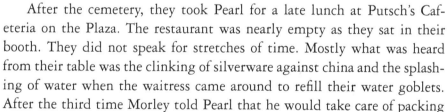

After the cemetery, they took Pearl for a late lunch at Putsch's Cafeteria on the Plaza. The restaurant was nearly empty as they sat in their booth. They did not speak for stretches of time. Mostly what was heard from their table was the clinking of silverware against china and the splashing of water when the waitress came around to refill their water goblets. After the third time Morley told Pearl that he would take care of packing up Henna's belongings and shipping them to her, she reached across the table and held his hand.

"You've told me that already, dear," she reassured him. "You take your time with everything."

That evening, they took her to the bus station and waited with her until she boarded for home. Teary, she thanked Morley and Edmond for everything they had done and quickly disappeared inside. They waited in the Ninety-Eight until the bus pulled away and disappeared into the night streets.

Driving back to the apartment, they didn't bother to turn the radio on to find out the Royals had lost 7-6 to the Philadelphia Phillies in Game 1 of the World Series.

CHAPTER 36

By Friday, the Royals had dropped the first two games of the Series to the Phillies, and every sportswriter and copy editor in the world had learned how to spell "hemorrhoids." Hampered by injuries throughout the season, Brett left Game 2 in the sixth inning, suffering from his sensitive condition. He had minor surgery the following travel day and returned to the lineup for Game 3. Brett's malady produced comic relief in the locker room and press box. With the Series back in Kansas City and Brett back in the lineup, the fans packed Royals Stadium, but not with the same level of excitement as they had shown during the playoff series with the Yankees.

It was as if all the energy in the city had been used up the previous week against New York. Even the sun seemed dimmer and cast longer shadows across the Astroturf, which now took on a more faded appearance. The fountains splashing and dancing in the outfield made the atmosphere at the ballpark more restive than energizing.

The somber mood at the stadium mirrored Morley's, stalking him as he walked the main concourse looking for color quotes from fans for a sidebar story he was working on. It was a story he thought he could dissuade the New York sports desk from wanting, but they insisted. All he wanted to do was file a brief game story, cull some quotes after the game, and go back to the apartment.

219

With every step he took amid the bustling crowd of fans, he thought of Henna. He couldn't go the stretch of a minute without thinking about her. He looked for her face in the crowd. It was all a dream, he would say to himself at times. She will show up any minute. He bargained with himself. Maybe if he thought of her enough, she would come back. God, if he existed, would bring her back, surely. *If only, if only* kept looping through his thoughts.

Walking along the concourse where the luxury suites were located, a figure caught Morley's attention. A familiar shape and movement that registered with him. The hot wash of adrenalin coursed through his body, starting from the waist and moving quickly up to his chest and into his face, which felt flushed. He could feel his heart start to pump faster, and the muscles in his arms and shoulders tensed and strained. He tried to control his breathing, unsure if he was seeing what he thought he was. Yet, in his very soul, he knew what was happening, and when he got closer and heard the voice he was certain.

It was Rhodes. He was dressed as if he were to report to the dugout for pregame batting practice. He wore a royal blue baseball cap and a silk warm-up jacket, beneath which was a game jersey sporting Brett's number. He was standing with LJ next to one of the suites, which Morley assumed was one of the perks of his family's business. Rhodes spoke loudly and appeared to be gesturing mockingly to the streams of people placidly walking by and ignoring him. He was drunk, Morley deduced.

In less than five steps, and without a clear thought of what he would do or what the outcome may be, Morley was on Rhodes, clenching his left hand tightly around his throat as he violently pulled him into the breezeway between two of the suites. Rhodes' face exploded into shades of red and purple, his eyes popping from their sockets in disbelief. LJ made no sound, but followed behind, a look of indifferent shock on her face. She was there for the show, not as a participant. By following them into the narrow space, LJ effectively blocked the view anyone might have of the combat taking place.

Morley tightened his grip on Rhodes' throat, cutting off his ability to breathe or gulp out a single word. Spit began to drip from his mouth, and mucous ran from his nose onto the shiny satin jacket. Morley pushed him into and up the wall until Rhodes was on his toes.

His mouth clinched shut, Morley breathed through his nostrils, the sound rushing in and out in regular intervals. He turned and looked at LJ so she would understand what was happening, then turned back to Rhodes.

"You raped her, and then you killed her," Morley hissed through clenched teeth. Then he turned back to LJ.

"He raped her and he killed her," he said. LJ blinked and shook her head in tacit agreement. When she did, the fear in her face triggered his memory of Henna and the promise he made not to say or do anything.

Morley closed his eyes for a second to wipe away the thought. He loosened his grip, and Rhodes slumped lower, though still unable to talk.

Morley drew his right arm across the front of his body and, leveraging all his weight, he swung and struck Rhodes in the face with the back of his hand. The slap hit with enough force that Rhodes' head ricocheted off the cement wall, and a large welt began to form.

When Morley let go his clutch, Rhodes slumped to the concrete floor and began to sob, just as he had outside the courtroom all those years ago.

❈

The buzzer on the elevator sounded, and the door opened to the Press Box level. Morley stepped into the bustling hallway as reporters and the team's media representatives scurried about to get everything in place before the game got underway. Morley was still shaking when he took his seat next to Tug, who scanned the crowd with a pair of binoculars.

"Where have you been?" he asked, without looking at Morley. "You don't want to miss the first pitch."

"I had some business to take care of," Morley said, pulling a fresh notepad from his valise.

"This is something, ain't it?" Tug said.

Morley didn't answer. When he opened the notepad, a small slip of red paper fell out. On it was scrawled in Henna's handwriting, "You're okay Morley." He picked the delicate scrap up and held it between his thumb and forefinger.

"So what was the best part of the season?" Tug asked, his eyes still glued to the field glasses.

It was an innocuous enough question, but Morley's thoughts fell backward through the hours, days, and months since he came home to bury his mother. He thought back over the spring and summer.

The answer wasn't about baseball, or the heat wave, or the harvest, or any of the many stories he wrote. The best part of the season was that he met an extraordinary woman who was beautiful, smart, and incredibly creative, and who thought he was beautiful, smart, and incredibly creative.

He remembered slipping on the flight of stairs and the look on her face as she ran to catch him. She was willing to sacrifice herself for him. No one had ever looked at him like that before. The memory made him short of breath.

He wanted to say he missed her. He wanted to say he missed her very much.

EPILOGUE

Despite Brett's return to the lineup, the Royals lost the World Series to Philadelphia in six games. In 1985, the Royals, under Manager Dick Howser, beat the Cardinals in seven games to win the Series that those people in St. Louis still contend should have been theirs, forever citing the bad call in game six by first-base umpire Don Denkiniger. At this printing, the Royals have not appeared in the World Series since, and no other Major League player has come as close to breaking Williams' record as Brett did during the summer of 1980.

Perceived by voters as an impotent leader for his mishandling of the Iran Hostage Crisis and the U.S. economy, Carter was tossed from the White House in a landslide defeat that November. The Reagan era was ushered in, and with it, a deepening recession that lasted several more years. Reagan's economic and foreign policies, heralded by the Republican Party and both Bush administrations, continue to be felt to this day. Historians, not journalists or novelists, will judge what Reagan imparted to the world.

LJ married an heir to a large regional bank. She is a dowdy, overweight society matron, living in Kansas City.

Rhodes died of AIDS in 1987.

Edmond is the head of the psychiatry department at Massachusetts General Hospital in Boston. He specializes in working with patients who suffer from post-traumatic stress disorder. Henna's portrait of Morley, covered in red slips of paper, hangs in his office.

Leo spent two years in Alaska and then reenlisted in the Marines. He retired from the service soon after the battle in Fallujah, Iraq, during the second Gulf War. The founder of a successful outdoor adventure company in Arizona, he has been sober since 1980.

Billy graduated from law school and moved to Los Angeles, where he is a celebrated entertainment attorney. He is on his fourth marriage.

Morley was killed in 2007 by a sniper while covering the war in Afghanistan. He is buried next to Henna. His funeral was the first time since 1980 that he, Leo, and Billy were together in the same place. Edmond attended. After the private graveside service, a small reception was held at The Pike. The wicker casket no longer hangs on the wall.